# A CA

## *Gentlemen of the Coast Book 2*

by
Danielle Thorne

First Edition
Copyright © 2020 by Danielle Thorne
Kindle Direct Publishing
Publish Date: April 2020 ISBN: 9798640726510
Cover Design: Bluewater Books, Inc.

# Quote

"No city could be more beautiful than Charleston during the brief reign of azaleas, no city on earth."

— Pat Conroy
*The Lords of Discipline*

# CHAPTER ONE

*Charleston, South Carolina*
*1794*

PHOEBE'S CLOGS SANK into a layer of sandy soil cluttered with oyster shells. Glancing toward the distant wharf, she dropped her sewing basket to the ground and slipped off her shoes. The arches of her feet relaxed as soon as they touched the sand through her stockings. The shore felt bitter cold.

She tugged the hood of her fur-trimmed pelisse around her neck, thankful she'd worn quilted petticoats under her linsey-woolsey dress for market day. The blue indigo skirt swished around her legs in a snapping breeze as she watched water lick over the narrow strip of beach.

Charleston. It pointed at the Atlantic Ocean like a finger dotted with palmetto trees. Either side of the harbor was protected by two islands within waving distance of each other. This allowed a narrow corridor of seawater to pass into the bay where Fort Wilkin observed the comings and goings of ships laden with rice, indigo, sugar, and molasses.

Squinting in the winter sunshine, Phoebe released a slow stream of air as a lingering headache subsided. Gulls spiraled around her with little effort, and she envied them. Life in her

2

narrow house on Beaufain Street was not effortless, but she was thankful for it. Her embroidered handkerchiefs were growing popular and helped sustain their meager income.

Papa had built the house and secured a land tract upriver for a plantation someday. She missed him—the smell of tobacco smoldering in his pipe, his boisterous laugh, and of course, the dry goods shop that had been an appendage to his merchant business. But the war for independence had come and after so many years, Mama, Phoebe, and her married sister, Winnifred, had to move on without him. So had Charleston.

Resolute, she untucked her mittens from the folds of her pelisse and slipped back on her clogs. They felt heavy as she plodded back to the street. Before she crossed, she hesitated, waiting for a handsome gig to bounce by. Its horse did a jaunty dance, and amused, Phoebe watched it slow to a stop and wait for her to pass.

She hurried across the road. A man in a heavy coat with lace at his throat and a bright jonquil-colored blanket across his lap leaned out. His English top hat looked ridiculous, nothing like the cocked hats worn by most of the men she knew these days.

"Ah!" he called and waved a gloved hand in acknowledgment. "Miss..."

She groaned inwardly when she realized it was the fetching but absurd son of Papa's old friend from Mount Pleasant. The one young man she had adored as a girl until she'd accepted that a planter's son would never settle for a late merchant's daughter of little means, especially one like her. "Good day, Mr. Hathaway," she replied.

"Oh, Miss Applewaite, is it?" he cried like he hadn't recognized her. He'd only asked her to dance at her very first ball, and what a disaster that had been.

He flashed her a brilliant grin like he knew the picture he made. His extravagant clothes were quite refined, and though she did appreciate the quality, this was just the port after dawn. Not a ball. The infatuation she'd once carried for him reared its sleepy head, but she pushed it back into the past.

Unaffected by her lack of enthusiasm for any banter, Mr. Hathaway touched his hat, and Phoebe continued her way up the wintry street with her gaze averted. She had no interest in entertaining the village fop. As if in reply, the snap of his whip sounded in the air, and she watched the gig lurch forward on to its destination.

Clearly, Mr. Hathaway had no interest in dallying with the unchaperoned Applewaite spinster, either.

JAMES HATHAWAY ENJOYED a good party, and the Twelfth Night ball made a perfect excuse to have fun. He hurried to the card room patting his pockets for his new deck and what remained of his allowance. Mama insisted he receive his inheritance by allowance month by month instead of annually. That was another reason to join the games. He needed a win.

He'd done his duty with the ladies in the drawing room. Earlier, he'd visited with Mrs. Quinton and her daughter and made them laugh, and then he promised Mama's friend, Mrs. Applewaite, that he'd dance with her daughter. But first, cards.

The pretty but overly serious Miss Applewaite would have to wait. She had a younger sister who was married, which had gained her a brother. The brother-in-law, Mr. Daniel Cadwell, was a good sort, although not known to be as clever as the late Mr. Applewaite. Not that James could remember. He'd only been ten years old and in poor health when war broke out with England. His bed chambers in the plantation house at Sandy Bank had been a prison for most of his childhood when all he'd needed for the suspected case of rickets was a little air.

He shook off the unpleasant memories of being confined to his bed by Mama, physicians, and the long war. What Twelfth Night revelers needed tonight was a smart game of Brag since a cockfight would not do. A smile crept across his face as he grabbed the doorknob. Cards or dice was the most leisurely way to make a little extra money, and he could amuse his friends at the same time.

He burst into the room. "Gentlemen. Your champion has arrived." A few guffaws erupted, but Benjamin Quinton let out a hoot. His best friend pushed out a chair using his boot. "Over here, Jamie. This table, yes?"

Pleased and since no one else offered, James ambled across the room greeting his parents' friends and associates. He was relieved to find Papa was in the library, probably smoking and avoiding the crowd, although the air in here still smelled pungent with tobacco and wax. With a quiet whistle, James dropped down into the chair beside Benjamin. Mr. Daniel Cadwell and the feisty old merchant, McClellan, completed the set.

"What are you playing?"

"Nothing yet," said Benjamin. "We took a break after Whitely left, so we need a new player."

"Brag?" suggested James.

Cadwell raised a brow. "You whipped me soundly last time. I was hoping for Piquet or Faro."

"Any will do," offered James, "but there's too many of us now for Piquet."

Benjamin called for Brag much to James's delight, and the gentlemen settled into their thoughts while sharing gossip from town or complaining about the others' bluffs.

When Cadwell tossed down a card in frustration, he mumbled, "My sister-in-law will box my ears if I lose too much tonight."

"Don't you mean your wife?" Benjamin teased.

"Her, too, I suppose."

"I pity you, poor man," laughed James. "A new wife, mother, *and* sister. How you must miss bachelorhood and answering to your father."

"Having Miss Applewaite over my shoulder advising my wife how to manage me is almost like having my papa here."

Benjamin pretended to groan. "Your sister-in-law is handsome, Mr. Cadwell, but Miss Applewaite has frightened us since we were in strings."

James caught himself before another laugh escaped. "Now, now. At least she is not silly like the new chits coming out and too old to bother us unreliable rakes. One must admire the confidence with which she takes pleasure in her own company."

Cadwell lifted his gaze from his hand. "I do, and I appreciate even more that she's better with figures. She would probably surpass me readying for planting season if it interested her."

Benjamin leaned back in his chair. "I would have thought you'd open a shop like her papa did what with their family's connections.

"You know I am a cabinet maker's grandson," Cadwell admitted, "but I am eager to work this plot of land that passed to me after marrying my wife."

"But back to your sister-in-law," said James, for Miss Applewaite lingered in the back of his mind like a shadow. This evening he'd spied her sitting across the ballroom all alone but could not bring himself to ask her for a dance. Yet.

"Why does she esteem the gentlemen of our society so poorly? I don't recall her ever being jilted if you don't mind me saying so."

Cadwell lifted a shoulder in a mystified shrug. "She's too bookish thanks to her doting papa and possesses these wild ambitions to be a shopkeeper."

"I'd rather be out in the fresh air," Mr. McClellan interposed, "but I do admire the clever lass."

"Me, too," agreed Benjamin, "but wild, yes. She's a lady. What lady belongs in business for herself?"

McClellan quickly differed, and the game halted as the men argued like squirrels over tree nuts.

"Come now, it is admirable in its way," said James, "and things are changing."

"What kind of shop?" Benjamin wondered.

"Milliner, of course," answered Cadwell. "The Applewaite women are hounds for textiles and trimmings. How they love their hats."

"A millinery shop," mused James. "Why, there are dozens of places like that, aren't there? Though I suppose a woman's interests are more suited in that direction."

The others made noises of agreement.

"So she would rather be a milliner than a wife?" thought Benjamin aloud. He gave a short, barking laugh.

James understood what it was like to want to be something different than what everyone expected. It was no secret among his friends he'd rather be a sailor than a planter's son—a captain than an heir. But who took James Hathaway seriously? No one. Not Mama. Not even Papa. Why else would he ask James to do nothing more than call on their business associates in Charleston or pass messages back and forth between Sandy Bank and the city's Exchange where business was conducted?

"Oh, yes," muttered Cadwell over the card game, "she wants to be independent and though I don't mind, the rest of her family does. She does need to get on with it soon though—either marry or open a shop, because as much as I respect her, my hands are full."

James understood Cadwell felt burdened. He'd married into a fatherless family and taken on a widowed mother and a spinster sister-in-law. Cadwell was not the businessman his father-in-law had been, and his new mother seemed the expectant sort. Had she not convinced James's own mama to encourage him to ask Miss Applewaite to dance?

The last card was called, and James frowned. Benjamin took the win and most of James's money. He was about penniless, and it was only January.

"Blast," he muttered slumping back into his chair, but then with a good-natured sigh, he laughed along with the others. The expected dancing invitation to Miss Applewaite awaited. That would get him out of this. "If you will excuse me, gentlemen, I think I will go in search of cake and try my luck at finding a pea or a bean. At least then I may be treated like a king during this revelry."

They began to tease him about ladies lying in wait across the hall, but he pasted on a resolute grin and trotted back out into the crowd in search of cake—and Miss Applewaite.

*"Miss Applewaite? That clumsy, orange-haired thing? No one will dance with her. She'll be lucky not to end up an old maid." The girls clustered around the spinet giggled behind their hands at Alice Quinton's prediction, and Phoebe, already into her second season, fled the room she'd entered to find solace someplace else—preferably without guests.*

Phoebe blinked away the memory. Had it really been that long since cruel peers had made her abhor dancing? Nine years later, here she was among some of those very same women, and they were married and she was not. The prophecy had come true. Stunning Alice Quinton, now Mrs. Alice Leonard, had snared the wealthy Leonard widower.

Music rang out over the Heyward's drawing room, and Phoebe pretended to be entertained as she gripped the edges of her chair. It was because of Mama's insistence that she had come out at all. Yes, her hair had been rather orange as a child, but it deepened to a shade of brown by the time she became a young woman. That wasn't why she was a spinster. She was single because she was too intelligent and reasonable to marry young or on a reckless whim. And shy. Truth be told, Phoebe didn't see the point in marrying at all. Mama had not married again, and she managed just fine with Phoebe's assistance, of course.

Phoebe glanced down at her silk taffeta bodice. One of mama's old gowns, it was a bit light for winter, but she'd repaired it with lace to cover the worn edges. It looked as fashionable as anyone else's. She straightened to stretch her aching shoulders and squeezed the fan in her grip. Her spindly chair rested against the back wall just beside the warming stove so she wouldn't be in anyone's way.

Mama smiled at her from across the room, and Phoebe returned it. Winnifred chatted with her friends in a corner. Daniel was nowhere to be seen. Her brother-in-law was probably in the card room where it was much quieter. She knew he didn't have the means to be gambling; not newly married to Winnifred and with his own low country household to run. For now, they had moved to the Applewaite's land upriver at Duck Point.

With a light sigh, Phoebe watched partners dance the reel. The women gleamed like polished gems. Without examining their overskirts, she knew the very weight of the silk damask and how difficult it was to sew and clean. She also understood what colors suited which complexions best. She would. A child born with a shocking shade of orange-red hair to a fashionable and sensitive mother would have to learn what to wear to survive in elegant society.

A pair of fitted green breeches came to a stop in front of her, blocking her view of the dancing. After impeding her view for too long, Phoebe looked up at the owner with her brows raised in chastisement. To her surprise, it was Mr. James Hathaway, and she had to steady herself to keep looking severe less he see through her act.

"I've just left a game of cards, and here you are, Miss Applewaite, just as your brother said you would be." He gave her an exaggerated bow then straightened with a beguiling grin.

Ignoring the square jaw that nearly touched his earlobes, Phoebe narrowed her eyes. Mr. Hathaway had a strong chin with a deep dimple that looked like someone had pressed a butter knife into it and left an impression.

He cocked his head in inquiry, and she realized his hand hung in the air. "You won't leave me standing here like a beggar will you, Miss Applewaite? I'm happy to dance, really I am. See," he turned his head and swept his gaze around the room, "everyone else is taken."

Phoebe swallowed down the absurd invitation. "Really, Mr. Hathaway, there is no one else? You poor man."

He realized his mistake and balled his outstretched hand onto his hip while chuckling under his breath. It was almost bashful, but not believable. "I only meant, see here you are, and I would be happy to take a turn with you around the room or stretch my legs with a hearty reel. Your brother-in-law says you hardly ever get a chance to take the floor."

Phoebe felt her spine snap when she jerked her chin. "I don't dance because I don't wish to." This usually sent away pitying dandies.

All but this one. Mr. Hathaway gave her a vexing pout.

Praying she was not flushed, Phoebe added, "You haven't spoken to me in at least a year by my estimation, yet you wish to converse as if we just chatted Tuesday."

"I'm sure I've tipped my hat." Mr. Hathaway's carefree grin tightened. "No. Wait. Did I not see you wandering around near the fort just after Christmas?"

Phoebe remembered his jaunty ride past her favorite strip of beach between the wharves and Fort Wilkin to watch the ships come in. She didn't remind him that he'd asked her to dance once before and how that ended. It was probably the last time they'd ever spoken besides the other week. It'd been years. In the meantime, he'd made a scoundrel of himself flirting with several ladies he did not marry and was known to do more scraping and bowing than any actual labor in his family's brick and shipping businesses. They had two boats now. Or was it three?

She looked up and found him staring with a cheap smile that looked almost roguish. The first notes of the next dance sang out over the room, and she sighed with satisfaction thinking it too late. "On the street, perhaps. I don't recall. We're hardly more than acquainted."

"Which I was trying to repair."

Would he not go away? Phoebe's mind raced furiously for a way to avoid having to dance with such a flirtatious and unaccountable coxcomb. "You will miss the rest of your card game, Mr. Hathaway, and we cannot allow that."

His smile melted into a curious line, and Phoebe didn't miss his light exhale of relief. "You're quite right, Miss Applewaite. That does fill me with great anxiety." He smiled at her in appreciation and strode from the room. Flickering candles made streaks of brass shine in his dark blond hair as he passed through the door.

No one seemed to have noticed their exchange, Phoebe thought with relief. It was a horrible, ungracious thing to do, but surely he had not minded it.

She watched dancers sashay down the line, some with their heads thrown back with glee. Really, what was there to be so exuberant about? A ball was just noises and smells with little space to move around and even less opportunity to think. *Bah!* She'd rather be at home hemming another handkerchief as tired as she was of stitching all hours of the day.

She glanced at the far end of the room where Mama and her gaggle of friends had settled. To Phoebe's horror, they were peering at her with grim lines around their mouths. She averted her gaze, but her throat tightened with questions. Had they seen? Did they know? Was Phoebe Applewaite so far gone at twenty-six that she'd rudely refuse a wealthy gentleman a dance?

James Hathaway was older now than when he'd flirted with all of the young girls at her coming out. He still looked dashing and was very much marriageable. Even more importantly, he was heir to the Sandy Bank plantation across the river near Mount Pleasant.

She peeked at Mama again. She glowered, and Phoebe's cheeks heated with shame. What did Mama care if she danced with silly and forever single Mr. Hathaway? He was a ridiculous, irresponsible rake who'd suddenly decided to take notice of her.

The rest of the night dragged by until she could bear it no longer. Rounding up her family by claiming a headache, they ended Twelfth Night a few hours before sunup at the tall, narrow house on Beaufain Street.

Winnifred and Daniel rushed upstairs. Phoebe followed Mama into the dim parlor. It was lit only by orange swaying flames in the fireplace. Roused by their clattering noises, Charity stuck her head into the room. A few years older and still single, the Applewaite's most trusted housekeeper and maid warmed them cups of chamomile tea.

Phoebe thanked Charity as she collapsed into her favorite tufted chair by the bright fire and then urged her to go back to bed. It was almost dawn, but Phoebe was too tired to do any sewing. Just the thought of it made her eyes ache. There were other things on her mind, what with the flirtatious Mr. Hathaway bowing and scraping at her knee at the party.

Mama, she noticed, said little on the carriage ride home, even with Daniel and Winnifred in their company. Her dark-haired little sister had only spoken to ask Phoebe with a giggle why she never danced. Daniel stared then chuckled, too. Phoebe had to clench her teeth to keep from scolding the young married couple for imbibing too much punch and wine on top of trash heaps of food.

She stared into the parlor's fire and tried to relax the knot between her shoulders. Phoebe had no tolerance for bad habits, not when peace and calm were the order of the day. One could not rise to any better station in life by drinking and dancing the nights away. Her great grandparents' aristocratic blood meant nothing anymore along the rich, sandy shores of South Carolina, especially since the war. Hard work and ingenuity, if not the right connections, mattered most now. It was a new country, a new government, and a new society, where almost anyone could make their dreams come true just like Papa had imagined.

Mama shifted in the chair across from her. Phoebe chided herself for staying too long and endangering her mother's health. "You are not to bed yet? Are you well?"

"Well enough I suppose." Mama's tone sounded unusually crisp.

"Did you not enjoy the ball? I'm sorry we stayed late. I should have urged Daniel to leave sooner or made him find an old nag to see his way home while we took the carriage back earlier with Winnifred."

Mama set down her teacup with a clink on the table beside her. "I am not quite so old that I cannot stay late at a ball," she insisted. "I am only in a mood because I believe you refused to dance with a gentleman tonight after sitting so long without a partner."

"I'm sorry if I upset you, Mama," returned Phoebe. "I did not wish to dance, and you know there were younger and more eager women there than me."

"Yes," Mama agreed in a beleaguered voice, "but you are so handsome when you try, Phoebe dear. Why do you refuse to make any effort?"

Phoebe kept her gaze on the fire. Mama would not stop now; she had her undivided attention.

"You are not plain by any means and have a beautiful mind. I did not educate you for nothing, but see," Mama's tired voice cracked, "you are too overly confident in yourself and have these ridiculous ambitions that are unseemly."

"Why is it so dreadful that I wish to make my own living? To have a shop like Papa?"

"You are not your father," retorted Mama, "or a gentleman. And you certainly are not so poor you need to scrabble for a living. The only thing you need to worry about is making someone comfortable and happy."

"A pudding and a bottle of port can do that," Phoebe countered.

Mama lowered her brows the way she did when Phoebe was a girl. "I have never been more ashamed," she confessed, "to see you refuse Mr. Hathaway after all of the maneuvering I did to encourage him to invite you to dance."

Humiliation drizzled over Phoebe in an unpleasant shower. "Please tell me you did not beg Mrs. Hathaway that her son should ask me to dance again."

"Again? I only encouraged it."

"Mama!" Phoebe's teacup wobbled, and a splash of chamomile wet her best gown. "Their pity ruined my coming out the first time he was forced to dance with me. I don't need you or the Hathaways meddling in my affairs."

"Who else will do it?" Mama protested. "Is your papa here? No. And Daniel is too preoccupied with starting a plantation although he's never planted an indigo seed in his life." She slapped the arms of her chair not caring if Charity heard. "I am the only one who cares about your prospects! If you do not marry soon, you'll be a burden to your brother-in-law as I already am. Meanwhile, our house is crumbling into ruin. Do you not see the curtains? The furnishings? They're fading like..."

The firelight reflecting off of Mama's over-excited cheeks made her look a bit mad. "They're almost as old as you, Phoebe. The carriage house leaks and smells ungodly, and in my chambers, the floor is sagging worse than my chin!" She fell back in her chair spent from the outburst.

Phoebe did not smile at Mama's exaggerations. She simply wanted the most comfort and security she could attain for both her and her daughters, but she couldn't see past the old traditions and ways of how to get them.

"I am sorry, Mama." Rather than meet her eye, Phoebe studied the shadows lurking in the parlor's corners. They seemed to mock her ambitions. Was she foolish? Should she consider a preposterous bachelor or mayhap a wealthy widower if Mama would not?

No. The thought of it made her stomach fold in halves. She was sewing like mad to help make ends meet. Wasn't that enough? She would not ransom herself to escape spinsterhood or even to finance a shop.

# CHAPTER TWO

James rented quarters from a widow who'd moved across the water to Mount Pleasant to live with her son. It was a good, sturdy house with windows that overlooked the harbor. Although his family had a home in town, he'd taken up residence in the widow's fine place as soon as he was old enough to leave Sandy Bank. There was no reason to stay. His mammy had died and there was no one left to shield him from Mama's suffocating attention.

From the upstairs windows, he could see the water. Two wide rivers wrapped around each side of Charleston: on one, the Cooper River skirted inland splitting off into smaller tributaries, and to the south, the Ashley did the same. Their gray-brown waters mingled in the bay with the ocean shoving white broken shells onto light brown shores.

A summons from Papa came Wednesday, less than four days after the Twelfth Night festivities, and James clutched his head as he tipped the messenger a coin. He shuffled back to the thick cushion of the widow's best chaise lounge and threw himself down in his banyan.

Last night's visit to Benjamin had started with drinks in his room above the tavern then leaked out into the street before ending at a club where they'd argued politics, which did not interest James except for the new tariff laws. Next came stronger

**18**

drink and bets, and he lost his grandfather's gold-trimmed snuff box, of all things.

James rubbed his forehead then broke open his father's seal. As his eyes scanned the page, he groaned aloud and flopped back onto the cushions. Not again. Word had got out. How did a man so obsessed with pinching extra coin manage to concern himself with the gossip around town? Didn't his parents understand that without James and his connections, the Hathaways would not be doing nearly so well?

The family did not operate a large agricultural plantation anymore, not like in his grandfather's day. Papa had turned to brick-making when he inherited the property and then invested in shipbuilding. The Hathaways were part-owners of two vessels with another on the way.

Almost three ships! And he was not aboard any of them. His heart wilted. All his life he'd explored the creeks and rivers whenever he could escape the house. He'd paddled his pirogue up and down the waterways around Charleston for years with Benjamin at his side until his friend outgrew the taste for salty, wet adventure. Later, Papa allowed him to take several voyages alongside him on the *Magnolia*. James had practically grown into manhood aboard the family's wooden vessels, and like the pirogue, they'd carried him far from mothers and mammies and blasted physicians, and his health bloomed. The sun and the sea cured him. He believed that with all his heart.

With a sigh, James crawled to his feet. He took his time dressing, waiting for his hired valet to slink upstairs to help him shave. Afterward and feeling rather handsome, he checked his jaw in the looking glass and found himself in good looks despite the previous night's raucousness. He hummed a little ditty he'd heard on the docks as he trotted down the stairs to wish the widow's old housekeeper a good day before taking the gig across town to his parents' house.

The day felt cold even for a late January day. Thin streaks of lead-colored clouds raced across the horizon. Whitecaps rippled the water in the harbor, and fishermen's boats heaved to and fro. It looked like fun to James, and what was the worst that could happen? Overturn and swim for shore? He'd catch a chill in the freezing water and frighten his parents to death.

"That's not a bad idea," he mused aloud.

Papa kept an office near the port although Mama felt sailors, with their baggy breeches and earrings, were too rough for his company, and James's, too. Pity, she did not understand his time aboard the *Magnolia* with Papa had been spent in their company where he'd been taught the ropes. He did love the order and activity of a vessel where every man knew his duty, his shift, and his hammock. There was nothing to hold one back but the weather gauge.

With growing courage, James stopped the gig along the docks and leaped to the ground determined to defend himself. He was doing nothing in the evenings less important than running communiques. He made connections in the card rooms, encouraged merchants to consider renting space on his family's ships, and made sure everyone knew the Hathaways and their partners did business above the board. Quality handling and safe deliveries were their primary aim.

He strode in with his chin up, expecting to find Papa waiting. His private secretary was in and motioned toward the Hathaway's office. With a grin, James straightened his coat and touched his cravat, and then gave a brisk knock.

"Yes," came Papa's patient voice.

James smiled at his serious, friendly tone, and let himself in. "Good morning."

"It's afternoon, James, and we expected you earlier."

James flopped down onto a narrow chair across from the small desk. He gave a flippant wave of his gloved hand. "I only just received your message, and here I am though I'd planned to ride out to the Quintons with Benjamin today. Did you know they are tilling up the indigo fields to try their hand at cotton this year?"

Hugh Hathaway glanced up from his ledgers. Like James, he was not exceptionally large but solidly built with a fine head of dark hair just beginning to gray at the temples. James admired the look. Bright, intelligent eyes hinted at the ability to carry on fascinating conversations. James envied that, too. A sensible man, his papa was patient and genteel in every way and loved for it. Especially by James.

"Cotton grows well enough but there is the labor to consider."

James nodded in agreement.

"But that is not why I asked you here." Mr. Hathaway removed a wiry pair of spectacles from his face. "I saw Mr. Whitely yesterday and understand you were at Shepheard's tavern until late."

Even as his stomach clenched, James shrugged. "Benji and I had drinks there and stayed for cards."

"You lost a great deal." Mr. Hathaway gave him a tired, disappointed stare, and James looked away. How could he possibly know about Grandfather's snuff box? "It was only a bit of fun, Papa, and yes, there was that unfortunate outcome."

"And the marching up and down the cobblestones chanting like deckhands until the authorities were called?"

James felt his cheeks color. "I drank a bit in excess."

Papa exhaled and dropped his gaze to the papers before him.

"I'm sorry, Papa. One must keep his companions entertained, and I did all but convince Mr. Whitely to consider us this year when the rice is harvested."

"Yes, we spoke," said Papa, but it sounded tinged with mild sarcasm. He folded his arms in front of him, and James met his steady gaze. It would be the same old scolding, although this time he probably deserved it.

"I want you to attend a dinner party this Saturday next. Your mother and I, as well as you, have been invited."

James gaped. He wasn't expecting this sort of punishment. "I did not receive an invitation to a dinner that I remember."

"Perhaps it's best that yours came to the house. Mrs. Hathaway has become very good friends with Mrs. McClellan, as you know, and I find the husband good company and an outstanding businessman."

"The merchant McClellans," mused James. Mr. McClellan was a great deal of boisterous fun in the card room. "That's it then?" It seemed a mild punishment for having his way about town, but his antics were nothing new. Heaven knew he meant no harm by it.

"The Applewaites will be there as well, I am told."

"Oh? And Mr. Cadwell—the son-in-law? We played a few rounds on Twelfth Night."

"So I hear." Mr. Hathaway took another breath. "No, it is only Mrs. Applewaite and her daughter who will be there, the unmarried one. They are special friends of Mrs. McClellan, and of course, your mama is fond of the widow."

"Hmm, yes, they seem to have become very good friends of late."

Papa had once done business with the late Mr. Applewaite. Their wives had remained friendly. James pictured the daughter—the very bold woman who about told him to take a dunk in the harbor when he'd asked her to dance. He grinned. "I know the daughter a little. She's not an eager conversationalist."

"Well," said Papa with a dip of his chin, "I expect you to remedy that and make her feel comfortable."

James inclined his head. "Me? It's not my party, but—"

Papa's meaningful look tripped him up.

"You want me to..."

Papa clasped his hands over the desk in a tight grip. "James, your mother and I are long past lecturing you. She is exhausted, and I am quite done. You are our only child, and our expectations haven't changed."

James blinked, quite unsure of what he meant.

"Your mama and I have decided it is time for you to settle whether you feel prepared for it or not."

James felt his jaw slacken. He'd heard this threat before, but this time it sounded weightier. Papa surprised him further by saying, "You cannot take on the family business until you are settled, and Mrs. Applewaite has a handsome daughter who is in need of a husband. You should start there."

A laugh coughed out before James could stop it. "Says who? Certainly not Miss Applewaite."

"Mrs. Applewaite has had many long talks with your Mama about her anxieties over her daughter's future. I've had a word with her brother-in-law as well."

"Cadwell?"

Papa nodded. "He is pursuing the idea of starting a plantation upriver on land passed to him from his wife's family."

"Yes, indigo, I know." James's mind buzzed with the implications of his parents' wishes.

"We spoke briefly of handling his indigo cakes and then his sister-in-law. I am of the opinion it would be wise for you to consider pursuing Miss Applewaite. She has a small dowry of land up the Ashley River as well, and she is—"

"I have no interest in marriage," interrupted James, "or land upriver." His hands jerked on reins that did not exist until he remembered he was not in the gig.

"Yes, I know," said Papa, "and that's why I called you here. It's time. If you cannot make your own choice, then as your father, I must encourage you to listen to your mama's advice."

"Nonsense," said James in a weak laugh.

Papa's razor-like stare did not look nonsensical.

"I mean no disrespect," James amended.

"You will soon be twenty-nine and then thirty by and by. I've decided you may partner with me here in the shipping company since you do not like the brickyard, but first, you must find a wife and start a family. It's time. You've let too many eligible ladies slip through your fingers."

"But Miss Applewaite?" sniped James.

"Anyone of good character and family will do. It's time to settle down."

"I don't want to work in an office or spend my life in a study," James reminded him. It was an old and rather tiring discussion. "Please, Papa. Give me a chance aboard a ship. You know I would make a better captain than a board member. Let me go to sea."

"James," said Papa in a tired voice. "I cannot trust you with a month's allowance, and you want to sail one of our ships?"

"I know I can do it." Feeling a surge of hope that maybe this time he would listen, James leaned forward in his chair. "I have more time on the books than any of the other investors, yet I always sail as a guest or advisor if I'm allowed aboard at all. I don't need to guard cargo or observe the crew. Let me lead them. You know I can sail."

Papa sighed. "There are midshipmen in the harbor with more experience than you."

"I have plenty of experience, and that's not true. If it wasn't for..."

James stopped. He'd almost revealed his bitterness toward Mama for locking him away for so long and keeping him from doing what he'd dreamed about. He would have been a fabulous midshipman in the Continental Navy, but they'd tucked him away during the war. It was his responsibility to carry on the family name, and the weight of it was too much for him to bear.

"I'm sorry, but you haven't proven yourself anymore capable of managing a ship than you are this office. Settle down," Papa advised with a sage dip of his chin, "and give yourself time."

James felt his shoulders slump as he sank in his chair. Why had he allowed himself to think anything had changed? "What good is it to chain me to some miserable, sharp-tongued spin-ster if it's not going to advance my own wishes?"

"Come to the dinner party," Papa encouraged him, "and entertain Miss Applewaite. Perhaps, after getting to know her better, you'll feel differently."

James felt his nose wrinkle. "She doesn't like me, Papa. She doesn't like anyone. It's a waste of time."

With a good-natured tone returning to his voice, Papa replied, "If you will court her or anyone else in Charleston of good family, it would please your Mama. And if your mama is pleased, so am I."

"Would you think more on it then?" James implored, un-able to stop himself from making one last attempt to get a posi-tion at sea. "Consider giving me command of one of the ships, or just get me aboard, and I'll find someone to be attentive to or at least be friendly to Miss Applewaite."

Papa stared in surprise at the blackmail-like offer, but James told himself it was only bartering. He just had to find someone to carry on a mild flirtation with until he got what he wanted.

After a long hesitation, Papa said in a tender tone, "If you can convince that intelligent, industrious, and rather pretty girl to pay you any mind, I'd consider recommending it. Perchance, she will be a good influence."

James could hardly believe his ears. He jumped to his feet and found his legs weak like jelly. A ship. His very own. He would do anything—even pander to the serious and rather mean Applewaite spinster. "Papa, I will see you on Saturday."

DINNER AT THE MCCLELLAN house was a rather formal affair for a chilly and wet January afternoon. There was no cold fish or ham but a delicious cut of venison with chicken and pheasant. Phoebe tossed honey-coated carrots around on her plate avoiding eye contact with the younger Mr. Hathaway. He had, for some reason, been seated right beside her, glistening in a royal blue brocade that made his green eyes brighter.

It was exasperating, considering before the meal he whirled around the drawing room smiling and bowing to his parents' friends before taking a stance beside her at the window. He then proceeded to flood her with inconsequential questions about weather and the previous Twelfth Night ball until she thought she would flop to the floor. She couldn't believe this was the young man she'd pined for so many seasons ago until she came to her senses. It didn't escape her notice that they were among the youngest guests there, either.

Mortified, Phoebe took miniature bites and chewed at length to keep her mouth full. The man beside her kept every-one entertained. He was as full of wit as he was air. Every time she glanced at Mama, she found her looking delighted at Mr. Hathaway's exaggerated humors.

"And then," he cried, putting an elbow on the table and leaning forward, "Mr. Quinton reached up to slap a branch overhead to celebrate his victory, but his sleeve became tangled up on a knot or something, so his mount when on without him to finish the race!" He cackled along with the other guests. "So, I won after all."

"Upon my word," chuckled Mrs. McClellan, her powdered hair trembling on her crown, "he's lucky he did not break an arm or a leg."

"It'll be his neck someday," murmured one of the other gentlemen.

Mrs. Hathaway bobbed her chin in agreement. "Mr. Quinton is a little too adventurous for his own good. It is lucky he did not maim himself." She gave her son a serious frown. "You are fortunate you did not come to harm yourself, darling boy."

"Yes, how would we all have managed?" murmured his father.

Amused, Phoebe caught the elder Mr. Hathaway studying her. His eyes brightened when Phoebe met them, and the corners of his mouth turned up. Phoebe shifted her gaze and grimaced inside.

"Miss Applewaite?"

She turned her attention to Mr. McClellan at the head of the table. His musical words carried the sounds of his Scottish legacy along like a pleasant song, and he sported the most fascinating thick mustache curled neatly at the ends.

"I understand you have a talent for predicting fashions?"

She gave him a questioning look. Certainly her gown tonight, far too leisurely for a dinner party and several years old, did not hint she was a woman of great income.

"I only mean I was at the tailor's this week past, and he mentioned you offered your confident opinion about a silk he'd chosen for new banyans."

Phoebe did not dare look at Mama as their host continued. "You informed him it would be much better suited for gowns and waistcoats, and he found in the end that you were right."

"My daughter enjoys fabrics and trimmings," blurted Mama. Her cheeks flushed, probably at Phoebe's audacity in telling a tailor his business or perhaps because she'd visited the tailor to sell their embroidered handkerchiefs and fichus.

"I do appreciate the textiles in Mr. Payne's shop although I'm fonder of the mantua-maker's windows," Phoebe explained.

"And we only have one of any worth in this port," insisted Mrs. Hathaway. "She is always scheduled weeks ahead and makes no time for my urgent requests." She gave a pert frown at the inconvenience.

"But you always look so lovely," Mama assured her.

While everyone gazed at Mrs. Hathaway with agreeable smiles, her son gave Phoebe a closer examination she did not like. True, he smelled rather pleasant and had good manners, and of course, he was as pleasing as ever to look at, but she did not want to be studied by the likes of him.

"Do you enjoy your needlepoint then? I'd wager you're quite good."

*Why is that?* she wished to ask but did not. She looked back at her carrots. "My needlepoint is passable, Mr. Hathaway," she replied.

"Oh come now," he prodded, "you are fond of textiles, so you must make the finest pillows in Charleston."

"My mother does," said Phoebe, annoyed at his false compliment. It shifted the attention to Mama, who beamed. "It's true," Phoebe insisted.

"Like mother-like daughter," declared Mr. McClellan, and he winked at her.

Phoebe smiled back. If they only knew that it was more, "like father-like daughter." Her mother had been a delightful, social young woman, happy with her near-love match and a marriage strongly encouraged by her grandparents. Unfortunately, Mama still embraced old traditions like romantic arrangements and found it unseemly for a woman to conduct her own business affairs.

A few glances shifted Phoebe's way, but no one asked her about "lowering" herself to an occupation such as mantua-maker. She stopped herself from snorting aloud. Someday, she'd open a shop and carry the finest silks and brocades abroad. She'd create patterns and designs, and all of Charleston would flock to her store to peruse her fichus and finely dressed hats among other things. Where was the shame in that? And why did she need a husband to do it?

She felt a soft nudge at her elbow and turned to Mr. Hathaway. His lips widened into a handsome smile, and Phoebe resisted the urge to pinch his cheek.

"May I say how comely you look tonight. Is that a new gown?"

"No," she returned in a flat tone, "it was my mother's many years ago, and I had it redone."

His embarrassed silence quieted him, and she looked back at her plate with relief. James Hathaway was so blatantly false with his attentions. How did others bear it?

After slices of warm sweet potato pie, the ladies excused themselves, and Phoebe nearly ran to the drawing room to claim her spot by the tall window that overlooked the street. The evening had settled into a pleasant shade of indigo after a final bout of misty rain.

Mrs. McClellan had fresh coffee beans from the Indies and insisted on serving everyone her best, so Phoebe accepted a cup willingly. Something warm in her hands on this damp night after all of the awkward pretenses felt rather comforting. She gripped the teacup, admiring the idyllic landscape painted in puce with a blue baroque border.

Mr. McClellan, who'd arrived from Scotland many years ago was doing well indeed. Many newcomers became merchants. The older families turned to plantations or shipbuilding. She glanced at Mrs. Hathaway dominating the conversation in Mrs. McClellan's drawing room.

As if feeling Phoebe's examination, Mrs. Hathaway settled her skirts toward the window. "Miss Applewaite, how sensible you are to wear that colorful, quilted overskirt. I do admire how well you know your brocade and silk."

"Linens and cottons, too," piped up Mama.

Mrs. Hathaway continued her study of Phoebe. "What a fine cut gown, too, although I must say a brighter blue would suit you better than flowery bouquets."

Phoebe grimaced. It was clear the fabric was old and refurbished.

"She's so inventive," Mama rushed on, "and does quick work with a needle. I have gowns that no longer suit me at all, and she has them redone in the most accommodating fashions."

"And frugal," approved Mrs. Hathaway. Her eyes seemed to calculate how serious and able of a woman Phoebe might be.

They were very rich, the Hathaways. Phoebe looked back at her coffee. At least the woman was gracious enough not to mention how her finances flourished while the Applewaites' had declined. Perhaps it was the war, she surmised. It had changed everyone, no matter their situation.

"Did you see my son's waistcoat? Now that's a fine cut of cloth," Mrs. Hathaway boasted. "He's a handsome lad, I must say." The women on either side of her tittered. Phoebe swallowed so that she did not groan.

"Every girl in town has her cap set for him," agreed Mrs. McClellan.

*Yes,* thought Phoebe, *ten years ago.* She let her gaze travel around the walls and appreciate the oil portraits.

Mama spoke for her again since Phoebe would not heap any compliments upon silly Mr. Hathaway's head. "Phoebe concerns herself so much with my comfort and her sister and new brother-in-law's happiness that she hardly does anything for herself."

"How devoted," murmured Mrs. McClellan, and Mrs. Hathaway looked pleased. Instead of replying, Phoebe took a sip of her cooling beverage.

"And modest," added Mrs. Hathaway. "Come now, tell us, did you enjoy the Twelfth Night ball? I thought perhaps you were unwell."

"Yes," choked Phoebe with surprise. She prayed the woman would not interrogate her for refusing her son a dance. "I should have not gone. I felt so fatigued."

"But I dragged you out," apologized Mama.

"Oh," Phoebe soothed her, "you must not feel bad. I did enjoy the music. It cheered me to be sure. It was just a long night."

"I understand," crooned Mrs. Hathaway. Her unspoken question appeared to be answered. No one mentioned Phoebe's clumsy coming out so long ago, or that she'd rarely danced since.

"Well, there will be more balls, and the weather will improve." Mrs. Hathaway smiled. "My son will be sure to attend them, for he does love a party as we all know." She chuckled like he was the most adorable man in America. "I would not have been entertained half my life if it weren't for my dear Jamie."

Mama and Mrs. McClellan beamed, too, like he was so full of life and fun that society could not do without him. Phoebe would not agree. She might have been fooled in her youth, but she knew he was the biggest flirt in all of Charleston and positively exhausting.

Approaching voices caught their attention and like a golden leprechaun, Mr. Hathaway appeared in the room after gliding the door back effortlessly on its hinges.

"My dear!" said Mrs. Hathaway with delight, and the gentlemen filed in. The conversation turned to the upcoming season and the latest engagements, and within only a few minutes, the younger Hathaway made his way over to Phoebe's chair and tried to converse with her again.

He was so persistent. It was like someone had told him Mama had advised her to encourage his attention, or perhaps it was his revenge on her because she'd refused to dance with him at the ball. She should not have done it. It was poor mannered and abominably rude. Now, he seemed determined to win her over no matter how much it discomfited her.

After a few minutes of silence, she began to regret she felt she needed to be impolite to put him off. Phoebe raised her eyes to meet his scrutiny. "How is the shipping business, Mr. Hathaway? My brother-in-law tells me you work with your papa."

Surprised at her inquiry, he leaned forward. "I do assist him," he answered, "in a manner of ways, but I am not too often in the office."

"You like to be in the shipyard then."

"Yes, that or the Exchange," he agreed, and something curious lit his eye. "In truth, I prefer to be in the open air watching the beams come together or overseeing our vessels in the harbor."

"You manage the ships?"

Mr. Hathaway's cheeks turned a little pink. "Well, not exactly, but I do pass information from the company to our good captains—two, you know—the *Magnolia* and the *Regina,* and on occasion, I join them on short trips down to Savannah or up to Boston."

"Yes," mused Phoebe, "I know you sail. Daniel has spoken of it on occasion."

"Well, not enough," explained Mr. Hathaway as if not bored with the conversation. "Usually I find myself on a fishing boat or in a pirogue, but we have nearly finished the *Lily,* our new vessel, and will christen her shortly."

"How fortunate," said Phoebe then she looked away so she did not stare too long at his charming face. There was a swirl of classical English with a touch of Carolina countryside around his eyes and straight nose. He did not wear a wig like so many of the older gentlemen still inclined to do so, and she appreciated that. Powder made her sneeze.

"Have you ever sailed?"

She took a breath before answering. "Twice that I recall and only as far as Savannah. I'm afraid I prefer home, although I confess I've been up the Ashley on occasion to see our land there."

"And there's a house?"

"Yes, a modest home, where my sister and brother-in-law live. Although," she admitted, "it's a wild and untamed place so they often come to stay with us in town to be more comfortable."

"That I can see with the winter chill and the summer heat," mused Mr. Hathaway.

"Oh yes," Phoebe agreed. "I cannot bear it in the summer, you know. I see no reason to be hot and miserable and eaten alive by mosquitoes for no reason at all. And the alligators..." She shuddered. Few things struck more fear in Phoebe's heart than those sinister reptiles.

Her companion chuckled. "Then you are a woman about town."

"I am most happy to take a walk along the harbor wall or traipse along the seashore on a fine day."

"Is that so?"

"Yes. I like the color of the sea where it meets the horizon." Phoebe stopped herself. What was she doing going on and on like an eager young miss? She didn't care what Mr. Hathaway thought about her habits. He would not understand how the tawny color of the sand reminded her of soft buckskin breeches or that the scarlet shades of sunset's final breath over the water made her think of rich brocades.

"And what's your opinion of the lush green palmettos and lovely oaks around town?" He leaned closer, emerald eyes beaming, and she glanced heavenward. "Really, Mr. Hathaway," she said, now in full control of her emotions, "if you're trying to imply your eyes are as colorful as the trees, they're well enough I suppose, but I've never been one for green, to be honest."

He laughed at her censure, and the others in the room looked their way. A moment's silence was too much to bear for his fun-loving nature. "Miss Applewaite does not like green eyes," he revealed, pretending to look downcast, and Phoebe saw Mama's cheek twitch.

"You have the most beautiful eyes in the world. Everyone thinks so," insisted Mrs. Hathaway. She looked around the room for the other women to agree as the men laughed.

"Tell me then," said jovial Mr. McClellan with his flashing blue eyes, "what color does tempt ye?"

Phoebe flushed, mortified for Mama who looked like she might faint. Mr. Hathaway's mother did not look amused, either. With all gazes pinned on her, Phoebe struggled to think. "My father had brown eyes," she mumbled, and knowing that she did, too, she flushed. What a vain creature they must think her.

"I like brown," said Mr. Hathaway agreeably, and the weighted moment passed. With a raised brow, Mrs. Hathaway returned to her quiet conversation with her friends, but Mr. McClellan caught Phoebe's eye and smiled so wide it stretched his mustache across his cheeks. Phoebe shifted her gaze back to the window.

"Mrs. Leonard has fine russet eyes like you. Have you noticed?"

"Mmm?" Phoebe kept her gaze averted. She did not want to talk about Alice Quinton—who was Mrs. Alice Leonard these days, and she did not want to engage in anymore flirtatious talk. "Yes," she grumbled at last when it became clear he waited for a response. "And I'm sure she admired yours until you ceased your attentions."

"Well!" exclaimed Mr. Hathaway as he repositioned his stance on the waxed boards beneath his feet. She threw him a sideways glance to measure his affront but found him staring at her with a wide grin on his face. "Touché," he whispered and gave her a wink.

Phoebe realized he was in earnest of playing their mothers' game. Did he seriously mean to consider her as a bride?

# CHAPTER THREE

J ames left his top hat and gig at the house and strolled north toward the company shipyard to enjoy the city sights. Charleston flourished thanks in part to the many artisans there; from cabinet makers to blacksmiths, jewelers to clockmakers, and of course, the many bricklayers who took advantage of the bricks dried and baked on the plantations along the low country's riverbanks. The streets were cobbled with old ship's ballast and crisscrossed town in a near-perfect grid between homes reminiscent of the architecture in London after the Great Fire. Many of these fine houses lined lower Church Street, including Mr. Heyward's town house where President Washington stayed during his visit only a few years ago. What an event that had been.

Enjoying the unnaturally warm day, James pulled back the cocked hat Mr. Albermarle had given him when he was a boy. His father's manager at the shipyard had been kind to him once upon a time. Besides shipbuilding, he'd taught him his knots, how to roll canvas, and most importantly, how to read the sky and interpret the wind. Things changed as James grew and moved on to other interests and responsibilities. The man hardly noticed him at all anymore.

A swallow-tailed hawk screeched overhead, and James looked up with a faint smile. It'd wandered too far from its inland pine tree, no doubt, and was anxious to return home. "Mr. Hathaway," called a family acquaintance from horseback, and James answered with a sweeping bow and then a salute. He was rather giddy to have business at the shipyard rather than business in town.

He sighed with pleasure as he looked out over the river. The *Magnolia* was out, but the *Regina* was in. He was blessed, he knew, to have this life, family, and the means he was endowed with, but there was still one thing that eluded his grasp and made him feel lost: he wanted a ship of his own. At this point, he would jig with joy to have a fishing boat, but he was poor at saving his allowance, a terrible spendthrift.

"Young Mr. Hathaway," croaked a sailor leaning over a barrel on the quay. James gave Pitty Joe a proper nod while secretly admiring the embroidered ribbon flapping in the breeze from his cap. It read *Regina*, and knowing he was one of his father's men, he tried to act serious.

As a man prone to friendliness and pleasing others, James knew it would be an obstacle in commanding a ship, but he just knew he could manage a crew. He would not be a cold or insufferable captain. The men would love him.

A few more familiar faces called *halloo*, and James hurried down to the yard to see Mr. Albermarle with whom he had an appointment. Albermarle oversaw the yard and much of the shipbuilding.

"Mr. Albermarle," he greeted him. "You asked to see me?"

Albermarle stood with his boot on a pile of thick, twisted rope. His fists rested on his hips. The generous room in his breeches billowed in the breeze making him look fat. A red and white striped kerchief around his neck was smudged with pitch and sweat. He glanced at James with an impatient look then back to the workers putting the final finishes on *Lily's* beams amidships.

"I did receive your message day before last."

Albermarle pointed a finger at one of the carpenters and shouted, "On the level, you donkey's backside! You ain't building a crab boat, ye know!"

James cringed and waited for the supervisor to finish his glaring and huffing then said, "Albermarle. You asked me to come down."

"Yes, why, thankee Mr. Hathaway for making time to visit," Albermarle drawled as if he had not sent a harried messenger to James that morning who looked in fear of his life. "My shipment of nails did not come in. I sent for them when the order come due, but they don't have no record of you asking after 'em."

James wrinkled his forehead. Mr. Albermarle had asked him some time ago about seeing to an order of nails. His mind raced to remember the exact day in his ledger but all he could recall was the very fine sketch where he'd drawn the *Regina's* stern leaving the harbor.

"You did order the nails, didn't you?"

"Of course, I did," James fired back. "I remember speaking with Mr. Bledsoe implicitly."

Albermarle growled, "He ain't bothered to come around here or reply to my messages, so if it ain't too much trouble..."

"It's no trouble at all," said James with gnawing worry in his gut. He'd spoken to Mr. Bledsoe many times, but had he about nails?

"I don't want to bring your papa into this." Albermarle gave James another sideways scowl, and he wondered when it was the man had taken a turn and decided to dislike him so.

"I'll see right to it," said James with as much respect as he would show Papa.

Albermarle was the backbone of the company. James owed him that much, and he knew he best find out what had happened to the nails he'd been asked to order for the yard. He hurried back toward the office, nearly diverting when he saw Papa at the door.

With a sinking heart, he strode up to greet him. "Papa."

"You are just in time," said Papa, dragging him inside. "I have two items of business I need you to see to, James."

James followed him inside the room, his feet echoing off the wood boards.

"Mr. Whitely is at Swallows. I was to meet him this afternoon to discuss the rates exchange for his rice, but I have a new customer, a man from England, who is interested in investing in our services. He has goods to distribute from Cornwall and needs a merchantman to carry them to Barbados."

"That's a voyage," remarked James, and his heart flickered with hope. "I've been to Barbados several times. I know the harbor well."

"Yes," conceded Papa, brushing him off, "but I'll take care of this. It will be a new route for the *Lily* when she's finished, and I must assure him of our safety record and other satisfied customers."

James forced a soft chuckle. Begging for a place aboard the *Lily* would do him no good. "I could do it."

"I need you to see Mr. Whitely," Papa encouraged him. "He likes you, and you know the rates of the tariff increases."

"Yes," mumbled James, of course he did, because he was the one who had to share bad news with clients when Papa felt a missive would not do.

Papa put a light hand on his shoulder. "You enjoy a good drink at Swallows and company more than I. Meet with Mr. Whitely for me and give him my apologies."

A few drinks at Swallows and some conversation did not sound so bad now that James had made his obligatory visit to the yard. "We'll get the exchanges all sorted out until Whitely is satisfied," James promised. It was better than seeing Albermarle's disgruntled face.

After a pat of gratitude from his father, James hurried back into the city where he quickly changed, grabbed his deck of cards, and called for his gig to be brought around. His horse, Dogberry, was a pretty gelding he'd won in a canoe race down Rathall Creek. He spoiled the horse, silly he knew, but he felt much like Mama when he did so and a part of him understood the pleasure of loving a thing to the point of insensibility. Together, they pranced back to Broad Street where James left him with a stable boy behind the tavern.

A few pleasant drinks and a smoke with Mr. Whitely ended too soon, and pleased with the man's understanding of the company's increased charges, James wandered into the card room downstairs not surprised to find Benjamin there.

"Don't you have a plantation to run? Supplies to purchase? Why am I always the one put to work?" James pretended to complain.

"That's what overseers are for, young Hathaway," joked Benjamin. "Besides," he grumbled, "I didn't ask for it. If my father would have minded the reigns better, he wouldn't have left me with the business to manage and a shrew of a stepmother."

"Oh, yes, I'm sorry," said James, although he knew Benjamin's many sisters loved the stepmother, and he was one less now with Alice married.

*Poor Benji*. He had a great deal of money and land but preferred to travel or hunt. The only girl who'd ever caught his heart was never accessible to him, and his parents had quickly sold the dark beauty back to the Indies. Rice, indigo, and corn—whatever could be grown along the Ashley, did nothing for Benjamin but disgust him.

"You should have been a fisherman," mused James, shuffling his cards. "You paddle as fast as me, and you're not too bad on the tide."

"I prefer fishing from shore where the ladies are, thank you," said Benjamin with a pipe between his teeth. "Speaking of fishing and shrews, how did you fare at the Scot's party? Are they still trying to match you with the Applewaite girl?"

"Ah, yes, Miss Applewaite." James thumped down the cards and leaned back into the leather club chair. Thinking of her filled him with a strange mix of amusement and dread. "It wasn't as bad as you said it'd be. She didn't snarl or stab me with her scissors—she's always toting that sewing basket around with her."

"An old seamstress in the making," snorted Benjamin.

"Yes," but James shook his head, "and no. She even mentioned she did not enjoy decorating pillows. It's a means to an end, I think, with Mr. Applewaite long gone and Cadwell living out on their land. Applewaite was a successful merchant and had a shop, too, so I think she has this inkling she would do just as well."

"I hardly remember him," admitted Benjamin, "though I must say they've a fine, old house on Beaufain. Did you know I asked her to dance once when she was a young miss, and she stumbled all over my feet and blamed it on me."

"Perhaps that's why she hates dancing. It's your fault."

"Oh, no." Benjamin picked up his hand and examined the cards. "She just dislikes people in general. Besides, aren't you the one who tripped her up her first dance at Drayton Hall so badly she fell and her petticoats flew over her head?"

James burst into laughter at the very idea until it became a picture and then a memory in his mind. His cheeks warmed a little, and he put his fist under his chin to distract himself. "Why, yes, I think you're right. That was me, and that was her, the poor red-headed thing. I'd completely forgotten." He made a show of wincing. "Are you sure it was her first dance?"

Benjamin nodded. "And probably her last besides a later dance with me. I only remember it because Alice found it amusing and still talks about it."

"It is us," joked James. "We are why she hates all men." Benjamin guffawed, and James decided not to tell him that he'd had a rather friendly conversation with her by the drawing room window. That is until Mama began showering down cannonades of personal questions upon her. It all became very unnatural and awkward then, and Miss Applewaite had snapped shut like a shy marsh oyster.

PHOEBE TOOK CAREFUL steps to avoid water puddles as she shielded herself from the chilly mist. Gray clouds hung low in the sky as if about to drop. Mama would be distressed when she learned Phoebe had not dragged out the old carriage and driver, but it was only three blocks to Mr. Payne's shop, and it wasn't freezing out, just damp.

She did not want to miss her weekly appointment with the tailor. Sometimes he made a large purchase of handkerchiefs, sometimes he did not. Phoebe always gave him a simple, curt nod, letting him know it made no difference. As far as he knew, she sewed for the pleasure of it and was happy to provide him with inventory if he fancied it.

A pair of horses cantered by, and Phoebe stepped back to avoid being run down. Across the street, the coffeehouse glowed from lanterns in the windows. It looked warm and cozy inside. She and Mama rarely visited the coffeehouses unless they were invited. Instead, they kept busy at home and made calls to old friends and neighbors. Socializing in some situations was a luxury they could not afford anymore.

Most of the citizens of Charleston did not know how close to destitute the Applewaites were, else they did not care. What was left of the family income was enough to feed them, and thank heavens the properties were owned outright. Phoebe's sewing made enough difference to fill in the cracks, and she saved whatever extra she could toward the shop she would open one day.

What a struggle it was, she thought to herself. Daniel had offered to buy her land upriver from Mama when he had the money, and she liked the idea. Phoebe had no interest in living anywhere besides Charleston, and the money along with her savings would be enough for her to rent a building and get started. It was only a matter of time.

Humming as she twirled her oil-cloth umbrella in the mist, Phoebe skipped over a mucky puddle that smelled suspiciously like horse manure then turned into the doorway of a green and gold-trimmed shop. Mr. Payne was not busy but leaned over an open book. The air smelled like cotton and wool with faint whiffs of wood polish. Smoky tendrils of burning oak drifted in from the warming stove in the back.

Phoebe examined the neat shelves behind the counter filled with inventory and a nearly-finished riding jacket displayed on a brass hook in the wall.

"Oh, Miss Applewaite," said Mr. Payne when he noticed her. "Why are you out in this poor weather?"

Mr. Payne was an eccentric sort, a ruddy-cheeked man who wore a turban wrapped around his head in the most charming way. Perhaps it was a fashion she might adopt someday.

"Why, it's cleared up a bit, and I needed to stretch my legs, so I brought you a selection of handkerchiefs and a lovely fichu my mother has finished this Friday last." Phoebe set her basket of wares on the counter and lifted the piece of oilcloth that protected her goods from the rain. "See here," she said and held it up.

Mr. Payne's eyes brightened, and he picked up the fichu to touch the delicate white embroidery. "She does have a fine hand," said the tailor, "and great skill." Then the pleasure on his face collapsed, and he set it down. "I'm sorry, Miss Applewaite, but I must tell you, I have a supplier from Richmond who has sent me two dozen of the same along with a roll of Irish lace."

As Phoebe's heart sank, he rummaged through his shelves until he found what he was looking for and held up the beautiful lace. "Between this and your kerchiefs, of which I still have a half-dozen, I am beautifully set for trimmings and the like. I don't need any more of your mama's fichus, right now, although she does them up beautifully."

Phoebe's throat tightened, and she did not trust herself to speak.

"Therefore," Mr. Payne informed her with a wistful smile, "I will let you know when I run short, but for now, we are well-stocked."

She swallowed the disappointment so she could answer. "That's wonderful news. I'm glad you are doing so well."

When the tailor's gaze lingered over her, Phoebe forced herself to look mischievous. "Truly, I am, Mr. Payne. And how does your striped silk do? Was I right? Was it better for waistcoats as I suspected?"

He gave her a guilty grin. "It was indeed, and whenever I am in need of a new assistant, I must warn you I may come a-begging to your door."

Phoebe knew he assumed an Applewaite lady would not lower herself to work as a tailor's assistant. How wrong he was. She did not mind what others would say although Mama and Daniel would be unhappy. No, she admitted, as she let herself back into the wet street after saying good-bye, Mama would be ashamed and appalled.

She sniffed in disdain. How fast people adapted from digging desperately for oysters to survive a war to behaving like helpless aristocrats as soon as they had a few new gowns. A sudden gust caught up her umbrella, and lost in her thoughts,

Phoebe's slight grip did not hold. She gasped in dismay as the wind carried it off over the treetops just as the rain began to sprinkle.

"Oh," she cried, biting her tongue to stop from using unladylike words. A carriage rolled by in a hurry, and the wheel splashed into the smelly puddle she'd avoided on her way in. A spatter of mud sheared off and washed over her like an ocean wave. It doused her from shoulders to hems, smearing her face and stinging her eyes.

"Oh! *Dash* it all!" She dropped her basket in dismay then lost her hat in another draft as the rain decided to pour. "Upon my word!" she sputtered. She used the sleeve of her cloak to wipe her cheeks and bent to the ground, finding that her things had spilled from the basket.

Mama's fichu lay sprawled over the dirty, wet cobblestones turning brown. Phoebe nearly cried at the sight of it, but picked it up with a groan and carried it limply in her hands in the hammering rain to protect the other handkerchiefs in the basket. Another horse trotted by, and she heard a laugh. The gentleman, if he could be called that, gave her a nod of sympathy but did not stop and offer to help. What did she expect? She was wet and covered in filth while lingering unchaperoned in the street like a mudlark. He probably took her for a lady's maid.

She heard voices across the road and glanced up to see the Leonards departing the coffeehouse. Their shiny black carriage pulled up to the door while an onyx-skinned servant held up an unsuitable silk parasol to keep them dry. Mrs. Alice Leonard spied her through the carriage window, and her dark eyes widened in surprise. Instead of pity, her petite mouth curled into a smirk. She raised a brow at Phoebe before looking away to face forward in the carriage.

Phoebe bit down on her lip. Fighting back tears, she slapped her wet hat back onto her soaked tresses and marched home in the downpour with her ruined goods, and without any extra money for the market or her savings.

LATER THAT WEEK WHEN James arrived at the family's town house, Mama wore a slight frown on her otherwise adoring face, and he thought he detected a warning in her eyes. Papa came in a few minutes later to join them before dinner, and the tense look of his usually placid expression filled James with consternation. He was grateful he hadn't interrupted him in the study. Their local clergyman, Mr. Riley, had joined them for their Sunday meal together, an appointment that Mama zealously guarded on her schedule as if she could not get to heaven without it.

Riley asked after them, and Mama told a rather terse story about a Mrs. M. and her candle-buying habits that left the Hathaways short of their usual order. She was a Catholic, Mama reminded them all, which made James's jaw tick as he did not understand the criticism between members of the different Christian sects any more than he did animosity between the French, German, and old English citizens.

Papa remained quiet. He did not laugh when James told them about the first mate of the *Wilhelmina* falling straight over the harbor wall on Friday eve, nor did he seem pleased when James mentioned that the Whitelys had decided to send *all* of their shipments through the Hathaways' merchantmen.

He'd had a rather productive week, he thought, only slipping into the gaming rooms three times and had not lost much over-all but come out on top.

James surrendered his attempts at gaiety and let Mama and the vicar chatter about Sunday services. He had seen Miss Applewaite. Of course she would have been there, they were Protestants, too, but he had actually noticed her today which was a new occurrence. He usually did not take much notice of anyone on Sundays, only the time and the weather.

"Gentlemen." Mama thanked them with a knowing smile, and James pulled himself out of the thinking cloud where he'd stored pictures of Miss Applewaite's smooth chin and the curve of her slender neck. Her hair... Was it brown? Red? Brick? *Cinnamon*, he decided.

Chairs scraped back, and James grinned at Mama as she excused herself and then tried to follow Mr. Riley who droned on to Papa about something that could have been settled before supper. To James's relief, the man didn't stay long, and as soon as the door closed behind him, James leaned back and clutched his forehead. "Really," he said with an exasperated chuckle, "must we entertain him every Sabbath? Shouldn't we share him with the rest of the flock?"

Papa stared across his crystal goblet now empty of port. His eyes looked heavy with disappointment—an expression James knew well. His heart did its usual shrinking as he folded his arms over himself. "I mean, I know he does not come every week, but we feed the man so often. If he would marry, he would have someone at home to dine with and not rely so much upon the good members of the congregation."

Papa's brows bent slightly. "It is a kindly effort and well-meant service on your mother's part."

"Yes, of course," James agreed.

Papa's gaze lingered on him, so feeling uncomfortable and confused, James turned to the first piece of conversation he could think of. "I saw Miss Applewaite at the church meeting today. I even tipped my hat when they rode off in their little wagon, *er* or carriage, of sorts." When papa remained indifferent, James added, "She didn't look irritated at all. In fact, I think she even smiled a little, although it may have been a grimace." His own joke amused him, and he smirked.

"Good Miss Applewaite? I almost regret recommending her to you," Papa muttered.

James's eyes widened in surprise.

Papa took a quiet breath then stood behind the table and stared at the rather good painting of the *Magnolia* on her maiden voyage. She was an old girl now.

"We had a problem at the shipyard this week," said Papa with his back turned. "A problem that has held up progress on the new ship and cost us money."

Sensing the seriousness of the situation, James asked in a low whisper, "What happened?"

His father spun and leaned his upper back against the mantle. He crossed his arms over his barrel-shaped chest. "Why, we ran out of nails, James. Nails, of all things."

James blinked.

"Albemarle warned me weeks ago, and if my memory and ledgers are not mistaken, you were tasked with making sure the blacksmith received the order."

The foggy recollection of intending to leave the shipyard to check his ledgers and call on the blacksmith about the nails rose in James's mind. He tried to pick up the loose ends of that day, but it faded into a swirl of confusion. Yes, he had talked with Albermarle but... He closed his eyes and rubbed his forehead. Yes, he was supposed to check his books. Had he ordered them after all? He had not checked back with the blacksmith, had he? He strained his mind to remember some worthwhile detail.

"Ah," he said looking up with relief when it came to him, "and then you asked me to meet with Mr. Whitely at Swallows. Do you recall?" He met Papa's gaze hoping for forgiveness.

Mr. Hathaway looked grim. "I sent a courier to the blacksmith yesterday and heard back before nightfall. You never made the order at all, nor did you follow up, but you assured Albermarle that you'd fulfilled his request."

Anxiety tossed a barrel of stones into James's chest, making his supper feel like flint in his gut. "I'm sure I did," he stammered. "I mean, I intended to check to make sure I hadn't forgotten, but—"

"Let me refresh your memory." Papa pulled his chair out and took a seat again. He clasped his hands in front of him on the polished mahogany table. "You beat Mr. Quinton in a horserace, I recall, the day you were sent to make the order. Let us presume that you were sidetracked from your duty and never wrote it down. Then, last week when you were advised to examine your books and check on the order, you visited with Mr. Whitely for a bit before spending the remaining evening in the tavern playing cards with Mr. Quinton until you made your way over to the docks to make bets on cockfights."

James tried to look sheepish. When it was put this way he sounded like an irresponsible idiot. "I did what you asked me to do, Papa, but yes, the evenings I like to think of as mine, and I did throw a few notes down."

Papa's cheeks became rather pale, and anger flickered in his gray eyes like lightning in a storm cloud. "I've warned you about your gambling and debts, and worse, the betting on dockside cockfighting. Your mama would faint with disgust."

James dropped in his chair. Animal fighting actually turned his stomach so much he hung back in the crowd, but other people accepted it as a gentlemanly pursuit, and he couldn't resist a bet.

Papa held him prisoner with a cold gaze. "While you've done us no real shame, you continue to embarrass your Mama with your excess and exploits around town, and now you've put the *Lily* behind schedule."

"I'm sorry, Papa," said James, mortified that he'd lost an order and put work on the *Lily* on hold. Papa and the brick and shipping businesses lived and died by schedules.

His father exhaled with great patience then gave James a grim look. "Your irresponsibility has cost us several weeks' delay and pay for our men. The *Lily's* christening will be postponed, and if we are affected by any more poor weather, we could miss the maiden voyage and let down other investors and clients." He gave James a deep frown that burned like a branding iron.

James swallowed as his chest stung with pain. He might as well be tarred and feathered. He couldn't think of anything encouraging or cheerful to say; there were certainly no jokes to tell. Forcing himself to offer some excuse, he said, "It slipped my mind. You're right. Twice. I've been distracted, more than ever I suppose, but I—"

"No more excuses, James." Papa breathed heavily now. His disappointment felt so palpable it made James want to run from the room. "I'm afraid I must let you go and hire someone else to represent us in town and at the Exchange. There will be a cut in your allowance."

The cut was painful, but being let go from his own family's shipping company felt humiliating. "Papa." James straightened and gave him a serious stare. "You know I am a good card when it comes to advertising the company. I can entertain and make a deal—discreetly. I'm very convincing."

"It's not your convincing that's the problem," said Mr. Hathaway. "It's your accountability and your behavior after hours."

The room became hot. James put his hands down and gripped the seat of his chair. He would never sail a ship now. He couldn't be trusted to carry an order from the shipyard to the other side of town. His jaw tightened.

"If you wish to stay on you may join Albermarle in the ship-yard."

"What?"

"As his assistant."

"Assistant?" James realized he would get dirty and work with his hands, which he rather enjoyed, but no more fine waistcoats or breeches. Then there was Albermarle's grumpy face. "I was tasked with that by the time I was twelve and mastered it by fourteen. Why, I—"

"That's your only option, I'm afraid," Papa informed him in a low tone. "It's that or the brickyard."

James detested making bricks, or rather, watching his father's "people" make them. That also meant being back home under Mama's wing. "What about..." James could not bring himself to say *ship*. "I can sail. Hire me as a deckhand, or—"

"No," interrupted Papa. "You'd be given special treatment whether you looked for it or not, and God knows how you'd represent us in the ports."

James sat back, stung.

"For the time being, you will assist Mr. Albermarle in the shipyard. Perhaps in time, should you develop a more professional and serious air, you can transfer to the office and work under me. Byers is close to retirement."

*A private secretary?* "Papa, I—"

"I refuse to discuss this any further. Your mama and Albermarle are in agreement."

They sat in silence until James looked away unable to bear any more condemnation. "Well, then," he said rising from his chair, "I will be in the yard first thing in the morning."

"See you're on time," warned Papa.

James's head buzzed with indignation. How had he messed up so badly this time? It was just a horserace that day, and smart, handsome Dogberry had won it.

"And James?"

He turned at the open door of the dining room and gave Papa one last look.

"If I had it my way, you wouldn't work for the company at all, but be shipped back to your room at Sandy Bank and put under lock and key."

AFTER A WEEK FETCHING like a dog for Mr. Albermarle, James rode Dogberry south several miles along the shoreline until he reached the streets of Charleston and the solitude of his rented house. He'd washed up in the back of the shipyard office, but his wrists and boots were still dotted with sticky, black pitch. He didn't mind his wind-chafed face or even the splinters, but his muscles ached and his backbone felt like there were pieces out of place.

He slipped upstairs after a quick greeting to the house-keeper in the petite drawing room overlooking the street. Deciding to leave his rather unreliable valet out of it, he packed his things. There was not enough money with a cut in his allowance to stay in this luxurious abode. He could rent a room over one of the taverns, which he preferred, or return home to his wing of the house. It would be better for Dogberry, but he hesitated to give up.

Of course, Mama had suggested he return to Sandy Bank with her, although it was hours across the river from the ship-yard depending on the tide. She'd also mentioned how it'd please their Mount Pleasant visitors who would come to call once she returned from Charleston. He knew she meant her friends, especially the ones with marriageable daughters. He flopped down in his chaise by the window and looked out over the water as far as he could see. The ocean view would be missed.

A message came to the door: Benjamin wanted to meet him at McCrady's tavern to share a pint. He bit his lip, knowing a pint could easily turn into a cask's worth in Benji's company, but he felt thirsty and dull. It was too quiet after hearing the wind and the hammering at the yard, not to mention Albermarle's loud, disgusted shouts.

After washing up again, James re-dressed himself, struggling with the cravat until it looked passable then hurried out to his fatigued mount. There would be no gig tonight; he did not have the desire or patience. Together under the fading sun, horse and master cantered back up East Bay from whence they'd come with a cold February sea gust chilling them to the bone.

As James rounded the corner to McCrady's busy street, he spied Daniel Cadwell and his sister-in-law. They came out of one of the shops, and a rather poorly-conditioned carriage seemed to be their destination.

He watched the lady. Most of the women he knew would sit down on the cobblestones before riding in such an antique around town, but Miss Applewaite didn't seem to mind. A boy from the stable took his reigns and led Dogberry off, but instead of walking down the tavern steps, James found himself striding across the street toward the brother and sister.

"Mr. Hathaway," bowed Cadwell.

James smiled. The sister-in-law dropped back behind them, watching from under the brim of a felt riding hat. He doffed his own and bent slightly. "Miss Applewaite. How do you do this chilly afternoon?"

Her dark brows raised, and James noticed her eyelashes were quite long, fanning across her brow bones as her pretty round eyes widened. "I'm quite well, Mr. Hathaway, and I don't mind a little cool weather."

He chuckled and admired her cloak. "If I had a cloak as fine as that, I'm sure I'd be less inclined to complain."

The corner of her mouth contracted. He wondered if she was making fun of him for attempting to make polite conversation even though he should not force her to stand and talk in the streets. He turned back to Cadwell, who watched his sister with a curious expression. "Are you coming in," James wondered, motioning toward the tavern with a tilt of his chin.

The man glanced at Miss Applewaite then shook his head. "No, not tonight."

Oh yes, he was married, James recalled. The poor dupe. Cadwell motioned back toward the storefront. "I was inquiring about seed, and Phoebe came with me to... Well, she had business of her own."

"Indeed?" James raised his brows to tease her a little although he remembered her interest in such affairs. He noticed she wore an attractive but sensible gown under her cloak, dark blue and rather loose. It looked heavy and warm and was probably pleated nicely between her shoulders. He blinked to clear his head when he caught himself thinking about her back.

She met his gaze without wavering. "I sell embroidered handkerchiefs to some of the shopkeepers in town on occasion."

"How very industrious." James wasn't teasing now. With his reduced income, he suddenly felt for her situation and admired her pride in her skills.

"Yes, well," said Cadwell with an awkward chuckle, "she likes to keep busy."

Miss Applewaite glanced at her brother-in-law as if his words annoyed her then returned to James's examination. "I see you will be joining the festivities at McCrady's."

He grinned at her attempted censure. "There is going to be a little play tonight."

"Oh?"

"Yes, I thought you had come to see it with your brother."

"No, we have business to finish as he said, and we're trying to get home by twilight." The horse harnessed to their carriage pitched around as if calling them to hurry. Cadwell excused himself and rushed over to see to it. Alone with James, Miss Applewaite didn't look certain what to do next.

"I hope your day was productive then." He offered a gloved hand, relieved that he'd worn them.

"Well enough," said Miss Applewaite.

She was so serious, so business-like. How could he ever win her over enough to satisfy his parents? Surely a proposal from him would be refused faster than a runaway horse. He could not even seem to make her like him as an acquaintance. "Tell me," James said on a whim, "do you ever sell them to single individuals?"

Her mouth pinched again like she was fighting a smile. "Are you in need of a pretty handkerchief, Mr. Hathaway? Or perhaps a lace-trimmed fichu would do?"

He laughed, impressed at her wit, and to his delight, her full lips widened into a broad smile that rounded the apples of her cheeks. James put a hand on his hip. "I dare say my trunks are heaping with fichus, but I was thinking about my Mama. I will see her in the morning to say good-bye, for she is returning to Sandy Bank soon, and it would make her quite happy to have something dainty and new to take along."

"I imagine so," Miss Applewaite agreed. Her eyes looked almost ebony in the fading daylight, but they still glinted with good humor. Torches lit up and down the street did not dance half so much.

After a small hesitation, the woman slid the basket off her arm and pulled back a coverlet. Her mitts stirred around in its depths until she pulled out a square piece of neatly folded linen with her fingertips. "This one has a lovely block flowered print that I've embroidered with curling vines. I daresay she'll admire the colors."

He took it from her and pretended to examine it although his mind was already made up. "And how much do you charge?" he asked, curious as to how savvy a vendor she would be.

"Three shillings," she said meeting his eye. "It's fine quality as you can see and a new cut of cloth, not a remnant that has been redone." A soft smile touched her lips, and he realized this was her attempt at humor—subtle with a point.

"That will do." He reached into his coat pocket, and they exchanged coin and kerchief. She seemed pleased, but he wasn't certain. As for himself, James felt curiously satisfied. "My mother will be delighted," he promised her, and she granted him another smile.

"She's complimented me on my embroidery, so I hope she is happy with it."

"You are an extraordinary artisan," said James then he realized he must not overdo it. She wasn't the sort that appreciated half-hearted compliments. "What I mean is..."

"I know what you meant," she said, her mouth sinking into its usual serious line, "and thank you."

"I was just trying to say that I admire your industry and ambition with something you enjoy."

"Oh," she said, with a small shake of her head, "I don't enjoy it."

"You don't?"

"Small and tedious detail? No. Sewing gives me headaches, painful ones. Really I find it difficult, although the final product pleases me. It's just a means to an end..." she said, fading off.

He'd been right after all. Almost word for word. "You intend to be a shopkeeper—to sell pretty hats and pretty silks and trimmings."

"You've heard?"

"I believe your brother-in-law once mentioned it." James appraised the felt hat she wore with its cheerful cluster of curled ribbons pinned to the crown. It framed her face which looked rather handsome flushed from the cold.

She eyed him for his examination.

"You do wear the most cheerful hats," he stammered and touched his own which was not quite warm enough for the weather. Then Cadwell approached, much to James's regret, for he was rather enjoying the chat with Miss Applewaite. He'd never known her to speak intimately to anyone of his close acquaintance. She preferred to hide behind warming stoves or in drawing room corners.

"We must go now, Phoebe, before your Mama thinks we are lost."

"Yes, and the cold is coming on," James agreed with a shiver. He looked around. Dusk had fallen over them and brightened the street torches' flickering flames.

"Enjoy your play, Mr. Hathaway," said Miss Applewaite in a pleasant tone as her brother led her to the carriage.

James quickly bowed then crossed the street with his mother's new handkerchief clutched in his fingers. "Good evening then, Applewaites," he called with enthusiasm he had not felt since facing Papa's quiet wrath in the dining room.

# CHAPTER FOUR

There was something pleasing about sunshine on a cool day, Phoebe mused, as she climbed the narrow stairs to her bed chambers. She found it necessary to stop at every window and press her forehead to the glass. White tufted clouds rolled across the blue sky, and birdsong made her realize it would not be long until the weather stayed decidedly warm and springtime *chasséd* in. Down in the narrow courtyard, cabbages in the vegetable patch were sprouting.

Phoebe tried to ignore the flaws. She knew if she looked hard enough she'd see white paint peeling in the corners of the eaves and under the windows. The iron railing on the upstairs porch leaned a little to the left.

She sighed, thankful that winter's blusters could soon be forgotten. It would make conducting business in the market easier, and of course, the parlor would be brighter for her sewing. She'd only managed two new handkerchiefs in the last week with her mind distracted by the dwindling food in the cellar and the household inventory lists. Thank goodness for their recent sales since Mr. Payne had declined the latest offerings.

She appreciated Mr. Hathaway's small purchase but had felt mortified at the time, certain he'd only bought it out of pity. She must have looked like an urchin standing in the street with her basket of delicate wares.

Not to be outdone, Mrs. Hathaway called on Mama just after her son bought the handkerchief from Phoebe. She bit her lip and thought with gratitude of Mrs. Hathaway's request for a fichu with the same embroidery, and Mama quickly agreed. As they were friends, Mrs. Hathaway gently suggested that she trade them two crocks of muscadine jam which was just as good as a few coins. As far as heaping Phoebe with praise, she only asked once if Phoebe enjoyed her brief visit with her son. She told her yes.

A door shut, and Phoebe jumped and grinned at Charity who hurried past her down the stairs. Phoebe slipped inside her room. Outside, a bird cooed, and she wondered if mourning doves were nesting in the eaves again. They were her favorite neighbors during the summer months. With a contented sigh, she turned to the bed where Charity had laid out her gown for Mr. Whitely's birthday party. His wife was throwing an extravagant gathering, and despite Phoebe's dread of singing and dancing, she looked forward to the dinner service.

Perhaps Mr. Hathaway would be there. She did not mind him so much now that he'd showed her a rather friendly and thoughtful side. Still, she suspected he would burst into gales of laughter and tease her relentlessly if she confided in him that she'd once been besotted by his bright smile and emerald eyes. With a nibble on her bottom lip, she worried that it might happen again.

Phoebe slid her fingers across the luxurious fabric of the gown. Daniel had bought a bolt of it for his bride, and Winnifred had cut Phoebe just enough to make a lovely robe and stomacher. An older underskirt and petticoat had been dyed a soft pink, and with some lace and ruffles from an older gown, she and Mama made a lovely set of clothes that looked perfect for a dance around the Maypole. She wouldn't wait that long to wear it though.

"I do declare," said Mama that evening as the rickety carriage rattled toward the Whitely home, "your hair is as lovely as ever."

Self-conscious, Phoebe patted the curls pinned up under her hat. She knew herself to have been a homely child because of all of the teasing over her orange, curly hair, but thank the good Lord, it'd darkened to an acceptable burnished brown now that looked scarlet in the sunshine.

Phoebe smiled. "It hardly coils anymore, not that I miss having it stick out in all directions like a lion." They had a good giggle until Mama complained hers was thinning at the crown, but before she could talk herself into hysterics, they were helped down from the carriage and into the house.

All of their friends were there. Those who would not attend dinner would crowd into the rooms later for dancing and punch. Phoebe listened to the words lofted around her as she concentrated on the turtle soup, oysters, and trout, and she answered all of her companion's questions—the young Miss Whitely, who had just come out—in-between delectable bites of steamed sweet potato and stewed corn. Just when she thought she'd have to loosen her stays, the ladies stood to retire to Mrs. Whitely's private parlor.

Phoebe stood at the small parlor window and watched the street swell with horses, carriages, and people who'd walked to the party. She could almost feel the house groaning to fit in all of the Whitelys' company. Even without anyone touching her, she felt crushed against the window panes, separated from all of the buzzing conversations like she was trapped alone in a glass jar.

As the party progressed, merchants and shopkeepers, officers and plantation owners, laughed and called loudly one to another from room to room. When the music began to play, the mass of friends drifted upstairs toward the drawing room's dancing, and Phoebe sighed with relief that she could take a chair now and just breathe. Forcing her mind to concentrate on the hordes of people around her drained her like a canal.

She scooted down into a soft velvet chair pushed against the wall and sat back to watch the candles flicker as guests tramped in and out the front door. Her full stomach and the warmth of the room tempted her to close her eyes, so she tried to concentrate on a beautiful walnut clock on the mantel. A jocular laugh from the hall stole her attention. Almost annoyed at the distraction, she caught herself gaping when James Hathaway trotted into the room.

"Mrs. Applewaite!" he said in delight, and Phoebe braced herself before she realized he was addressing Mama in the opposite corner.

Mama snuck a peek across the room at Phoebe. *Oh, no.* Mama had rattled on for days, glorifying Mr. Hathaway with ridiculous amounts of praise for purchasing the handkerchief until Phoebe wanted to walk out of the room every time she heard his name.

Mama's companion, Mrs. McClellan, looked up with a flattered smile and conversed with Mr. Hathaway for a few minutes while Phoebe returned to the window, or at least as much of it as she could see while sitting in her low chair.

She hoped he would not notice her gown or her attempts to fashion her hair prettily. He was so inclined to be delighted and loud over every little thing he would draw the attention of everyone in the house to her appearance. Several moments went by without hearing his booming tone in her ear, and her shoulders relaxed. She looked back at Mama with relief, but Mama was whispering to Mrs. McClellan again from behind an open fan.

On the other side of the fire, just a few feet away from them, Mr. Hathaway leaned against the mantel with a hand on his hip staring at Phoebe like he was in a trance. It was so pointed and obvious it made her blush, and the others in the room who noticed burst into guffaws at her surprise.

Phoebe forced herself to smile so she did not look grumpy. He laughed suddenly, clapped his hands, and strode across the room. "Miss Applewaite, I am only teasing," he said with his charming grin. He gave her a bow, and she resisted the urge to groan. He was so friendly it was exhausting, and he was exhausting because he was so...

She looked up into his pleasant face. His green eyes glowed with some unconfessed thought. She wasn't sure, but they looked somewhat hesitant instead of flashing with obliged charm and enthusiasm. It made her warm and calmed her nerves in some odd way.

She widened her smile. "Mr. Hathaway, I'm sorry, I did not mean to stare. You caught me off my guard."

"Oh, I entirely meant to stare," he laughed, and she caught her lips twitching. "But I'm only joking," he added, moving near the window to lean against it. "I'm surprised to see you here, although I know you are friends with the Whitelys."

"Yes," said Phoebe. "My father and Mr. Whitely were friends. He did business with them."

"Your shop, you mean?"

"My papa's dry goods store."

"That explains why I seldom see your mother without Mrs. Whitely or Mrs. McClellan at her side—besides yourself."

"Well, it's just Mama and me now since Daniel and Winnifred have returned to the house upriver, not that I mind it."

He pursed his lips. "What a good situation that you enjoy each other's company so."

"Yes, I suppose..." Phoebe could not explain exactly how they'd become close as mother and daughter since Papa's death, nor how their friendship had become strained with Daniel and Winnifred staying often at the house.

"She says you do not ship your lovely handkerchiefs out," added Mr. Hathaway with a curious look. "I just assumed since your papa shipped with the McClellans once upon a time, they sold your goods for you as well."

"What? Oh no." Phoebe smiled at his erroneous thinking. "We do not make enough handkerchiefs to export out of Charleston. It is just Mama and me. Our little hobby." She wondered if this was a lie. It wasn't a very good one. "Besides, anyone can hem a handkerchief. I'm sure there's no great demand in other cities."

"Oh, I see. Pity then." Mr. Hathaway lifted his brows. "But you are not thinking outside of our waters. The West Indies is in want of anything and everything from the colonies."

He folded his arms, and Phoebe watched with interest as his rather social expression shifted into the more intimate and serious countenance she had begun to notice with him. "We ship to the Indies, you know," he said dipping his head when their eyes met. Phoebe glanced away. It was too difficult not to admire him standing so close because there was little to dislike on the outside.

"Why, even if you only had a dozen, one of our ships could carry them down for you. They'd be easy to sell off and at twice the price you ask here."

"Really?" Phoebe sat up taller in her chair. "Don't most textiles and trimmings come from England and France or the East Indies? What would they want from Charleston besides cotton and livestock?"

"Well," said Mr. Hathaway looking very serious, "they make their own indigo, of course, but are happy to take in linen, wool, and yes, cotton. A few pretty aprons and handkerchiefs wouldn't be as costly as East Indian silk or muslin, and besides, they hold up better if you ask me."

She wondered how he knew, usually dressed in such fine breeches and waistcoats. As if hearing her thoughts, he leaned closer and grinned. "I don't always wear silk and damask."

"Do you not?" she wondered. He glanced around the room. She thought he might sit down across from her, but instead he stepped closer.

"Did you not hear?" he asked with a reluctant shake of his head. "I am assigned to the shipyard these days. I work under the shipyard master, I'm not even a lowly secretary." He pretended to look depressed before breaking into a smirk.

"I did not know," confessed Phoebe with some surprise. She didn't listen to gossip, and Mama had said nothing although Phoebe suspected she might know something of it.

"Yes," said Mr. Hathaway. "I no longer represent Magnolia Shipbuilders, especially not in the smoking room or at the game tables. I have been lowered to hard and filthy labor—which I do not mind, to be honest."

"A good day's work," Phoebe approved, although it was rather common work for a man who fancied himself an English sort of dandy.

"My papa put in his time before taking over. Of course, he never sailed like Grandfather did, but... it's just he prefers the office and his study, you see. Figures and the like. Much like you, I understand."

Phoebe raised a brow. "And what is wrong with the efficient organization of one's business?"

"Nothing at all," soothed Mr. Hathaway. "I've also heard not only are you an artist with a needle, you have a talent for figures. Your brother insists that you manage the house and family income, if you'll forgive me, better than he and an accountant combined."

"Yes, well, there's something to be said for building a ship. Do you miss your gig and lap blanket?" teased Phoebe.

"No." He chuckled under his breath. "I'd prefer to be on the water. I did my duty and learned the craft when I was a boy, though I still love seeing a vessel come together just so—water tight and able to catch the wind. I always fancied myself aboard a ship someday."

"As a captain?" Phoebe guessed.

"Why, yes, exactly that," he said, and the tops of his cheeks flushed.

"Why not then? You have several ships, don't you?" Phoebe was amazed at his genuine enthusiasm and plain speaking.

"We mostly repair or build vessels for the local fisherman and such; but yes, we have two merchantmen of our own, the *Magnolia* and the *Regina*, and this winter we are building our third."

"That you hope to sail."

"Oh, it is obvious?" said Mr. Hathaway, and his jocular smile turned upside down. "I'm afraid my father doesn't believe one can run a company from a captain's cabin. My lot is working from land, whether I'm in the office or warehouse or courting business in town."

"That's an admirable occupation, managing a shipping company." Phoebe didn't know what else to say. Why shouldn't Mr. Hathaway sail one of his own ships if he wanted? A career was a career no matter what it entailed as far as she was concerned. "Some people enjoy letters and numbers," she declared, "and others hammers and awls. I daresay it shouldn't matter one way or the other as long as there's food to eat and a roof over your head."

"Well said." He met her eyes as if trying to see inside of her mind. Feeling Mama's gaze from across the room, Phoebe turned back to the window realizing she'd been leaning forward in earnest.

Mr. Hathaway glanced over his shoulder. "Ah," he said in a low tone. "I see I have forgotten my manners. We should have a dance, Miss Applewaite."

"You do not have to ask," she murmured as heat rose to her cheeks.

"Oh, no, my new friend," Mr. Hathaway insisted, "you have refused me once already, and I am in a great deal of trouble with my mama for loitering around town instead of making any useful attachments. I am practically cut off!"

The thought of dancing with everyone's eyes upon her filled Phoebe with dread. "Mr. Hathaway," she murmured, catching his eye to show she was most sincere, "I cannot bear for you to feel obligated to dance, and besides, performing in that way does not come easy to me."

He completely ignored her excuses. "Yes, I know you are the serious sort, stoic even, when brought to anyone's attention, but everyone's dancing, they won't even notice. Besides, Miss Applewaite, I want to dance with you."

Phoebe felt the stone wall around her vanity crumble, but said, "I'm sure they have not forgotten the last time we danced."

He smiled, making her cringe at the realization that he remembered it. "My goodness, you must have been what? Fifteen? I was only doing my duty when I asked you to take the floor, and I certainly did not mean to pull you around so violently that you fell."

Phoebe felt her face blaze just imagining the view he must have had of her flailing ankles and underthings."

"Come now," he said, patting her arm, "I'd forgotten it completely until you rebuked me on Twelfth Night. I'm sure we are much better dancers now." His touch abated her resolve further and sent imaginary sparrows fluttering across her belly. "Everyone else here is either ten years my junior or twice as old—babies and crones."

A giggle gurgled up in Phoebe's throat.

"They are!" Mr. Hathaway exclaimed, and a laugh escaped even as Phoebe *shushed* him.

"*Shh*! Really, you can't make such a scene. Surely you know by now I abhor such a thing."

Persistent Mr. Hathaway stepped up to her chair, bowed, and held out a hand. "Do come dance with me, and we will talk about sending small shipments of your pretty things to the Indies aboard one of our vessels for a modest fee."

Phoebe found herself up on her feet before she could think it through. She knew she was blushing but did not care. If there was an offer to ship her handkerchiefs, she told herself, then she wanted to take Mr. Hathaway's arm and talk with him more. He was quite tolerable when it was one on one, and besides, the surprise on the faces of the other ladies in the room when she stood amused her and made her feel tingly and bold all at the same time.

JAMES LED MISS APPLEWAITE through a crowded hall and upstairs into the large drawing room vacant of furniture except for a few spindled chairs. Pine wood planks on the floor shined in the candlelight. Damask curtains hung from the windows, blocking the stealthy cold air from seeping in although the dancers made enough heat to warm up the room.

The formalities of the evening were slipping away. A musician announced a reel that made the chatter in the room increase to a dull roar as eager young women tried to contain their excitement.

James pulled Miss Applewaite to the center of the room and noticed her face flooded with color. Her eyes were downcast, staring at his pumps, and he realized at once that her rather iron exterior protected a soft, shy shell. He clapped his hands together as the dance began, deciding to make the best of it. He did love a reel, and she was very pretty. All of the gentlemen knew it, although she was no great temptation to anyone looking to climb the social ladders in Charleston since her father's demise. Her rather cross demeanor at dinner parties and ballrooms, not to mention her age, dissuaded the attentions of most gentlemen. She would not inherit a working plantation, and she wasn't exactly silly or fun. Or was she?

Her chin went up and with it a lock of hair escaped, snaking down her neck in a delicate spiral. She raised her brows and gave him a small smile like she was actually enjoying herself as they sashayed down the line together. Her lovely gown whipped to and fro.

James spun on his heel, his mind whirling at the picture her dark eyes made against her dusky peach complexion. She reminded him of a young deer; intelligent, watchful, on guard, and very beauti—

James snapped his head back and pushed *that* thought away. There was a handsome girl around every corner in Charleston, girls of all colors and in a rainbow of temperaments. He laughed as he skipped by Mr. McClellan, who shouted with joy in his strange accent while the bright thatch of red hair on top of his head glistened with his enthusiasm.

James turned to find Phoebe again right where she should be, and without fumbling to catch her hands, their fingers met, and he winked at her with approval. She glowed now, with a natural, unexpected grin beaming from her cheeks. She looked like she was having a good time, and he realized she was quite a proficient dancer since she wasn't worrying about it so much.

He glanced away after a pause when their eyes met, not wanting to let his gaze linger less she see inside his head. James suddenly felt very aware of himself, an odd sensation, and wondered if Benji was about or even Mama, watching him admire Miss Applewaite while he danced with her.

He felt nearly breathless when he clicked his heels together and gave the woman across from him an exaggerated bow. Rather than roll her eyes as she usually did at his antics, she laughed and shook her head in surrender. His heart warmed in a queer, pinching way. Her approval and pleasure made him feel rather lightheaded and pleased. Before she could escape, he reached for her hands and drew her close. They felt warm and familiar in his grip.

"Come with me to the dining room," he begged. "Did you see it? There's petit fours and macaroons and cider if you wish, and I heard there is syllabub if you know the right person to ask."

Her smile stiffened, and she pulled at the lock of hair that had come undone. "Come," James urged, wondering what kind of fun he could get her into now that her guard was down. They moved into the hall and traipsed downstairs and through another sitting room crowded with mamas and grandmothers and a few young wallflowers. Two-double doors opened into the room with the punch table.

Mrs. Leonard was standing near the door in an expensive-looking gown the shade of claret. Now wed, Benjamin's sister belonged to one of the biggest plantations near Sandy Bank, and she made sure everyone knew it was flourishing through her attire. Glistening earbobs sparkled from her ears.

She gave James a wink, and he chuckled under his breath as he slipped by. The silly wench was a year or so his junior, and she had married young—and well. He'd ignored her flirtations growing up; he would never cross his best friend in that way. Her shrill voice caused him to halt as his shoes hit the swathe of carpet leading down the hall.

"Mr. Hathaway," she called after them, and he brought Miss Applewaite to a stop behind him. "What are you playing at? Do you not know there is dancing upstairs?"

"Why, yes," he said, nearly breathless from his former exertion. "See, we have just finished a reel and are looking for refreshment."

Her eyes, which had been examining his arm linked with Miss Applewaite's, snapped up to her and widened in astonishment. As if caught off guard, Mrs. Leonard stuttered, "Oh, I see. How very, very kind of you." Her tone sounded charitable, and he laughed lightly, not knowing what else to do, since everyone would know Miss Applewaite did not care to dance. As he turned back, she added, "I do hope you didn't trip this time."

Miss Applewaite froze. Her smile dropped from her face. He closed his hand around hers like a protective shell around a hermit crab, but he felt her fingers go limp.

"Come along," he said forcing himself to sound more cheerful than he felt. A strange unseen current shot through the hall. He almost looked up to see if a wave had washed over them.

Miss Applewaite dropped his hand and hurried forward until she disappeared, and James followed her into a lovely room painted the brightest green with large, long windows and a set of louvered doors that opened out into a courtyard. Even in the dripping candlelight, the room looked fresh and cheerful as happy guests chattered over their punch cups.

She hesitated, and he drew her over to a small tea table. "Let me get you some cider," he coaxed, hoping whatever had crossed between Mrs. Leonard and herself had passed. Perhaps Mrs. Leonard's comments had been too kind, or perhaps sensitive Miss Applewaite had misinterpreted her words.

She gave him a jerky nod and looked down at her hands. James hurried over to the punch table to fetch her something wet and cool. A small stack of dishes offered cheese and dried figs and dried apples that were not too far gone for the season.

"For you, he said, setting the treats before her. She glanced up at him with a grateful look.

"May I?"

She nodded.

James took the chair beside her, so close their knees almost touched. He felt a draft from a nearby window. "Are you cold? Should we move?"

She swallowed and set down her cup. "No, it feels lovely with all of the heat in this place."

"It will grow warmer yet with springtime on the horizon."

"Let us hope," she said with a faint smile.

He studied her quizzically. "You like a walk along the shore, don't you? I mean, I see you on occasion walking near Fort Wilkin beyond the port."

Her lips allowed a half-smile tinged with sheepishness. "I spend a great deal of the day in the parlor sewing with Mama. Even if I do not have a good reason to wander down to the market, I'm often tempted by the fresh air. It's nice there since it's quiet."

"Yes," he said, understanding completely. "Do you ever go upriver to your family's house?"

"I have on the barges on occasion, and that's nice enough, but sometimes we take a wagon across the low country and ferry over although it takes much longer."

"Yes. Upriver is much easier when the tide is right."

"I get a little jumpy," Miss Applewaite admitted. "I worry more about the alligators than I do the currents."

James laughed. "I can understand that. They wander upriver into the shipyard on occasion. That always gives one a shock."

She shuddered. "Do they have alligators in the Indies?"

"A type, I believe. Although I can't say that I've seen them. They have turtles, enormous and beautiful things, more than I see here, and of course, porpoises and whiprays and the like."

"So, it's not too different than here, I suppose." She took a nibble of cheese. "How often do you go?"

"Me?" James almost felt ashamed for some reason, but he realized it was regret. "Why, I've been at least a half dozen times, and I'd be happy to go more often, but..." He hesitated. "My work is in the shipyard for now, perhaps the offices later."

Her eyes widened slightly with sympathy. "That's a shame. You mentioned before you'd prefer to be aboard one of your ships."

"It's not forever," he blustered while managing to hold back his bitterness. After all, she seemed to prefer the same things his father enjoyed—the business end of things.

"How much do you think a dozen handkerchiefs would go for in the Indies?"

"Hmm." James put a fist to his chin. "Well, I'm sure the milliner in Bridgetown would be happy to take them off our hands."

"Oh," said Miss Applewaite, sounding pleased. She bit down on her lip like she wanted to say more, but glanced away with a flush instead. James realized she felt indelicate discussing business with him here on this occasion.

"Perhaps I should call on you this week next, and we could discuss it. I'd be happy to if..." He left the question dangling in the air.

"Why, yes," she said and gave him a grateful nod. "And thank you, also," she added, "for dancing with me because you did not have to."

"Miss Applewaite," he chided, "you act as if you aren't a worthy partner, and you were quite enjoyable."

"Enjoyable? Really? I would think you would have both been quite nervous," interjected a jarring voice.

James looked up to find Mrs. Leonard peering down at them. She was quite tall, but of course he was seated. He jumped to his feet, and she tittered, as did the group of women trailing behind her.

"Ladies," he said, giving them a quick bow, "have you come to steal my chair and take over Miss Applewaite's table?"

Mrs. Leonard's face seemed to harden. Her eyes shined, but her mouth was no longer smiling. "No, Miss Applewaite is not interested in the tiresome affairs of us poor married things with our husbands and households." She glanced down at Miss

Applewaite's gown. "Or tasteful gowns and trimmings and the like."

James blinked, sensing a line had just been crossed. "Well, then, I shall keep her all to myself then, and your chair, too," he retorted with a strained grin. She smirked at him and pushed by with her friends following like ducks in a row. James let a breath of relief escape, but when he glanced at Miss Apple- waite, she was staring at the table with her cheeks a shade of pink he'd never seen before.

She cleared her throat and looked at him with a tight smile. "I think I'll return to the parlor," she blurted.

James could not agree before she jumped to her feet. He rushed to offer his arm, and they bumped into one another making the table rattle and spill her punch. It left a trail across the tabletop, and she gasped, reaching for the cup, but it slid from her hand. The remnants of it made an ugly splash down her gown.

"Oh, no!" she cried, and James tamped down a chuckle, but the room did not. A few snickers escaped from those seated around them. Across the room, surrounded by her confidants, Mrs. Leonard and her ladies broke into sympathetic laughter. At least he assumed that's what it was, but it only multiplied and became louder as Phoebe made a few angry swipes over the stomacher of her elegant flowered gown.

Mrs. Leonard's voice echoed across the room. "Why, Miss Applewaite, I do believe you've had far too much dancing and more than sufficient refreshment." Her friends chortled with delight.

Rather than laugh with them, Miss Applewaite's neck and cheeks deepened to a lobster's shade of red. "Come now, it's only cider," said James, aghast at her embarrassment. He handed her a napkin, afraid it would be unseemly to help her dry her bodice. She took it in her fist, stumbled back against the chair behind her, and fled the room.

James looked at Mrs. Leonard in confusion. She was nearly doubled over with amusement. Someone had surely had too much spirits, and it wasn't Miss Applewaite.

He relented to their amusement with a small smile, wishing that it had been he who'd had the accident for he could laugh with the best of them. Then he hurried out after his companion. Her rose-streaked hair bobbed through the crowd as he tried to follow it, but it disappeared, and he did not find her in her corner. Whirling around, he did not see her mama either, so he slipped back upstairs to the drawing room. Miss Applewaite was not in there, either.

"Hathaway!" someone called, and James saw Benjamin leaning from a doorway. He jerked his head toward the room behind him, and James realized he was missing cards. He could suddenly use a stronger drink than cider.

With a sigh of surrender, he scanned the upper and lower halls one more time, then assuming Miss Applewaite had retired to one of the private rooms set aside for the ladies, strode into a card room to escape the wild and loud festivities.

PHOEBE STRODE SEVERAL blocks home in the cold darkness, stomping across the uneven cobblestones and dirty patches of road that were unpaved. She had not informed Mama that she was retiring early, but perhaps nasty Mrs. Leonard would be happy to share the news. Phoebe realized her eyes were damp and not from the sting of the bitter cold. They seeped with humiliation and wrath.

She had stumbled at her first ball in her first dance, and Alice Leonard had been there to laugh and remind everyone about it again and again. Ever since, her antagonist managed to find flaws in Phoebe's deportment, clothes, and even her family.

Alice Quinton Leonard was nothing more than a bully; it was all she'd ever been, and at this rate, all she'd ever be. No one had the nerve to stand up to her. Phoebe caught herself about to wish the homeliest and stupidest of all progeny upon her, but that would be unfair to the children. She sniffled, her nose tingling in the cold as she looked ahead for anyone loitering suspiciously in the street.

Really, where had it all began? Long before balls, the snobbish Alice Leonard had ruled over all of the girls their age. She'd never liked Phoebe. Mama had always said to pay her no mind; that she was only jealous because Phoebe was not easily swayed and that she was pretty, prettier than Alice, although she was sure she was not. Phoebe been teased for so many years for her hair that when it finally darkened and matured she still saw only orange when she looked into the mirror. That and the few scattered freckles here and there on her face like constellations in the night sky.

She reached the steps in front of the house but strode past them to the tall iron gate that led to the back courtyard. Finding it unlocked, she clanked it shut behind her and hurried down the narrow passage missing the scent of curling honeysuckle blooms. Summer seemed so far away. When she turned the corner, she saw lamps lit in the brick kitchen house, so she skipped the privy, slipped inside the back door, and rushed up the flight of stairs to her bedroom.

It wasn't long before Charity rapped on the door, and Phoebe slid off of the ticked feather bed and rearranged the frown on her face. The housekeeper held a tea tray. "I kept the water hot for when you returned," she said with a hesitant smile on her face. Her walnut-colored hair was pulled back under her cap, and her porcelain complexion made Phoebe envious.

"Thank you," Phoebe breathed. She widened the door and let her in. "You do so much for us, Charity, I don't know how you manage." Between cleaning and meal service and even helping Mama and her dress, Phoebe was amazed at how the Irish girl managed all she had to do. They simply could not afford any extra help besides Matildy in the kitchen who eased Charity's load.

"You came without the carriage?" Lines of concern crinkled across Charity's forehead.

"Yes. I walked."

"Alone?"

"It was quite safe. Mama will be home soon, I imagine."

Phoebe remembered with a pang that she had not told anyone she was leaving. Perhaps she should send a message, but with who at this late hour?

Charity set down the tray, and seeing what Phoebe suspected were her red cheeks and wet eyes, said, "Is anything wrong, Miss Applewaite?"

Phoebe turned her head to hide the truth. "No, I'm well enough, and thank you for the herb tea."

"Should I help you undress?"

Phoebe allowed Charity to help her slip off the stained gown as she explained the accident. After waiting for the woman to loosen her stays, she collapsed into a soft chaise in front of the small hearth, and drank her tea in her shift covered only by Papa's silk blue banyan that she'd pilfered from his trunks before Daniel could find it.

*What must Mr. Hathaway think?*

The thought came unbidden into her head, and she widened her eyes at her vanity as she stared into the low, burning fire. What did it matter? He only thought about himself. He adored attention in any form; he had not minded her accident at all, in fact, he'd practically made light of it.

And then of course there was Mrs. Leonard. Mean thing. She looked for opportunities to make fun of anyone. *But if only he had not seen.* Phoebe was not clumsy by nature, but when she was the center of attention she became as stiff as the bones in her stays.

She squeezed her eyes shut. Mr. Hathaway had not seemed to think anything of it. If not for Mrs. Leonard's insult, Phoebe could have quietly excused herself to clean up the mess. Flying out of the room must have looked awkward and silly. What had he thought of her dashing out like a frightened cat? Did he think anything at all? Probably not.

Phoebe stretched her neck and forced herself to shrug. What did it matter? He'd been as polite and attentive as perhaps his mother—and her's—had encouraged him to be. Her departure probably gave him a good excuse to find his friends and play his games or whatever nonsensical things he entertained himself with.

Perhaps they might become good friends if other people stayed out of it, but not at a ball, no. She shouldn't have danced with him. Everyone had stared. Perhaps there were whispers, too. He would laugh at such a thing and never understand how she could not bear it.

Phoebe rubbed her lips to taste the sweet tang of the honey stirred into the tea. Mr. Hathaway had mentioned shipping handkerchiefs for her. If she could sew faster and encourage Mama to increase her fichus by the month, perhaps they might make enough embroidered goods to send to the Indies on one of the Hathaway ships.

It could be a first step, she mused, a way to open her own millinery shop with hats and trimmings. With Daniel's connections, she also could import hosiery and shoes and maybe even trade with a jeweler. Really, it could be so much more. She smiled to herself.

A door slammed far below, and Phoebe tensed. Mama was home. Yes, she heard her mother's trilling worried tones. Setting down the small tea cup, Phoebe jumped to her slippered feet, tied Papa's banyan around herself, and scurried down the stairs careful not to fall.

Mama marched through the arch in the middle of the hall, ignoring the parlor in her beeline for the stairs. Phoebe met her at the bottom while Charity struggled to help her out of her fur wraps.

"Phoebe Applewaite, I do declare!" scolded Mama while flapping her arms, "you almost made me faint, leaving the party like that without a word. Why, if Mr. Hathaway had not seen me looking for you on the stairs, I'm sure I would have never known."

"I'm sorry, Mama," said Phoebe. "There was an accident. I soaked my gown and felt I should leave immediately."

"You could have come to me or gone upstairs." Mama hesitated as her brows lowered with concern. "How bad was it?"

"Just a spill."

"But..."

"I'm sure that Charity and I can get it out. The gown isn't ruined, I don't think."

Charity murmured her reassurance as she passed them to climb the stairs with her arms heaped in muffs and capes and beaver hats.

"But how did you get home?" Mama's earbobs swayed as she shook her head in disbelief. Phoebe took her hand. "Come, let's go upstairs to your room and settle you in."

Mama dug her heels into the boards of the floor. "Phoebe? Who escorted you home?" Her face brightened. "Was it Mr. Benjamin Quinton? Did he leave early? Or did... well, I don't suppose Mr. Hathaway helped you back for we met on the stairs."

"No, Mama, but we did have a dance, and he sat with me and drank a bit of cider."

"Yes, I heard." Before she could say more, Phoebe encouraged her to walk up the stairs.

Later in her bed, Phoebe stared up at the worn ruffles drooping between the bed posts. Sleep hovered in the wings, but the party still whirled around in her mind. She'd enjoyed the dance and the conversation with Mr. Hathaway. If she was honest with herself, she liked him very much, again, but she wasn't a silly young thing anymore. He had changed some, at least when he wasn't worrying about making everyone else smile and laugh.

Phoebe squinted her eyes in the dim light and turned toward the glowing fire. She could not bear to shut the curtains around her bed, even in the winter, because she felt like she couldn't breathe. Besides, she liked to watch the flames wriggle and writhe.

Mama had questioned her thoroughly tonight, and though Phoebe admitted to the dancing and cider, she kept any new feelings to herself. Their talk turned to the machinations of Mrs. Leonard, and true to form, Mama reassured her that Alice Quinton Leonard had always been a jealous thing who had once set her cap for Mr. Hathaway and had no luck.

It made Phoebe admire him a little more, that he should be so sensible as to avoid Mrs. Leonard's pursuit, but she did not admit it to Mama. She could hardly admit it to herself. Instead, she shuffled it away and thought about the possibilities of exporting fine trifles from Charleston to the Indies. At least she hoped Mr. Hathaway was serious about that. She shouldn't expect it though. Perhaps it had all been meaningless puffs of air.

# CHAPTER FIVE

James bet little and won nothing at Whitely's, but that was the way of things. The party and Miss Applewaite's attendance there lingered in his mind for more days than he dared to count. Even more strangely, he found himself looking for her at church every time he was there.

The day before, as his mind wandered in circles during the sermon, he glanced over his shoulder across the bodies behind him, acknowledging each young woman with a silent tick. He found Miss Applewaite at last, to his right and several rows back with her mama. She'd looked straight ahead, her neck long and rather lovely with her hair up on her crown, but her gaze seemed distant as if she was thinking of other things besides humility and repentance. Her mama caught his eye, and he'd turned back around fast.

"Mr. Hathaway!" The cry from the end of the pier shook James from his reflection. Shivering, he raised a gloved hand at the *Regina's* bosun directing traffic on and off the ship. Dash it all, he would have to hurry back to the warehouse to ready the next load of the crew's supplies. He crossed his arms over himself and bustled through the crowd of sailors and traders along Charleston's wharf, thankful at least Gadsden's was further north so he did not have to see or hear the Africans being unloaded like cargo as if they were not human beings. It rent his heart in two to see other people acting as if this was a normal, Christian thing to do.

He was almost done for the day. Papa and Albermarle had sent him from the yard to see to business in the port. The captain of *Regina* and he had paperwork to finish, and then he was free. Dinner, of course, would be at Shepheard's. He knew Benji would be there. But he had promised, he reminded himself, that he would call on Miss Applewaite in regard to her pristine goods. He glanced up at the overhead sun, and thinking it not too late after noonday, decided it wouldn't be out of order, not if he at least took a card.

He wondered if she'd refuse to let him in, and he almost grinned. She did not enjoy splashing cider down herself, but really it had been a funny thing. If she had not jumped up to leave and if he had not jumped up to be so proper for Mrs. Leonard, they would not have bounced into one another so heartily.

After business was settled, James hurried down East Bay to his simple apartment not far from the taverns and wharves. He discarded his old boots, changed his shirt and breeches, donned his favorite waistcoat embroidered with peafowl, and slipped on his finest riding boots—two-toned and polished to a luster. His hair looked tangled so he set it right with a little pomade, then donning his silk plush hat, hurried out to take his gig up to the market and across the way to Beaufain Street.

The sun appeared in full force. It chased away the iron clouds as Dogberry clopped toward the house. At the carriage stoop, James hopped out, tied off the horse and gave him a bite of peppermint before skipping up the steps.

The coastal climate had not been kind to the Applewaite house. The shutters needed a fresh lick of paint, and brick pavers leading to the back garden were dappled with moss and beginning to separate. Sympathetic to the women living here without a husband or papa, he tapped his cane on the door and waited, wondering why he felt rather anxious instead of eager to converse with someone other than one of his father's workers who looked down their noses at him.

A charming girl wearing a crisp white linen apron and cap opened the door. She was as fair as a princess, he decided, with rather light eyes that made her mousy hair rather nice. James fumbled for his card and passed it over with a quick introduction. Obviously, none was needed. She seemed to know exactly who he was and allowed him into a long hall with mahogany wainscoting and oil paintings. The young housekeeper slipped into a room on his left, most likely the ladies' parlor, he guessed, and was pleased when the door widened, and she motioned for him to go in.

"Mr. Hathaway," said Mrs. Applewaite, "what a very pleasant surprise."

Miss Applewaite and her mama stood. Hoops holding cuts of cloth were tossed onto a comfortable looking settee with a low back. Both looked surprised, and it amused him. He gave them a sweeping bow.

When Miss Applewaite looked less than impressed, he widened his grin until he felt it touch his ear. "Please, ladies, do sit down. I did not mean to interrupt your commendable toil."

"Oh, they're just little projects," insisted her mama.

Miss Applewaite seemed drawn and serious. She looked away when James examined her then sank down into her seat. Mrs. Applewaite indicated for him to take a chair, and rather than stand, he pulled a fine side chair from the wall with a country scene painted on its back rest.

"How charming. Did you do this?" He looked from mother to daughter."

"Oh no," answered Mrs. Applewaite, "there are no artists here. Not quite." She smiled. "They were commissioned. I have a set of four."

"How handsome," repeated James, realizing all of the subjects he'd thought of to carry on a conversation here were disappearing out of his head faster than he could retrieve them. He cleared his throat. Miss Applewaite looked like a hare about to bolt. She wore a colorful frock with jaunty stripes he admired, but before he could say so, her brown eyes sparked with something like uncertainty.

"Why, I promised you I would call," he said, stiffening his back. "Our business arrangement," he reminded her, and her mama looked over at her in surprise.

"You are still interested in purchasing some of our handkerchiefs and fichus for export?"

James raised his chin at Miss Applewaite's query. "If you are still interested. I think it would be best to ship them at a prearranged price, and I would like ten percent."

"Ten percent?"

Mrs. Applewaite was speechless, her eyes snapping back and forth between James and her daughter's caller.

"Are you certain that's fair to you?" asked Miss Applewaite.

"You don't want me to be generous?"

The corner of her mouth twitched, and James found himself admiring it. Her lips were full, but not heavy.

"I expect you to be fair," she insisted, "although ten percent would be a wonderful rate."

"It would be more if it were heavier cargo," he explained, "or took up a great deal of space, but it's such a small thing."

"I suppose the more I export the higher the rate?"

He shrugged, realizing Papa was far better at this type of negotiating than himself. "I don't see your goods taking up any more space I don't already have."

"That would be generous of you, Mr. Hathaway." Miss Applewaite granted him a smile and reached for the tea table beside her. It was stacked with perfectly aligned handkerchiefs. "When would you need them?"

"Well," said James, dropping his gaze to think, "the *Regina* departs tomorrow on the first tide. She is destined for Bridgetown where I think your goods will be snapped up rather quickly."

Miss Applewaite riffled through cotton, linen, and a few silk squares. "I'm not prepared to give you a substantial amount at this time."

"My goodness," he teased, "they'd easily fit into my ditty box."

"Oh," she answered, "we have more upstairs. Are you going this time around?"

James felt his heart wrinkle. "Why, no," he admitted, "I am still working at the yard, you see, or sometimes down at the docks."

She fell quiet. It became obvious Mrs. Applewaite knew nothing of his change in responsibilities when she looked sideways at her daughter. James chuckled under his breath, saying nothing about his penance, because it would certainly get back to Mama.

"Well," blurted Mrs. Applewaite, "it is getting on, and I forgot to offer you something to refresh yourself. Perhaps something warm?"

He smiled in appreciation before realizing she hoped for an excuse to leave the room. "If it's on," he suggested.

"There is always water on," she insisted, "and coffee ground, too." She glanced at her daughter with curiosity then hurried out leaving the door cracked rather than ajar.

Miss Applewaite's cheeks flushed. "You have made my mother happy today and probably for the entire week."

"My, my, how our mothers will talk. And by the by, I did not get to wish you a good night when you hurried from the refreshment room at the Whitely's, and it's been almost a fortnight. I did say I would come."

"Yes," remembered Miss Applewaite, "I haven't thought much about it."

James jerked his head back. "You did not take me seriously? Or you do not wish to export your handsome things?"

"Oh, no," she answered in a rush, "I do, Mr. Hathaway. It's just I didn't know for sure that you were in earnest."

"You don't take me seriously, do you?" he asked, thinking how often she looked bemused with him like his mammy did.

Miss Applewaite folded her hands in her lap. He thought she might be fighting back a smile.

"You may be frank with me, Miss Applewaite," encouraged James, leaning back against the chair to study her. He folded his arms. "So few people are truly honest and forthcoming with their thoughts. I can hardly tell the difference when one is sincere. It makes me a poor judge of character on occasion."

She smiled at last, and it crinkled the delicate skin around her eyes. "I'm afraid I am *too* forthcoming and honest, Mr. Hathaway, and it discomfits others."

"I challenge you to discomfit me," he teased.

A quiet laugh escaped her sweet mouth. It was a gentle, breathy sound. Slender fingers tucked a dark auburn curl of hair behind her ear. "I could easily win that challenge," she promised him. She crossed her feet together at the ankles, and he admired her embroidered little slippers that looked far more comfortable than his boots.

"You see," she continued, "I am anxious to invest in some type of commerce that would benefit my family; if not for my mama, for myself in the future. So I can in no way refuse such a bargain from you, especially when it is such a small amount of inventory and hardly worth your time."

"But," James pointed out, "one must begin somewhere."

"I agree, and I appreciate your eagerness to help."

"They're quality pieces, your handkerchiefs," he praised her. "I'd buy a dozen and sell them myself if I had the time."

She smiled openly now, and it reminded him of their dance. She'd seemed pleased then, and dare he think it—comfortable with him.

"I am happy to do it," he assured her. "Our fathers worked together on the banking board so many years ago besides doing business together, and the Applewaites are known to be as good as their word."

She beamed. "Thank you."

He caught himself grinning. "Will you be dancing again? At the next ball, I mean?"

Her expression seemed to crisp. "What ball? We have nothing but an invitation to dine with the McClellans next week. I'm afraid a widow and her daughter do not receive invitations to every party."

James caught himself pulling at a loose thread on his cuff. "Mama will have a spring ball at the plantation house in a month. Surely, you have been invited to Sandy Bank."

Miss Applewaite looked past him. "I suppose, but I'm not certain. We do not leave town often I'm afraid, and we've had to decline invitations in the past."

"You could travel across the river with me. I know an excellent ferry to Mount Pleasant."

Her gaze flitted about the room. James could see her thinking. It would mean staying at the great house on his property, away from her hidden fortress, her sewing, and the private places along the shore she snuck away to.

"I..."

"It would please our mothers," he joked with a wink.

Her cheeks pinkened, and it made his chest quiver. Why, how silly. He was only teasing.

"About that," said Miss Applewaite with no warning. She glanced toward the door and lowered her voice. "I know my mama and Mr. Cadwell are quick to encourage any bachelor to pay me compliments because of my age and situation, but the truth is, Mr. Hathaway..." She flushed to a crimson red that made her hair look darker. "I hope you understand you are not expected to pay calls or ask me to dance just because our mothers have lately become better friends." She took an unsteady breath. "I have no expectations. I understand this is a business call only."

A surprising stream of disappointment trickled down James's spine and made him feel hot and uncomfortable. She was such a handsome girl, and intelligent, too, but she had no interest in the likes of him. But that was not new. She'd never shown an interest in anyone. He thought of her rapid withdrawal from the Whitely's party after her hand felt so fragile and soft in his. Unable to hold back a flirtatious inclination, James replied, "What if it's not?" He felt his brows wrinkle as if he was asking himself.

Her eyes widened with the familiar amusement he was now accustomed to seeing. "I know you are not here for any other reason, and I'm sure it's for the best."

"Is it?"

"Yes?" she said as if confused. "You have aspirations to go to sea, and of course, there are certainly girls of more interest and... well, equal to your station in life at Mount Pleasant than a late merchant's daughter living in blessed spinsterhood with her mama on Beaufain Street."

He slanted his head at her. "Do you really find singleness a blessed state?"

Her amusement faded, and her gaze returned to the window behind his head. "Yes. Don't you? If I ever marry, it will not be for anyone's convenience or my mother's whim."

Was he a whim? James blurted, "What about love?"

She made a noise in her throat. "I'd never let myself fall into that trap," she assured him. "I have a mama and our home to care for. Perhaps I did when I was young and silly, but it was just vain imaginings."

"I have a very good imagination, Miss Applewaite," baited James, "and I think a dose of infatuation or falling in love on occasion serves one well."

She flushed but answered, "Well then, Mr. Hathaway, you fall first."

To his surprise, James liked the idea, and he liked the idea of such a thing with her. He caught himself grinning again, but she did not take the hint, merely blinked and looked away.

A clatter on the other side of the door made them both jump. Mrs. Applewaite and her housekeeper burst into the room juggling trays and cups. "Here we are, Mr. Hathaway," she said in a breathless voice. "We do not drink English tea in this house anymore, but there is coffee."

James clapped his hands together in pretended delight while he snuck a peek at her daughter. The red-cheeked Miss Applewaite was studying him like a ledger.

MR. HATHAWAY TOOK ALL of the inventory Phoebe had stored upstairs. She packed over a dozen handkerchiefs in a small watertight trunk made of sturdy oak. When he promised to return it—it had been Papa's—she gave him a solemn nod. She had a few kerchiefs left she saved for market day but waited a few days for Mama to finish the latest fichu she had been embroidering with birds and French knots.

It felt warm and pleasant for February. The sun shimmered, and the wind felt less biting. Phoebe all but melted with contentment as she strode out of the Pilchers' shop, satisfied that the woman shopkeeper had bought from her what Mr. Payne would not.

She was deeply appreciative. There were more than a dozen women in the city with their own businesses, from dry goods to dressmaking to millinery. Seduced by the fair weather, Phoebe tightened the ribbon under her chin and strolled to the busy corner of the Exchange then turned south toward the fort at the end of the peninsula. As she walked past row houses one up against the other, she surveyed the busy wharf through the branches of naked trees waiting patiently to bud.

It made her think of Mr. Hathaway. He'd surprised her by showing up just as he said he would, to collect her handkerchiefs for the next merchantman out. It was kind of him. Generous. He certainly didn't need the small amount of money, not with his inheritance, but perhaps he was trying to impress his father. Maybe he didn't care for his labors in the shipyard as much as he pretended. It seemed to keep him out of trouble though.

She caught her cheek pulling and fought back a smile. His arrival left her speechless the first few minutes because she'd convinced herself he would not come. Not to mention, he was so handsome and effervescent, it'd felt like the lighthouse on Morris Island had cast one of its long stretching beams through the window and into the room. He quite made her forget her determination not to be distracted by the other sex.

Sunbeams sparkled like diamonds over the scuttling bay. A few soldiers practiced formations in the distance. As the street widened, she diverted from the cobblestones onto the familiar footpath that led to the narrow strip of sand along the sea wall. She set a silk and linen drawstring bag inside her basket and dropped them onto the beach. Off came her shoes.

The barrier islands shined in the distance, and she stared hard between their arms to gaze out to sea. Movement in the expanse made her squint, but it was not runaway boats. She smiled at silver porpoises leap-frogging in the distance.

"What are they running from, I wonder," said a smooth voice behind her.

Phoebe nearly jumped out of her stockings. Gazing heavenward with relief, she put a hand on her heart. "Mr. Hathaway, you nearly caused me to faint."

He grinned at her from beneath a worn cocked hat that shielded his palm-green eyes from the sun. "I do have that effect on the occasional woman."

A gushing laugh erupted from Phoebe's throat. "I said faint, as in with fear, not swoon," she corrected.

He laughed and stepped nearer, so close their elbows touched. They watched the vessels in the harbor scurry from island to port to river mouth, dodging sandbars and one another.

"A fine day," he remarked, and Phoebe snuck a glance at his profile before returning to her examination of the Atlantic.

"Quite fine," she agreed. "It almost feels like spring will stay, but I'm certain it's a jest. It will be raining by Thursday and frigid by the Sabbath."

"That is the way of things, but we do have the most delicious season once it settles in."

"Yes," she murmured. "I'm eager to see the tulips and azaleas bloom, but of course the vegetable patch would be even better."

"I miss a good ripe melon from the farm," bemoaned Mr. Hathaway. "We have a small hot house at Sandy Bank, and they have a few good ones at the port, but it's all fish and rice until I'm sick of it."

"Captain Russell has returned from the Indies," Phoebe informed him. "Did you know? Mama said he stuck a pineapple on his front gate—speared it right through and what a shame for the birds were at it."

"Yes, well, I suppose he has some to spare."

Phoebe caught herself licking her lip just thinking of the sweetness. He nudged her lightly. "Do you like a rare pineapple, Miss Applewaite? It's not apples then, is it?"

"Really, Mr. Hathaway, there is not an apple joke you can tell I have not heard, and yes," she admitted, "I do love pineapple very much although they are expensive and hard to come by. It's almost enough to tempt me to hop aboard one of these ships heading out."

"Now that would be a sight," teased the man beside her.

Phoebe noticed he wore plain breeches and a loose shirt with only a dark waistcoat over billowing sleeves. "Aren't you cold? It's pleasant but not that warm."

"I get overheated in the yard, and it is a pleasant day as you said. I'm afraid my coat is at the warehouse."

"Have you come to the fort?" Phoebe looked around.

"Not exactly," Mr. Hathaway smiled. "I was hurrying home for a document I forgot, and I spied you ahead and thus bypassed my intended destination."

"Oh, dear," admonished Phoebe, knowing his tendency to become distracted, "I'm flattered you would walk all the way down Bay Street just to follow me, but do not let me distract you."

"Why not?" he returned without hesitation. "This is a much prettier view."

His flippant words struck Phoebe's heart like an arrow. She grit her teeth to keep from showing that she'd felt them. When had she become so susceptible to such things?

"I mean the bay," Mr. Hathaway stammered, clearing his throat. "Tell me," he added as her cheeks flushed at his clarification, "would you like to walk a bit? Just through the neighborhood?"

Phoebe glanced up the street. "I could," she admitted, "but I don't want to pull you further away from your address."

"Ah," he scoffed, "it's just an apartment across from the wharves. I have plenty of time, and in all seriousness, I think they breathe a sigh of relief in the yard when I leave."

"Yes," retorted Phoebe, "I'm sure you're a cruel taskmaster."

He laughed but not as heartily as she expected. Again, she surprised herself. When did she grow so comfortable with James Hathaway that she would tease him and make jokes?

Taking her elbow, he scooped up her basket and led her back up to the street. They walked arm in arm discussing the new houses being built in the outlying village and the brick floated downriver from his plantation.

"I presume it's a great deal of weight for shipping," mused Phoebe as they walked along.

"Yes," he agreed, "not like your pretty handkerchiefs."

"I'm anxious for the *Regina* to return to see the outcome although I understand it will be some time."

"Oh," said Mr. Hathaway, "do you need an advance?"

Phoebe's cheeks smarted. "No, Mr. Hathaway, I'm just curious to see if your merchantman will be able to sell my trifles is all."

"You must not worry. I'm surprised that all of the milliners and tailors in town aren't scrambling for your goods."

"There is competition," she insisted, although his compliments were gratifying. "It's an easy enough endeavor for anyone to do herself."

The man beside her raised a gloved finger into the air. "Not everyone enjoys working a needle." It was as if he actually recalled her mentioning her headaches.

"I can't imagine not bothering at all," admitted Phoebe, meaning that she could not imagine being so rich and lazy that even a little needlepoint was too much a task. "Although you must know our embroidery is favored by a great many gentlemen around town."

"I'm sure it is," he replied. "You and your mama are very skilled although she makes light of it. I don't wonder that you prefer to open your own shop."

Phoebe raised a shoulder. "Mama is peculiar about what is appropriate for my situation."

"Bah!" Mr. Hathaway exclaimed. "Look at me! The heir of Sandy Bank, reared with a mammy, schooled by the finest tutors, and civilized by the most popular dance masters. Yet, I am working in the shipyard like a carpenter and the warehouse office like a secretary, not to mention, running up and down the docks like an errand boy."

Phoebe tightened her arm against his. "It may be your most valuable education yet."

He smirked. "My mama is aghast, and Papa has no shame. But I believe you're right. Anyway, I have no desire to waste my days away doing near to nothing back at home. That's why I prefer town. I've always loved it." He scrunched his lips while nodding to himself. "I like the activity—the sights and sounds and smell of it—the bakery especially, but the harbor view is preferable to the brickyard."

"I like the creeks and marshes upriver," mused Phoebe. "They're peaceful, but yes, I must agree the quiet would puzzle me after a time, or perhaps I would grow to love it, I don't know."

"Well, there are no shops in the low country," he warned.

She sniffed to cover a chuckle. His mama probably ordered most of her things from across the sea.

"Speaking of marshes and creeks," Mr. Hathaway continued, "you do intend to come to Sandy Bank for the ball in a fortnight, don't you? My mama received a letter from yours."

"Yes," relented Phoebe, "and of course we meant to stay in Mount Pleasant, but they have contrived together that we will have one of your rooms saved for company."

"Then I can give you the grand tour of the place," said Mr. Hathaway, and Phoebe thought he sounded rather eager. "Especially if you love the marsh. We're set right along Rathall Creek, you recall, where even the alligators crawl into our freshwater pond."

Phoebe shivered. "Now those do not interest me."

He laughed at her shudder. They turned a corner, and she gazed ahead at her aging home that would probably fit three times inside his manor at Sandy Bank.

"Alligators or not," he continued, "you must promise me a dance, and I promise to keep the cider far from your gown."

Phoebe managed to chuckle while hoping Mrs. Leonard would not be there.

"I'll scrub the tar from my fingernails."

"Well then," she said finding herself in a playful mood and not dreading the ball so much despite the outcome of the Whitely party, "I suppose I can risk a dance if you'll go as far as to do all that."

His gaze met hers, and the impish grin on his face loosened into a faint smile while his eyes lowered to her mouth then dropped further to scrutinize her neck. Phoebe felt herself blush and looked away. What was the man thinking? He was such a puzzle—one moment flirting and the next pondering his worth and future.

"Here we are," he declared, and Phoebe stopped at the stoop, unsure if she should invite him in. He tapped his hat back down on his head like he meant to be off. "I should hurry back I suppose and find the papers I've misplaced."

She understood that he probably tended to misplace things since his thoughts seemed to ricochet from one thing to the next. "Thank you for the escort."

"I know you could find your way from the fort and back wearing a blindfold, but thank you for the stroll and conversation. I'm much less worried about the celebrations at Sandy Bank now."

"I'm sure a ball at your family home is the last thing that would ever give you cause for concern, Mr. Hathaway," chuckled Phoebe. "You'll be in your element."

He broke into peals of laughter, resting his hands on his hips. "Now, Miss Applewaite, why do we put off our parents' encouragements when you know me so well?"

This abrupt change of subject caught Phoebe off guard. Her teasing spirit withdrew, and she felt her face tighten. Did he know he had reignited a flame in her heart that must never burn down her walls?

Her throat tangled into knots as her mind frantically searched for something to say. Feeling her cheeks grow hot as he waited, she could only shrug her shoulders and murmur, "Good day, Mr. Hathaway. Do let me know when the *Regina* returns." And then she dashed inside.

TWO DAYS LATER, WITH his mind flitting about with thoughts of the charming Miss Applewaite, James met Papa at the Exchange to discuss business with a rice merchant connected to some of the old families upriver. He later accompanied him and his cronies to Swallows.

Benjamin was not about, so James forced himself to focus on the discussion of market prices and new government tariffs, understanding that these things would be an important part of shipping goods—or running a plantation if it came to that. The latter thought made him forlorn.

Papa lingered at the table and reclined in his seat. "Your mama is anxious for you to return to Sandy Bank in time for her party."

James spun a tankard in front of him in a circle, admiring the gleam of light against the German silver. "Yes," he said, somewhat hesitant to reveal his intentions. "I have promised

Mrs. Applewaite and her daughter I will accompany them across on the ferry and ride with them to the house."

"I can send a carriage."

"That will do."

"Your mother will be pleased you've agreed to accompany them. You were quite attentive at the Whitely's party before we left town."

If they were happy with the improvements in his conduct, it was difficult to tell. He did not remind Papa that he'd rented the family town house out to someone else rather than let James move in. Not that he really minded. His little apartment over the wharf was cheap and closer to business. With all of the work and distraction, he'd had little time to gamble, and his savings had increased. James was proud of that but still confused.

What was the purpose of it all if he was to be an heir? Especially when the common folk in the warehouses and at the docks struggled for every last pence while the rest of Charleston pranced around in luxury. It was a wealthy city, but not for everyone.

As if curious about his son's silence, Mr. Hathaway continued: "I meant Miss Applewaite. Such a handsome girl. And you danced?"

James looked over the rim of his ale then straightened in his chair. The business talk had shifted to a personal interview. "Yes, and I called on her not long ago. We took a turn about town and then a promenade through her neighborhood." James forgot the importance of impressing Papa and began to muse aloud: "She's pretty to be sure and has the land inheritance upriver, but she's also clever and industrious. She has a quiet mind and appreciates simple things, even the harbor view—I know—because I find her there frequently."

He bent his elbow and put his chin in his hand. "She doesn't shy away from discussing commerce with the shopkeepers, and she has the most wry sense of humor that amuses me." He gazed off at nothing over Papa's shoulder. "You can't put anything past that one. Slick smiles and oily compliments only push her shoulders back and make her jerk her chin."

James realized he'd quite prattled on and met Papa's gaze sheepishly. A lazy smile spread across his father's face, as did a light of approval in his eyes. "I see your weeks in the yard have slowed you down and helped you think more clearly."

"It's only been just over a month, I know, but yes. If you mean the gaming tables though, why, I don't have the time. Was that your plan?"

Papa's grin widened. "I only meant to keep you busy and hoped to inspire you to reflect on more serious things. Besides, if you want to commandeer a ship, you must know how things work between the warehouse and the wardroom."

James doubted that Papa was ready to give him a ship or a small position for he was no closer to settling down with anyone. Miss Applewaite had brushed off his subtle hint about their parents' wishes. Still, Papa seemed pleased with his progress. He might as well try his hand.

"So you would consider it now? A ship's command? Even if I don't find anyone to marry right away?"

His father studied him. "I may. We launch in a few weeks. Considering your improvement, I'm convinced you are not a lost cause, just a little off course."

"Thank you, I think."

Papa chuckled. "I only wanted to get your attention before you ended up meandering listlessly through life like Mr. Quinton."

James would not speak ill of his friend, but he understood Papa's meaning. Papa leaned forward. "Now then, I'm delighted you find Miss Applewaite amiable, and I hope you'll continue to explore those possibilities. Meanwhile, I will try to find you a ship's position if you do come to Sandy Bank for the ball and please your mama."

James blinked. It was impossible. Incredible. A teasing possibility dangled in his mind. "And if I were to convince Miss Applewaite to marry me, perhaps... you would consider me for the captain's command?"

Mr. Hathaway straightened in his chair. "Jamie, if you marry that lovely girl with the land tract along the Ashley, I will promise you a first mate's post on the *Lily* and heartily fight for you to commandeer her—in time."

James felt himself grow lightheaded. It was the possibility of being an officer and sailing his own ship someday, he told himself, not the idea of wedding the rosy-haired Phoebe Applewaite. *Why*, snuck a sudden thought into his head, *she could run the warehouse on her very own...*

The muddled clouds of his future swept away. It looked like a bright star now, shining across the dark sea of his impenetrable hopes and dreams. A life in Charleston right along the bay, not sequestered in a hollow plantation house upriver. And with a girl, a handsome, smart girl who enjoyed town as much as he—and business—which he did not. James jumped to his feet and leaned across the table resisting the urge to plant a kiss on his father's forehead. "Papa, you have a bargain!"

# CHAPTER SIX

The waters of the Cooper River looked choppy even though snowy white clouds hung calmly overhead. Phoebe waited beside Mama as Mr. Hathaway made certain their trunks were loaded onto Watson's ferry. Mama had a satisfied smirk on her face every time Phoebe addressed their escort, who'd generously made the arrangements for them to travel to Sandy Bank for his family's spring ball. He'd even paid the toll.

As the ladies were helped onto the ferry, Phoebe felt her stomach revolt against the rocking motion that only made her nerves worse. She disliked balls, although not as much lately. At least there would be an extravagant meal with a music concert.

Mama leaned over to whisper in her ear once Mr. Hathaway made sure they were comfortable. "Did you see? Mr. Quinton is along, too. He will not be too much of a distraction, I hope."

Phoebe held her gaze straight ahead. "They are very good friends, Mama. Why should they not enjoy their time together?" She glanced at his dark, curly-haired friend. His long face was rather attractive, but it was widely known he was an even worse rake than Mr. Hathaway.

Mr. Quinton caught her studying him and smirked. She tried to make her cheeks dimple into a pert smile before looking away. One curious, charming flirt of a man was enough, and thanks to Mrs. Leonard, she knew she was not rich or connected enough to ever interest a Quinton. She certainly didn't need their pity.

Phoebe found herself taking sniffs off Mama's smelling salts to calm her stomach before the ferry slid into its moorings at the causeway of the large isthmus of Mount Pleasant. The docking made the ferry rock more violently than ever.

"Whoa, there!" called Mr. Hathaway as Mama let out a small cry. Phoebe staggered onto her feet and reached for her mother's arm. Together, the men helped Mama out, and before Phoebe could take the hand of the ferryman, Mr. Quinton appeared and offered his hand. He gave her a wink as her boots hit solid earth, and she hesitated, uncertain of how to react. If was as if Mr. Quinton knew her opinion of his friend had changed, and he wanted to change her mind, too.

The fine carriage with the Hathaway family crest on the door rolled through the parish as Phoebe tried to act unruffled. The covered windows and the close quarters made her feel tense. To be stuffed in a cozy compartment with two handsome fellows and her mama was a unique type of torture.

"Have you been to Sandy Bank before?" Mr. Quinton jerked her attention back to the conversation.

"Twice with my father when I was little," answered Phoebe in a pleasant tone. "Once up the Wando River and once across the Cooper like today."

"You have been up Rathall Creek?"

"Such an unpleasant name," interjected Mama.

Mr. Quinton laughed, but Mr. Hathaway said, "Yes, but it has the most beautiful salt marshes.

"And the trees—the pines," Phoebe added, "how thick and lush they grow."

"Yes." Mr. Hathaway seemed pleased with her observations. "Palmettos and magnolias grow thick on our property, and I must boast that we have an orchard of fine pecan trees in very neat rows."

Phoebe listened with interest, her heart tingling every time Mr. Hathaway looked her way while speaking. She wasn't certain if it was to include her in the conversation or for an entirely different reason. She'd received such looks before, but not from anyone who turned her head. Her head was turned now, she admitted to herself, and it didn't turn easily.

Mr. Quinton startled her by tugging on the drawstring of her shade. It curled up into a neat roll as they made a wide turn onto a pitted road lined with luscious scarlet azaleas. Phoebe had a glimpse of a great house in the distance. It stood tall like its city counterparts but wider. Stacked three stories high with wooden eaves, it had two large porticos, both up and down, and was painted a cheerful mustard shade of yellow that stood out against the deep red bricks. A smoother dirt drive for carriages circled the front with budding gardens on either side of the house.

The carriage rattled and rolled, nearly twisting in half as the gentlemen laughed, and Phoebe hung on for life. Cool afternoon breezes gusted through the window, and she drew her wrap around herself with one hand. She knew they were near their final destination when they passed a neat row of small houses made of mismatched brick with faded planked doors. A few small children lingered in the yards, and she heard the distant rhythmic murmurs of the Africans enslaved there.

The voices were at once beautiful and melancholy, and her stomach returned to the unsettled feeling she'd endured crossing the water. Phoebe tried to look past them as she had been taught and studied the distant marsh lying on the other side of their cabins. The homes were separated from the marsh by the swift-moving currents of Rathall Creek.

The team of horses jingled to a stop, and the door beside Mama swung open onto the carriage stoop. Mr. Hathaway and Mr. Quinton climbed out, helped Mama, and when Phoebe reached the door, she found Mr. Hathaway waiting with an outstretched glove as his friend escorted Mama inside.

"Thank you," Phoebe murmured, surprised he had not helped Mama and left Mr. Quinton to assist her. It felt strangely formal like she was a special guest. He smiled at her, his real smile, not his flirty, silly grin, and motioned toward the open door where a servant in white linen waited.

"Welcome to Sandy Bank. Again," he added with a quiet laugh, "although I'm sure I don't recall having you here before."

She took his arm as he led her into a wide, open room flanked on either side by an open library and an enormous dining room. In a circular grand hall, an impressive, round staircase floated in the air as it climbed up to the next level. Phoebe gazed around the familiar Prussian blue-painted walls.

"It's as lovely as ever," she confessed then realized their arms were still linked. She dropped her hand, and he hurried to help her from her cloak, a red wool piece lined in silk with a charming hood that Mama insisted she wear. As he handed it to the waiting housekeeper, she heard him say in a low tone behind her ear, "What a fetching color to wear with your ruddy locks."

The apples of her cheeks warmed, but she reminded herself this was nothing but a polite welcome from the heir of Sandy Bank.

Mr. Hathaway took her into the front parlor, a room clearly used for visitors with its impressive book collection, great hearth at the south end, and a harpsicord positioned between two windows that reached floor to ceiling. The room was sprinkled with early guests, some still wearing their traveling clothes.

"Do come in," said Mrs. Hathaway, and Mr. Hathaway led Phoebe across the room like a footman.

Mama was seated along a tufted bench beneath the books within reach of conversation with Mrs. Hathaway. She beamed at Phoebe as if today was the most exciting day of their lives. Phoebe pasted a polite smile on her face as soft conversations around her dwindled into silence. She swallowed as she made a curtsey to Mrs. Hathaway.

"You have arrived safe and sound, I see. Did my son keep you safe on your passage over? He's such a comfort to me when I take the ferry."

"Yes, quite," Phoebe assured her.

The lady gave Mr. Hathaway a nod of approval. "I congratulate you on delivering two of my favorite friends safely to Sandy Bank. I knew we could count on you."

Phoebe never felt worthy of this woman's notice before. The changes in her social position since being asked by Mr. Hathaway to dance at the Twelfth Night ball were curious. What had she been thinking refusing him when he was really so charming?

She refocused on Mrs. Hathaway's thin lips as the hostess explained the schedule for the evening. Afterward, when

Phoebe joined Mama on the bench, she realized Mr. Hathaway had walked away to converse with another man in front of the windows.

She felt lost. Occasionally her gaze swept back over to Mr. Hathaway, and once she found him looking her way. Their eyes met, and as if sensing her discomfort, he gave her a small nod that made her inhale deeply.

Phoebe dipped her chin back in acknowledgement and forced herself to relax. She turned her attention back to Mrs. Hathaway's story about her worst party ever and joined in the sympathetic gasps, although she was certain Lily Hathaway had never thrown a terrible ball in her entire life.

THE NEXT EVENING, JAMES grabbed Benjamin's arm and hurried him upstairs. The time to relax would be short with the concert Mama had planned. Since St. Cecilia Society's concert season was over, she'd invited a popular English violinist in town to travel to Mount Pleasant to play. Four local girls, rather young to come out, would be singing, except for Miss Whitely, who was clearly more gifted at the spinet than conversation or dancing. *Unlike Miss Applewaite*, James thought to himself as he climbed the steps.

Benjamin let out a satisfied sigh when they slipped into the near-empty room. Most of the other gentlemen had returned downstairs to the ballroom for the concert on the arms of their companions. Patting his stomach, he groaned, "I thought we would never get away from the table," and James chuckled.

They took two yellow chairs pushed together on one side of the flickering fire that cheered the dark green walls. Benjamin draped his long arms over the chair's rosewood arms. "Miss Applewaite is in good looks tonight."

James rubbed his chin, surprised he would bring her up so soon. Did Benjamin sense she was constantly on his mind; either floating around in the back of it with dark eyes and bright locks or at the forefront as he sorted through the possible scenarios of becoming a "tenant for life."

"Did you see her lovely gown? I do love the colors so bright and flowered like summertime."

"It isn't the attire I admired, no," chuckled Benjamin. "If one can get past her persistent frown and distant gazes, she's a lovely thing."

"I always thought so," admitted James. He could do much worse than Phoebe Applewaite, and not much better when it came to her true disposition.

"And you did not mind being asked to accompany them here?" Benjamin arched a brow. "Your mama does not ask for things unless she has a motive, you know."

"You've puzzled her out." James realized it was probably time to admit there was a plan brewing in his head, too. He accepted a cigar from the case passed around and then scooted back to watch the fire glow. "I was happy to do it, you see, as I've already called on her a time or two. We've walked and talked."

Benjamin looked at him in surprise.

"I see her on East Bay on occasion when she's wandering through the market."

"She should not be out without a chaperone," remarked Benjamin.

"Well, yes, but she's nearly our age, and everyone knows the family. Plus, as you've mentioned, she's rather independent and too careful of a person to let some rogue lead her off down an alley."

Benjamin clamped his teeth around his cigar. "Then you enjoy her company although she refused you on Twelfth Night."

"It was only a dance," James dismissed, wishing he had not confided that, "and do you blame her?"

"No." They laughed at themselves, and James took a deep breath. "To be honest," he whispered as he glanced around the room, "Papa is champing at the bit to get a piece of land on the other side of Charleston, and the Applewaites have a tract right up the Ashley not far from Duck Point.

"Yes, but Daniel Cadwell has that piece and is living out there with his little lawful blanket," Benjamin reminded him.

"Not all of it. There are a couple hundred acres in reserve for Miss Applewaite. A dowry, I believe."

"And you know this how?" Benjamin looked interested, if not concerned.

"I suppose it's something Papa knew through her father. They don't have a great deal of income since the war and Mr. Applewaite's untimely death, but—"

"Who can be poor in Charleston?" shrugged Benjamin. "One can buy anything the heart desires."

James hesitated. From his lofty position lording over the enormous Quinton estate, Benjamin did not rub shoulders with those who had little to their names. James returned to Miss Applewaite. "She is, as you have heard, more interested in becoming a professional than a wife."

"A milliner or something?" snorted Benjamin. "There's dozens of those."

"Yes, but she has connections with Cadwell's modest attempt to carry on the family merchant business, and besides cutting and sewing like a mantua-maker, she knows how to acquire and move inventory."

"Ah, yes," Benjamin drawled, "her little kerchiefs? I admit she has skill with her embroideries and such. I purchased a handkerchief from Mr. Payne last time I was in, and he told me it was her work, but..." He licked his lip. "Jamie, is that why you asked me to dissuade old Leonard from bringing my sister out? You know she has concerns about your interest in the Applewaites."

"Your sister is rather unkind to Miss Applewaite. I see no reason for it."

"You don't really want a woman who manages a shop, do you? It's a step down for you Hathaways."

"There are dozens of highly respected women managing their own enterprises in Charleston," James reminded him, "I think it's rather modern of them. Besides, if I'm at sea it would keep her occupied."

Benjamin's eyes widened in alarm. "Are you seriously considering chaining yourself down?" He skimmed the room, leaned forward, and whispered, "Then the old master has made up his mind, has he? Is he still dangling a ship? Let me guess, he will let you go to sea if you submit yourself to the altar."

James resisted the urge to pat his friend's hand. "Listen, you old rogue elephant, if I don't find something to do beside play cards and drink you under the table every night, I will never be anything more than a pathetic dependent, and I don't want to end up back at this place." He shot a look around for emphasis. "She's handsome, you know, in good health, and strong. I know

I amuse her although she'll never admit it. And look, when I have a ship under my command someday, people will take me seriously and then she will, too." He sat back and cleared his throat.

Benjamin stared at him like he was mad. "What do you care what people think?"

James shrugged to hide the fact that he did care, a little bit. Thinking about Miss Applewaite and the rather pleasant benefits of marriage, not to mention his very own ship, made his chest burn inside in a queer way, like the first time he'd ever noticed a pretty girl.

He shook off the silly, boyish sensation. "It's like this," he said in a hushed tone turning back to the fire, "*if* I marry Miss Applewaite, my mama is pleased to see me settled, my papa sees the family acquire land up the other river, and I..." he leaned over and said with emphasis, "will get an officer's post and someday captain the *Lily*!"

DINNER DID NOT FEEL too much like torture, admitted Phoebe. She sipped a cup of punch while standing on the fringes of the modest-sized ballroom dripping with elaborate ivory chandeliers. Servants moved chairs against the walls. A harpsicord was tugged back into a corner since the musical performances of Mrs. Hathaway's guests were complete. Shy Miss Whitely had sang in her beautiful falsetto and rippled chills down Phoebe's arms. It'd been a good distraction since Mr. Hathaway had not reappeared.

Standing just inside the door, Phoebe studied the contrast of the blues and greens of the upholstered furniture against the white walls. Soon, the dancing would start, and the smiles and painted fans would flick and flutter as the evening flirtations began—if they had not already. She hadn't noticed.

The first dance was announced, and Phoebe felt herself sink against the wall behind her as if she could melt into it like a ghost and pass through to the other side. Mama and other ladies sat in circles around Mrs. Hathaway's empty chair near a window that overlooked the back lawn. Partners lined up in descending order of rank, and the strings scratched out sounds of preparation.

Phoebe noted with an odd sense of satisfaction that Mr. Hathaway had not taken the floor beside his parents as flames danced up and down on their wicks. She wasn't sure how she'd feel seeing him partnered with someone else, and that was ridiculous. He had not claimed her. She had not claimed him. Besides, he was such a flirt, he'd probably begged a dance from every single woman there.

With a sudden jerk, two doors flush with the long wall to her left pulled apart, and a few older gentlemen slunk into the room. Next was Mr. Hathaway in his bright spring fineries, and then the sophisticated and very rich Mr. Quinton with his dark hair and eyes.

She watched the handsome pair shoulder their way through the crowd. Unfortunately, Mr. Quinton seized her attention with his searching gaze first. There was something sly about the upward stroke of his sharp smile.

When she looked back, he was no longer beside Mr. Hathaway but weaving through the crowd. Her stomach lurched with suspicion as he came closer. With her back against the wall, she felt trapped behind the throng of guests on both sides.

He probably had a question regarding something she'd mentioned to Mr. Hathaway or perhaps Daniel. Surely, there were no other intentions.

"I said, 'Good evening, Miss Applewaite.'"

He smelled of pungent tobacco and was quite tall. Phoebe looked up. "I'm sorry, Mr. Quinton, my mind was elsewhere."

"Even though you saw me from across the room? Or were you looking for someone else? Mr. Hathaway, perhaps?"

His words stung. "I beg your pardon?"

He chuckled. "I apologize, I'm only teasing. You must not mind it, for see they are ready to start dancing, and I have no partner whilst my friend has many."

Phoebe jerked her gaze back to Mr. Hathaway. Two women hovered on either side of him, smiling, chatting, and flapping their fans like they'd forgotten how to use them. He laughed, not the least bit concerned about where she might be. Something heavy plunked into the pit of Phoebe's stomach. A hot ripple of nausea followed. She felt her back teeth come together and swallowed to keep from locking her jaw—her usual response. It would not do to look jealous. *Jealous*?

Mr. Quinton made a shallow bow then waved toward the center of the room. "I know you are not fond of dancing, for it is widely known, but I did see you dancing last month at the McClellan's and I can assure you, I've had my share of hours with the dance master. There will be no tripping or falling tonight."

Appalled at his reference to her accident in the past, Phoebe forced herself not to glare. He grinned like she imagined a dark warlock might and stretched out a beckoning hand.

With a sharp inhale, she took it. His brown eyes flickered in surprise.

"Well then," she murmured, her heart shrinking, "I suppose you deserve a partner of some sort." She could not wait for Mr. Hathaway to ask her. She must at least pretend to enjoy herself—for Mama and Mrs. Hathaway's sake. Mr. Quinton made a noise that sounded like a snicker as he led her to the floor.

Phoebe found it hard not to watch Mr. Hathaway as she was maneuvered past others waiting for a partner. When she took her position across from Mr. Quinton, she glanced toward Mr. Hathaway and saw him watching the line take shape while the women around him chattered on like chickens.

His gaze met hers and lightning struck. Phoebe caught her breath and wondered at the jolt she felt when they connected. Mr. Hathaway's eyes widened when he saw her on the floor with his friend but then he looked away. She wasn't sure if it was in question or surprise. Moments later, she watched him cross the floor leading one of the women by the elbow to the front of the room. He beamed like it was the best night of his life.

Phoebe's damp hands began to tremble. She felt a frown escape. Glancing at Mr. Quinton, she saw he'd noticed the entire event and an amused grin spread across his face.

Chiding herself for being distracted by her fickle friend, she turned her attention back to Mr. Quinton and gave him a pretty opening curtsy. The music then proceeded to blur in her ears as she moved through the steps.

"You dance well, Miss Applewaite," murmured Mr. Quinton as he circled around her, "and not often enough."

She raised a brow, not certain if he was trying to be friendly or flirtatious. She moved around him, careful to keep her balance and tried not to notice Mr. Hathaway and his pretty partner smiling at each other.

A shadow fluttered over her heart like a dark crow and another scowl sank into her face. What business did young women seething in flattery have to do here at Sandy Bank anyway? This was a celebration of spring—of music and the planting season—not a coming out.

Her shoulders slumped as she realized her thoughts sounded vain and presumptuous. Most of the guests were from the upper ranks of Charleston society—plantation owners, bankers, and politicians. Then there were the wealthy or affluent merchants, and some of the older and respected families like her own.

It was, Phoebe knew, a privilege to be a week-long guest at Sandy Bank. She took another breath to keep dizziness at bay and wished her stays were not so tight. She'd allowed a lady's maid to help her dress quite fancifully tonight: a new gown remade from a silk frock of Mama's in the softest shade of shell-pink with a darker petticoat. She'd let down a thick lock at the nape of her neck and split it into two neat curls that draped over her shoulder and around her throat.

Mr. Quinton caught her eye and gave her another quick wink. It disconcerted her so much that she nearly tripped over her toes. Phoebe caught herself and managed a final pirouette before her curtsy to her partner and then the gaping onlookers. With a pounding heart, she searched the room for Alice Leonard, then recalled she had not come and let out a sigh of relief. Hopefully, no one had seen her stumble. Across the room, women sitting in Mama's corner leaned into one another and whispered behind their fans.

"It looks like people are talking," mused Mr. Quinton as he took her elbow. She could not run away, so she let him lead her toward a small punch table across the room.

"People are always talking," returned Phoebe in a quiet tone.

"Yes, they are," he agreed but did not set her loose.

She waited for him to pass her a crystal glass brimming with refreshment.

"You do not seem the sort to mind it."

"I do not," she pretended and took a sip of the delicious tangy citrus and spiced drink.

Mr. Quinton put a hand on his hip and examined her rather rudely. "I suppose that is what earned you your reputation. You're quite respected and independent they say."

"Who says?" wondered Phoebe. Had Mr. Hathaway spoken about her?

"I've heard," said Mr. Quinton with a brittle smile, "that you have some useless ambition to be a mantua-maker or something of the sort. Or to dress hats."

"Most ladies dress hats," Phoebe informed him, "and do a great deal of sewing. There is nothing low about it."

"Ah," he said as if she did not understand his meaning, but she did.

"I happen to know there are a great many ladies in Charleston who do not have the time or skill to sew silk or damask gowns, and the mantua-makers can't keep up."

"So you are thinking of going into business for yourself although you have a fine home already in town and land up the Ashley?"

His voice sounded disdainful, and how did he know Papa had left land for her in Mama's hands? Phoebe slanted her head and managed to stand taller in her bow-laden heeled shoes. "Tell me, Mr. Quinton, what is it that you find low about a person's ambition to be industrious?"

He was silent for a heartbeat then said with flashing eyes, "I meant no offense, Miss Applewaite. It is only I believe birth to be a privilege and an honor and do not know many ladies of your rank with their eyes on business affairs."

"Well," said Phoebe in a biting tone, quite tired of Mr. Quinton now, "I've often found that privilege comes without any effort and requires little character."

He looked stung for a moment then his face widened into a grin. "Aren't you wild, Miss Applewaite? And what will be next? Your own indigo farm? Or a new crop that has never been grown in Carolina soil?"

"If you imply I'm to be compared to Mrs. Eliza Pinckney, God rest her soul, because I have a mind and abilities suited to commerce, then for that I thank you, Mr. Quinton."

Phoebe raised her empty goblet into the air and let it hang, and as soon as he took it, brushed past him like he was a servant. She nearly collided into Mr. Hathaway who had just approached them. His eyes looked quizzical as if he'd seen the private tête-à-tête between her and his friend.

"Miss Applewaite – Mr. Hathaway," they said at the same time, but Phoebe did not stop less she berate him for telling his friends all about her. Probably they had laughed over it earlier as the port was passed around the table. It seemed she was an amusing topic of conversation Mr. Hathaway used to entertain his companions. He did it so well.

She whisked through the door and into the hall, ignoring the looks of surprise at her hurry and most likely flushed face. Storming down a back passage to a garden room, she hurried out a set of open doors into the back courtyard and chilly March night.

# CHAPTER SEVEN

James only needed seconds to see that Benjamin had stirred up Miss Applewaite into some kind of tempest. He balked when Benjamin broke into laughter after she fled. "What did you say?" he demanded in disbelief.

"I questioned her about her little shop that you mentioned, and she took offense at my opinion that ladies of her class bring themselves no honor engaging in business."

A few women glanced at them from behind their fans, and James felt a chill in the air. "I'm sure you have forgotten the household accounts upon which no gentleman could better manage."

He said this loud and with a grin, knowing it was true in most cases. A few smiles shot his way, and he gave Benjamin a shake of his head. "And now look," he added, feeling devilish, "there is Miss Whitely, and she has heard you insult her most reliable and capable sex."

James escaped as Benjamin turned his head to find Miss Whitely watching them from a narrow side chair where she sat alone. James felt a little guilty drawing everyone's attention to the quiet girl, but she needed a partner or at least a kind word. Though Benjamin Quinton might be a rake, he would not insult a lady by seeing her addressed and then ignored.

James trotted out to the front hall nodding *hello* to his neighbors and his parents' friends. Daniel Cadwell stood across the room and raised a glass in acknowledgment. James hurried over.

"I say there, Cadwell. Have you seen your sister about?"

Mr. Cadwell shook his head, but an unmistakable spark of interest flickered in his eye.

A man beside him motioned toward the back door of the hall. "I believe I saw her just moments ago. She seemed in a hurry. Is that the ladies' room?" he asked himself.

"Perhaps, but I think my wife said there was a lounge upstairs," replied Cadwell.

"Yes," agreed James, "on the top floor and very private," he told them before leaving with a pat on Cadwell's shoulder as if he hated to go.

He did not, in fact, hate to go. His mind wasn't interested in conversations about crops and exports but concerned for Miss Applewaite's comfort. He'd planned to ask her for the first dance. It would set the tone for his intentions, he thought, for the rest of the week. People would catch on if they were observant, and perhaps all this nonsense talk that he was spoiled and unaccountable and acting like a London dandy would cease. No one, in his memory, had ever softened bristly Phoebe Applewaite. She liked him, he believed. Surely he had a chance to convince her to marry him. His future depended on it.

Mama thought she was brilliant and beautiful. Papa liked her temperament—and her land. Best of all, James liked her most for a myriad of reasons. She was pretty and serious and clever and...

Why had Benjamin asked her first, dash it all? He did not like the idea of James settling down, that was much clear, although he still cared for his mother, younger brother, and a gaggle of sisters. Odd that a man of his responsibilities was never censured for galloping up and down the coast letting his house and land run to ruin.

Benjamin really had very little else to do. Rice and cotton were like silver and gold in South Carolina, and with his property and assets managed by others, poor Benjamin wandered around a wealthy and free man. No wonder he was bored.

The thought struck James his friend might have insulted Miss Applewaite as he hurried into his mother's conservatory and saw the open doors leading out onto the brick-paved courtyard. Gardens flanked the sides of the house and stretched around the corners to the back where Mama's flowerbeds made a lovely oval with walking paths and statuettes. A few roses hearty enough to flower early perfumed the air along with the salted breeze blowing through the oaks and willows across the creek.

James wondered if Miss Applewaite had come outside after all. She wasn't afraid to walk to the market or the shore on her own. He squinted. The moon hung full in the sky, and candles and lanterns shining from the windows aided his ability to search through the darkness. He strode down the narrow paths, familiar with their confusing abrupt turns and passed the occasional sheepish couple, alone, arm and arm, and lost in conversation.

*Ah*. There she was, poised on a narrow bench beneath an unfurled tulip tree with her back to him. He crept up behind her, noticing how her neck looked with her hair pulled up. A dark lock of hair hung down past her neck, and he resisted the urge to slip his finger under it and curl it around his hand.

She sat motionlessly, but he could see her breathing. Her gaze was on the egret-white moon dappled with silver scars. Unable to resist, he leaned down to her ear and found himself tempted to kiss it. Instead, he said, "Are you lost?"

The contemplative woman jerked so hard he erupted into a fit of giggles. "I'm sorry," he gasped, covering his mouth and snickering at her violent stare. "May I?"

There wasn't much room. It was narrow and short, his mother's seat when she came out to pick at her flowers. To his surprise, Miss Applewaite scooted over to one edge.

He sat next to her and tried to ignore the awareness he felt so close to her shoulder, her arm, and her side. She angled her legs further away. He lowered his hand to rest it on the small space between them, but it landed on hers. She didn't move it away, but she jumped again.

"I do not mean to disturb you. You look so peaceful sitting out here alone."

"Not peaceful enough," she murmured and turned back to her study of the moon.

"Shall I go? You look cross." His chest prickled, and James wondered what he would feel like if she told him yes. Benjamin must have said something to her to make her quite upset.

"No." She gave a curt shake of her head. "I needed some air. Do I look angry? This is how we're taught to sit, stiff and straight, and there's little choice with our... bindings."

"Stays," mused James, not shocked in the least she would bring up such a thing. "Yes. I've had my share of bindings. Not in so many years, but when I was little."

She looked at him in question. He shrugged in the dark.

"They believed I had rickets when I was small. I was a sickly thing," he admitted. James twisted his neck to glance at the house behind them. "I was kept indoors most of my childhood and in bed."

Miss Applewaite turned back to the moon, but her eyes looked alert as she listened.

"You can see the marsh from my room—can look across the creek and almost all the way down to the river mouth. I used to stand at the window and watch the barges go down, laden with the indigo, bricks..." He fell silent, remembering the first time Mammy had let him go out with her son in one of the pirogues, while she hopped from one foot to the other in fear he would be harmed.

"I didn't know that about you," Miss Applewaite admitted. "You look to be in full health these days."

James felt himself smile. "Why, Phoebe—I mean—Miss Applewaite, I do believe you paid me a compliment."

She made a noise of amusement. "Which surprises even me, Mr. Hathaway, and since you asked, I am a little angry after all, but perhaps I am too sensitive."

James's heart wavered with concern. "About what?"

"Mr. Quinton is an elegant dancer, but less than charming when he converses."

"Good heavens, what has the dolt said now? And you're quite right. He possesses all of the manners and charms required of a gentleman but drives even me half-mad with his jests."

She lifted her chin like she understood. "It seems my reputation has evolved, from one of sharp, bitter spinsterhood into avaricious, unladylike business ambitions." There was something earnest in the way she held her head, forward and tilted, her eyes looking intently into his as if the moonlight could reveal what was inside of his mind.

"No one of my acquaintance has ever called you bitter," James assured her, "though perhaps your talents and abilities have been noticed a little more often of late. You do have a remarkable acquaintanceship with Mr. Payne and a few of the dry goods merchants in the market."

"My little handkerchief business?" She bit her lip, eyes still focused on him. "How did Mr. Quinton know I intend to open my own shop in the future? He mentioned it as if I were a hoyden for wanting to make my own money rather than grovel at the feet of every single man of wealth in the low country."

James blinked. "I'm sure that was not his meaning."

"I'm sure it was," she replied. "Unless..."

"What?"

She remained silent and looked away.

Her distress made James feel uneasy. "Please accept my apology," he said with sincerity. "I did mention your plans to Mr. Quinton, for he is my very good friend. But it was shared with the most ardent admiration, for I do, Miss Applewaite," James cleared his throat, "admire you."

All at once, her expression became silvery and fairy-like in the moonlight although her jaw still looked tight. James went on. "I admire how hard you work and how confident you are in what you want and your aim to get it."

Dash it all, he was babbling, but he couldn't stop. "You seem to have an enviable sort of contentment, not only with yourself but for the little things. I wish I was as comfortable with my mama as you are with yours, and I have no brothers or sisters to speak of, so..."

He fell silent for a pause then Miss Applewaite said in a gentle tone, "I'm sorry you've had your own difficult circumstances, Mr. Hathaway. Please understand that I do appreciate your enthusiasm and support for my endeavors. Shipping our little trunk of kerchiefs to the Indies was very generous indeed."

He'd forgotten all about that. "I'm sure your dividends will arrive soon. You are a pleasure to do business with, to converse with, and even..." He looked up toward the house again, listening for the echo of music, "to dance with."

Their gazes met again, and James remembered they were quite alone. He could kiss her, but she did not seem the sort that would let him get away with it. He best not. It would lower him in her esteem, and for some reason, that mattered to him.

"I quite intended to ask for your hand for the first dance," he admitted, "but Quinton beat me to it." Her dark eyes widened in the indigo night. "Do come inside and dance with me, Miss Applewaite, and we will set old Quinton straight."

THEY DID DANCE, AND the following days for Phoebe became more enjoyable than any others she could remember. Under the watchful eyes of the mamas roosting at Sandy Bank, Mr. Hathaway took her riding to see land lush with green grass, dainty azaleas, and palmetto trees. There were also thickly-wooded pine forests and sprouting straight rows in the fields where the vegetables grew. They spoke of the futile attempts to raise silkworms by their ancestors, and Mr. Hathaway went on to explain the trade routes between the East and West Indies as they pertained to the Americas. Phoebe found it all very interesting.

The next morning, the women of the party remaining at Sandy Bank attended the small parish church, jostling up and down on the rough roads in their Sunday best while the men rode their horses alongside the carriage. Mrs. Hathaway acted kindly, but Phoebe felt undeserving of it because she understood the lady's expectations. Mama fairly glowed. It was as if a great burden had been lifted from her shoulders, and she was chattier and livelier than her usual self.

On Monday, looking quite dapper in dark breeches and a woolen waistcoat with no cravat, Mr. Hathaway took Phoebe to the brickyard. They stood without speaking, watching the workers shape and carry bricks to line up in the sun to dry. They were turned every so often by little brown-skinned children who belonged in nurseries or at their mothers' knees.

It soon began to drizzle, and Mr. Hathaway joined Phoebe in the library to read although he did not last for long. She saw him later walking the rutted road past the back of the house with his papa, who spoke while pointing across the marsh. His son watched the ground, only occasionally nodding in the wet, misty air. He was bound heavily in an overcoat—an effort, she suspected, to please his mama.

After another fine dinner and good conversation in the drawing room thereafter, Phoebe decided she would walk down to the small dock in the morning to see where the bricks were loaded onto barges and moved down the creek into the Wando River. From there, she knew, they would merge with the Cooper and float down to Charleston's port.

She'd seen Rathall Creek in the distance. It was confided to her that this was where Mr. Hathaway escaped to as a boy whenever he was let out of the house. He knew all of the fish, waterfowl, and plants by name—some the Gullah interpretation—but they were, he hinted, at one time his only friends that carried him down the waterways and protected him as he came and went in his mammy's son's little pirogue until he got his own.

It was dry and surprisingly tepid the next day. Phoebe dressed the best she could without help so as not to wake Mama. The sky glimmered with lavender suggestions of dawn as birds nested around the house began to murmur. She walked down the carpeted grand staircase wrapped in her scarlet cloak, a simple morning dress, and the good boots she'd worn on the ferry, avoiding the household staff moving silently in and out of the rooms on the ground floor.

Boldly, she let herself out the front door, took the side steps down to the lawn, and slipped into the garden, seeing that some of the flower buds looked about to burst. The morning air felt brittle, anxious for sun, so she pulled the hood over her head and lifted her petticoats to keep them dry in the damp grass.

Down the drive lined with holly trees, she avoided the mud. Horses nodded across the road. A light mist slipped across the pasture and curled its fingers around the fence posts. Hearing the low murmurs of the enslaved people risen for another day, she continued until she reached the narrow road rutted with wagon wheels. It led to trees lining the creek. A large boarded structure with a slanted roof stood sentry over the wooden dock and its pilings.

Hearing the rushing sound of water, Phoebe wandered over to the small dock as an enormous pelican glided by overhead. The narrow creek was rather high but looked like it might ebb soon. A few wobbly-looking boats were tied off at the last piling.

Phoebe wrapped her arm around it and studied the western sky still draped in darkness. It was peaceful here, but different than her favorite shore where the mouth to the sea yawned opened in the distance. Here, she admitted, was a sense of comfort one couldn't find in the clattering streets of town.

A distant splash made her look upstream. Turtles or fish were moving around with daybreak. She squinted through the lifting shadows and remembered the danger of creeping alligators. Her stomach dropped, but then she saw the figure of a man sitting on the grassy bank. It was probably still muddy, and she wondered that he did not take care to protect his breeches.

Upon closer examination, she saw it was young Mr. Hathaway, her companion for most hours of the day at Sandy Bank, and though she had just seen him last night, her heart soared. The poor man must have felt obligated to see to her entertainment during the day when she wasn't with the other ladies in Mrs. Hathaway's private parlor, but how she enjoyed it. And him.

She found herself crossing the dock and wading through the grass above the creek's muddy waterline. Mr. Hathaway stared over the creek into the distant marshland. His legs were bent and his arms wrapped around his knees. The rising sun had chased away the gloom around the creek, but with his eyes on the distant clouds still untouched by morning, he did not seem to notice her.

She crept up beside him before he saw her from the corner of his eye, and his face bloomed into a brilliant, toothy grin. She only just turned up the corners of her mouth, and at her quiet composure, his grin melted into a more natural and relaxed smile. He moved to get up.

"No." She held out a cold hand. "Please. I don't mean to interrupt your solitude. I just wanted to wish you a good morning."

"It looks like we had the same idea."

"It's so busy during the day I wanted to see what it was like at dawn," admitted Phoebe, "and to see if I could hear the marsh the way I hear the sea."

"It's much easier to listen out here," agreed Mr. Hathaway, and he removed his coat. He spread it on the ground and patted it. "Sit next to me."

Phoebe touched her lips together, thinking. His green eyes creased in the corners, and she decided his invitation was sincere. She pulled down the hood of her cloak. "If you're sure."

"I am," he insisted, offering his hand to help her to the ground. It felt soft and mushy beneath her as she folded her legs and sat down. "I'm going to ruin your coat," she worried.

He waved off her concern. "It's an old thing I wear to the fields and the brickyard, what I throw over a shirt if I want to paddle upstream."

Convinced, Phoebe relaxed and loosened the ribbon around her throat. "And how does Rathall Creek look this morning?"

"Satisfactory," declared the man beside her. "The barges from Boone will come down soon. We do not have a load going out today, so it's peaceful for now." His mussed hair ruffled in the breeze. He looked like a young farm boy without a hat or cravat.

"I like it here," Phoebe assured him. "You were right. The birds far outnumber what we have in town and sound prettier, too."

"Yes, chatty things."

She quieted, but he turned to her without warning. Almost arm to arm, his face was so close it had a startling effect on her. She blinked, inspecting his eyes as he studied hers.

"You have handsome eyes, Miss Applewaite," he said. "Some people would say doe-like, but they are rather oval and slanted with golden flecks that remind me of a dog I had when I was a boy."

A laugh gurgled up in Phoebe's throat. "So, I remind you of your favorite dog," she said, both amused and somewhere in her heart, aghast.

He chuckled at her censure. "She was a most loyal and trustworthy friend. Queenie lived a good long life until she turned twelve years old. How I cried when she passed on."

"I'm sorry," faltered Phoebe, feeling sad for him. "I'm afraid we never had animals in our house, they irritate Mama's congestion, so I settle for the mourning doves in the windows, the cranes on the shore, the nag in the carriage house, and the occasional kitten in the alleyway if it isn't too wild."

"Ah, yes, some of them are," he agreed. "Cats are screechy-scratchy things. I much prefer a terrier for a mouser like they keep aboard some ships."

"You know a great many things about sailing, Mr. Hathaway, and running a plantation. Who would think that you carted around so much knowledge and experience in your mind? I underestimated you."

He returned to her examination, and rays of morning sunlight stroked his crown making him look princely. "I have learned a great many things, too," he admitted, "just this week alone."

She thought he might mean her by the way he regarded her with such a warm expression. It looked like the affection she felt for him and made her tremble. She clasped her hands together, sorry she'd forgotten her gloves.

"Miss Applewaite?"

Phoebe swallowed. "Yes?"

"I like to think we've become very good friends."

She raised her head in a half-nod while studying a ripple in the flowing creek below.

Mr. Hathaway fell silent again, and she peeked at him from the corner of her eye. He stared at her in a way that made her stomach lurch like she'd fallen from a tree. She knew him now to be more than handsome. He was a good man with charming, sincere airs when he chose to be himself.

As if sensing her thoughts, he murmured, "You know I wish to sail, and I know I'm fortunate to have this lovely home. But I do not wish to live out the rest of my days here, especially on the backs of others."

He was quite the abolitionist, she thought.

"I hope to inherit my parents' house in town, and if this land passes to me as I expect it will, I'll probably sell it if I do not keep it as a small farm. Does that shock you?"

"It is a great tract of land and well developed. Safe, I suspect from storms and intruders."

"Far safer than Charleston but not immune from attack. We're fortunate it survived the war, and Papa has added onto it in my lifetime, but..."

"You hear the siren of the sea," guessed Phoebe, "just as I have dreams that make no sense either."

"Come now," Mr. Hathaway chided, scooting closer, "your dreams make perfect sense. I've made a few inquiries out of curiosity and found there is always a shortage of seamstresses and supplies when it comes to garment-making and such. I quite admire you for aiming to have a shop like your papa."

"Even though I'm a woman?"

He glanced past her as if embarrassed to meet her eye. "It's not like it's a tobacco shop or a tavern, either. And you did say you would only manage it."

"Yes," agreed Phoebe. "And not that I believe it a low occupation, but I'm tired to death of stitching, Mr. Hathaway. It seems I have had a needle in my hand since my papa died, trying in some way I suspect, to replace his absence, to comfort my family, or to be industrious and prove myself worthy of him."

"Yes, and I admire that." He pushed his fingers through his hair then slanted his head and smiled at her. "I suppose your family assumed you'd marry as soon as you came out—being so handsome and all."

She bit her lip pensively. Had he just called her handsome? Her? Little Phoebe Applewaite who could not dance the minuet without falling on her face. "I did not come out so well, you know."

He raised his brows. "Just because of a fall? *Pfft*. We've all done it."

Phoebe felt inclined to be honest, even if it sounded like she disagreed. "I did not have any close friends, and there were others who weren't very kind to me. It caused so much distraction that I couldn't think straight or dance well at all, and with one disaster after another, I just avoided the ballrooms and kept to myself."

Mr. Hathaway cupped a hand over his mouth as if thinking. White sunlight shimmered off of the creek's streaming current. "Do you mean Alice Quinton? Mrs. Leonard, I should say. You were never friends?"

"No," Phoebe cringed. She'd never complained to anyone about Alice Quinton Leonard except Mama, but since they were speaking intimately, perhaps she could make Mr. Hathaway understand how she felt about his best friend's sister.

"Mrs. Leonard has long liked to criticize me. My attempts to dance and perform at dinner parties were her favorite amusements. How she liked to point out my flaws." Phoebe sat back. "She has always disliked me, and I know of no reason why."

Mr. Hathaway chuckled. "But of course you do. She and all the girls of that set are not as sweet. They were always laughing and flirting—quite false. Why, they all married quickly, didn't they? I'm sure it was jealousy. She doesn't like to be around anyone with more money; I imagine she disliked you because she felt second to your looks and charm."

"Mine? Oh, no," denied Phoebe, although a wave of pleasure washed over her. Did he really think so? "I'm sure I had neither of those. I was practically orange-headed, you remember, and too shy to be found charming."

"I always thought you were charming," Mr. Hathaway insisted. "You answered kindly and intelligently although you kept to the corners of the rooms. That is until you became older and cross with me and the others."

"*Hmph*," muttered Phoebe, "you would have too if you were me."

To her surprise, Mr. Hathaway reached out and pulled a lock of hair from behind her ear then wound it around his finger. "In case you haven't noticed, Miss Applewaite, you no longer have fiery orange locks which were adorable anyway. Your hair is russet now with streaks of scarlet and gold that well-near take a man's breath away."

Phoebe almost choked on laughter but managed to say, "How kind you are Mr. Hathaway. All I see is tangerine."

He made a noise of dissent in his throat. "For someone so sharp-witted and observant, my darling, you overlook yourself completely."

Phoebe's breath caught in her throat. She liked being addressed as *his darling*. Bold but... She wanted to believe him, to believe that when people looked at her they did not think of widows and orphans and orange-haired homely children. Or spinsters.

She faced him and found their chins only inches apart. It gave her the wild desire to bend her forehead over his lips and rest it there. She shifted her gaze to his eyes and found him staring deeply into hers.

"Do you really think so?" she wondered at last to break the spell.

He gave a curt nod. "You have worried far too long about what others think of you. Really, people are so busy thinking of themselves, they hardly spare a thought for anyone else."

She could not tear her gaze away. Her breath danced in her chest.

"Miss Applewaite," the man whispered, and Phoebe's heart made an arching, graceful dive like a bird into the sea. Everything around them blurred. She could not move. The world around them felt paralyzed as if waiting for something.

How could this be? How could Phoebe Applewaite have such violent feelings of affection alongside her strong attraction to this man? How had they come so far and so fast since he'd first teased her in the drawing room at the McClellans? He was not at all what she'd always thought him to be. Perhaps she was just as wrong about herself.

As if he understood her feelings, Mr. Hathaway leaned forward and brushed his lips across hers. Heat washed over her in a delightful shower. She thought she would faint if she did not fly up to the sky. She felt his hand rub over her cheek and dared to watch him examine her skin, her sparse scattering of freckles, and she suspected, her scarlet cheeks.

To her relief and mixed disappointment, he leaned back, but his fingers trailed down her arm and took her hand. Together their hands felt warm.

Watching her intently, he whispered, "I'm afraid I have grown more than fond of you, Miss Applewaite, in ways I can't explain. Do you really think it's such a bad idea, this prompting and prying from our mothers? You must know that I think I—" he hesitated, and his cheeks flooded with a dark shade of red. The boyish look and what he'd almost said made Phoebe's eyes brim with tears.

"I think it would be a handsome idea," he suggested, clearing his throat and squeezing her hand, "to consider an arrangement between you and me." His mouth clamped shut like he needed to hold his breath.

Phoebe's mind spun as she tried to make sense of his words. She suspected she loved him, did he know? He reached up to swipe under his eye as if trying to distract himself from some inner agony.

"Do you mean?" she began, trying to sound non-plussed and not like her heart was floating somewhere up above them in the scattered clouds.

"A union," he whispered. "I know you wish to have your own opportunities, and I fully support that."

His accommodating words on top of the unexpected proposal made Phoebe want to throw her arms around him. How could he know this scene was an answer to her young womanly dreams—hopes she had given up on long ago with no papa, wealth, or popularity. Not trusting her tongue, she forced herself to give a small nod.

James continued like he thought she needed more convincing. "I know it's odd I have no desire to manage a plantation and that I prefer town."

"But so do I," she blurted, a possible future falling into place before her like colored bricks.

"I mean to sail somehow, even if I have to buy a commission in the Navy or find another shipping company if our own won't have me."

Wanting to reassure him, Phoebe offered, "I daresay a merchantman captain and a shopkeeper about town would make a very handsome couple."

"Indeed," he agreed, "and a pair that gets on so well. You could organize my books, and I'd..." He hesitated as if not sure what he could offer.

"You could take me to parties and balls, and then I wouldn't feel so inclined to hide in the corners. Why," she breathed, "I wouldn't hide at all, because I enjoy your companionship and conversation."

He looked amazed. "You do? I thought you were of the opinion I was the most ridiculous thing to ride a gig about town."

"Well..." A smile tugged at the corners of Phoebe's mouth. "As I said, you were a bit misunderstood."

"As were you, Miss Applewaite."

Phoebe let herself grin. Affection for this charming, friendly soul flowed through her. She adored him.

He leaned over again, so close their noses touched, and she held her breath. "Would you marry me then, Miss Applewaite? It would make us both happy, I am sure, and please the entire city of Charleston including Sandy Bank."

It felt like a dream, and though it made her dizzy and trembly, Phoebe made herself whisper, "Yes," paying no mind to the argument in her head that this could not be true.

A lilting, sing-song call echoed over the water, and she looked up at the interruption feeling shy. A barge came floating down the creek, low in the water with a half-dozen white and dark-skinned men chanting a melody to themselves.

"Here come your neighbors," she murmured, feeling the dream slip away. They were holding hands now, warm as a summer day, and James—might she call him James now—didn't let go as he climbed to his feet.

He helped her up. "What poor timing," he said in a playful tone. "Should we tell them the silly fool of a boy from Sandy Bank has convinced an Applewaite to marry him?"

# CHAPTER EIGHT

Mr. Hathaway's study at Sandy Bank was situated in the corner of the large library on the first floor. It was there he conducted his business and private conversations, one of which James initiated that evening.

After meeting Miss Applewaite along the creek and her warm acceptance of his proposal, James's enthusiasm for their attachment blossomed throughout the day like the early roses in the garden. They walked along the fence that corralled the horses and shared their opinions on future market demands.

In agreement that limited trade with Britain was a lucrative opportunity to resell goods to the French-held islands and Spanish Florida, they found themselves at odds over one principle: James was a believer in life's necessities; Phoebe felt certain it was the luxuries of life people would buy.

Together, they came to a scenario of a shop filled with American and British goods acquired through Daniel's merchandising efforts with the unsold inventory shipped to the Caribbean. Aboard their southbound ships could be brick from Sandy Bank and bolts of cotton now that Whitney's cotton gin made production faster.

Mr. Hathaway listened carefully, his eyes sparkling with amusement at times and at others, staring steadily at his son as if he was impressed.

"See now," finished James, "in the end, it benefits us both. I have a plan for the future and a partner I admire—"

"She's very handsome," agreed Papa, although he'd pointed it out more than once.

"Yes, and everyone else will be satisfied. Mama sees me settled, I get a post aboard a ship, and the Applewaites no longer have to worry about their unmarried daughter."

Papa's attention dropped to the desk and his ivory-colored clay pipe. He stuck it between his teeth. "It sounds promising for the most part," he agreed, "but that leaves little time for you to take over things here."

James's heart skipped a beat. "You are as healthy as can be, Papa. You don't need me here. I know the business at hand—I grew up on this land."

"Then why hurry back to Charleston? You can't leave a wife alone to fend for herself while you wander the seas, and Miss Applewaite seems to like Sandy Bank."

James clasped his hands together in a show of patience and set them on the desk. "I have never wandered, Papa, not far. There's always a destination. It's not like it's India." James heard himself pleading. He tried to change his tone to confident. "Miss Applewaite completely supports me in the idea as she has her own ambitions."

Something like disappointment flashed in Papa's eyes and caused a heavy feeling to drop over the back of James's shoulders.

"What if she falls ill or needs aid? Who would be there for her if her husband is not?"

James's mind galloped ahead. "Her mama is in town, her sister and brother-in-law are only a few hours upriver, and of course, you and Mama are here at Sandy Bank."

Papa didn't look convinced.

"And there's Benjamin," added James in a rush. "He's always in town."

"Yes," said his father in a wry tone, "more often than not." He breathed loudly through his nose as if sighing in surrender.

James found himself balancing on the edge of his seat. "What do you think of it? I can speak to Mrs. Applewaite in the morning or perhaps in the drawing room tonight if she hasn't excused herself."

Papa's gaze drifted out the tall window beside them where twilight twinkled from the light of a thousand glow-worms. The house seemed quiet all of a sudden, and James could hear his pulse in his ears. His hands felt damp, so much so that he wiped them on his breeches.

"Well, then," said Papa at last. "I admit I hoped you'd fall in love, wildly and madly and give up these aspirations of sailing, but we did have an agreement."

James's heart leaped with excitement. He could hardly believe his ears. Papa's soft gray eyes looked reflective as he stared outside. Around them, the pine floorboards, waxed mahogany desk, paper, ink, and the faint tendrils of tobacco made James's head swim, both at once familiar and overwhelming.

Papa finally looked over at him, his face awash in subdued amusement. "Mr. Albermarle has lost the first mate hired for *Lily* since we changed captains. I will send a missive at dawn, and you will be aboard for the maiden voyage."

"First mate? Oh, thank you, Papa!" James didn't know whether to laugh or cry or to jump with joy, so he sat there in a mild stupor.

"Don't thank me yet," Papa warned. "It's a new captain and a new crew on a new vessel. It won't be easy, even with your persuasive charms."

"I understand."

Mr. Hathaway turned the pipe upside down and tapped it on the edge of the desk. "That leaves me with nothing more to do than to congratulate you." He nodded in approval. "You know I like Miss Applewaite, a great deal. She is mature and level-headed, except for this shop-keeping nonsense, but I presume after a few months' time she will see the difficulty in running a business and a household and turn it over to a manager. You should have someone in mind."

"Yes, Papa," agreed James, although he knew in his heart his father was wrong. "Thank you," he repeated with a heartfelt look, and Papa climbed to his feet and came around the desk. He gave James a momentary embrace then clapped him on the back.

"And don't you worry about the land along the Ashley River," Papa said in a satisfied tone, "I have just the man to oversee clearing the timber. We can move some of our people across the peninsula."

James could only lift his chin in a show of agreement. Miss Applewaite would not like that, for she'd said she wished to keep it as an investment for her brother-in-law, although she would no longer control it once they married. Cadwell wanted to buy it. It would certainly cover the cost of a new business.

He smiled again when Papa gazed at him with affection. Really, these expressions of true happiness came easily. He'd won over Phoebe Applewaite and would soon be at sea and practically in command. He would be a captain in no time.

MAMA BURST INTO THE room where Phoebe and one of the maids were packing her things. The sun shined as bright as a narcissus and there wasn't a cloud in the sky. Phoebe looked over her shoulder when Mama clapped her hands and skipped across the room with her arms outstretched.

"My darling girl," she cried, shaking her head in awe. "Why did I ever worry so about you?" Phoebe gave her a sheepish smile, aware Mama was as much excited as she but for different reasons.

She gave Phoebe a tight embrace and held her there. "We won't ever have to worry about the future again," she whispered.

Phoebe wondered if she meant her own or Phoebe's.

Mama took her by the elbows and stepped back. "I have given my permission," she cried, "and before the autumn harvest, you will be a Charleston bride. My," she added, as she looked around the bright bedroom, "this will all be yours someday." She returned her regard to Phoebe. "Of course, you will need to keep a room for your old mama."

"Mama!" chided Phoebe, resisting the urge to shush her, "that is a long way off, and you know Daniel has plans for you when he and Winnifred take over the house."

"Yes," said Mama, looking almost regretful. "He will refurbish the house once the crops make a profit. Winnifred can't bear living out in the countryside even when it's hot in town.

It is nice though," Mama hinted, "to have other options." She flounced down onto the thick featherbed like a little girl. "I imagine it's very cool here at Sandy Creek in the summer." She had the grace to look thoughtful, although it began to feel calculating to Phoebe.

She folded a green shawl in halves and rolled it neatly. "I daresay we won't spend an inordinate amount of time out here, what with a shop to keep up and Mr. Hathaway at sea."

"At sea?" Mama exclaimed. "Why would he want to leave you, my darling girl? And don't be silly, you have no need for a shop now." She looked up from the bed. "All I ever wanted was to see you safely settled, and look, you will soon be a wealthy woman. You'll never want for anything."

Phoebe tried to conjure up a smile for her face. Humming to herself, Mama leaped up and dashed into the hall, presumably to find more help to help her pack. She seemed to have become helpless since arriving at Sandy Bank, letting everyone do everything for her.

Such was the way, mused Phoebe with a shrug. She dropped onto the bed. She had slept little last night, what with the announcement the day before and a long afternoon yesterday of preliminary celebrations. Mama and Mrs. Hathaway practically had the entire engagement party planned, and yet it had just been decided.

She felt her mouth twitch into a reluctant smile. Mr. Hathaway—James—he insisted she call him after losing to her in a game of Spillikans, had been quite the good sport. He cheerfully listened to their mamas, smiled in agreement, and even made suggestions. Although Mrs. Hathaway was happy to have another reason to throw a ball, they narrowed it down to something small and private at their home in town.

Phoebe rubbed her fingers together, looking down at her hands now well-rested from the hours of sewing she was so used to. She hadn't had a headache in weeks. Sandy Bank had been a nice distraction, but it was time to get back to work.

She worried her lip, her mind turning this way and that. She'd spoken with Daniel again about the land, about buying her share so that she could use the money to lease a store. She had explained this to James, as she did not want him to think she expected his family to set her up. Marriage would not magically give her a shop on the corner of East Bay and Church. She'd learned long ago that one had to make her own magic if wishes were to come true.

Brushing away her concerns, Phoebe climbed up and started to pleat her handsome ballgown for the journey home. She dismissed the solemn maid who'd come in to help. It made her uncomfortable, the service of a person who was not to be paid, and worse, who had no choice in the matter. The halls and grounds of Sandy Bank ran like a very efficient man-o-war; no wonder James was so inclined to sail.

She could understand how the serious, rigid business of the plantation made him uncomfortable with his hopeful spirit and need for cheer but wondered why he would go to sea when life aboard a wooden ship was much the same. Sandy Bank was a busy hive of worker bees in a beautiful Eden, but even here, every moment of the day was scheduled on the calendar—and romance was arranged.

DANIEL AND WINNIFRED met Phoebe and Mama at the mouth of the Wando River to accompany them home. As the ferry sloshed along the fast-moving Cooper, Daniel came up beside Phoebe.

"Your mama has Winnifred ridiculously excited."

"I know," murmured Phoebe without looking back at them. Instead, she watched tall trees on the opposite side of the water slip by. "It's not like it's tomorrow, it's many months away. We haven't quite decided although it will be before harvest time."

"You're happy then?" he probed, and she smiled. He smirked at her.

"Really, Daniel," she reproved, "Mr. Hathaway is a good person and a charming companion. Don't underestimate him."

"To do what? Buy a bigger carriage perhaps?"

"Bah!" Phoebe fluttered her fingers to wave away his disdain. "He just likes to make people laugh, but he does have a serious side."

Daniel made a choking sound like he didn't believe it.

"Honestly," she huffed, "how well can you get to know a man playing cards? Although he's at the shipyard now, he worked for his papa at the Exchange for some time. Not to mention, he's quite the fishmonger in his own right—for brick I mean. Their businesses do quite well."

She slid her brother-in-law a sideways look to see if he understood. "He's always wanted to sail, and perhaps in time and with more experience he may commandeer a vessel, maybe one that carries our exports—and without fees!" She liked that idea.

"Your mama says he has been offered a position aboard the *Lily*."

"Yes," acknowledged Phoebe, "as a first mate."

"You won't see much of one another then," mused Daniel. He eyed her with some deliberation, and she gave a half-shrug. "That's all well and good. I'll be busy with my shop."

He laughed. "You are still willing then, to sell your land tract to me? Hathaway approves? I can give you an advance, enough to find a place to rent. We can do it in my name if you like, and Mr. Hathaway can change it over once you're wed."

"I've mentioned it to him." Phoebe bit her lip. Was this the moment she'd been waiting for? It seemed as if the stars had aligned for her and James. They would both get to taste of their dreams and enjoy them—together.

JAMES FELT AS JAUNTY as he was sure he looked as he trotted Dogberry to the carriage stoop of the Applewaites' home. He rapped on the door and waited for the comely Charity to open it. Once she allowed him inside, he found Phoebe sewing in the front parlor where the light was good. She looked as beautiful as ever as her petite frame jumped up to greet him.

"Good morning, Mr. Hathaway," she welcomed him. Her peach complexion glowed in the rays of the late morning, and dark brows curved over her handsome eyes just so made him want to kiss both eyelids one at a time. Perhaps he should refrain, he told himself. She'd think him a fool in love rather than a partner in a very affectionate arrangement.

"Tomorrow is the day then," she remarked, slipping back down onto the settle. He sat beside her and took her hand and kissed it.

"It is," he beamed. A flush on her cheeks filled him with giddy satisfaction that she should be so happy for him. "I shall be gone a month at least plus a few more days I'd wager, but it all depends on the weather gauge." James saw the sewing she'd set aside. "You are working at a frantic pace as well, I see."

Phoebe looked satisfied. "Mama has less time to assist me, what with her excitement for our engagement party. I, however, have an order from Mr. Payne, and there are things to prepare and put away as inventory for the new shop."

"Yes," James agreed. "I suppose we should look for a place," he murmured, realizing now would be a good time to put things in motion.

"Daniel is already on the hunt. There is the leather shop in the market that no longer does business. He is looking into it and will let me know."

"Your mother will not like it," James said, wagging his finger.

"Pish, my dear," she said in a serious tone, "I may have a space acquired before you return."

"Is that so?" he questioned her in surprise. He could not be any more impressed. "Do you need any assistance?"

"No," she said, and he watched her hold back a smile of pride. He'd assumed he would be providing the income for this endeavor; had thought it an upspoken condition of their marriage although she'd suggested selling her land. Had she saved enough to do it all on her own?

"I shall have enough, thank you," she continued. "It will take time to get it furnished and stocked, but I'm in no hurry now, what with the lovely weather and our plans."

To think she would do such a thing all on her own. James could not reign in his admiration. He must have looked like an idiot staring into her eyes. "You make me very determined," he promised, "to succeed handsomely at my new command."

"I'm sure you will do wonderfully," she assured him. "I believe in you."

"You do?" He let a chuckle escape. "You have never seen me paddle a pirogue or hoist a sail, but you believe," he repeated in wonder. "More than others I must say." He suddenly wanted to kiss her again; not like he had at Sandy Bank but harder and deeper to show her how much he loved her.

*Love?* The thought of it rattled him for the briefest moment then it settled across his shoulders like an embrace and warmed him to his toes. He swallowed a lump in his throat. "Thank you," he mumbled.

The apples of Phoebe's cheeks turned pinker. James watched a sunbeam from the window behind them make her hair shine like sunset. "You are the most beautiful girl I have ever seen."

A laugh warbled out, and Phoebe chided him with, "I'm sure that's not true." Before she could say more, he touched the deep crease above her lip to quiet her.

"I've always thought you to be handsome even when you were small with your freckles and orange hair," he teased, "but now that I know you, which is a privilege, by the way, I have the happy advantage to study your lovely dark eyes, your soft skin that glows like apricots, and your thoughtful little mouth that takes my breath away when you smile."

"Now, James," said Phoebe, trying to sound serious but failing miserably as her blush deepened, "it's not my first dance."

He would have laughed, but he meant every word he said, and he wanted her to know it. She never frowned at him anymore, and this had changed everything. "I may be a little thick with my compliments from time to time," he admitted, "but I have never meant it more than I do now. You are a beautiful and strong woman. It makes me..." he stammered, "I mean I feel all grown up at last, Phoebe, and well, like I'll never meet a better lady or want anyone else at my side."

She bit her lip, and he saw the yearning in her eyes to believe him. "It's true," he promised and then forced a laugh. "I'm afraid I've quite fallen out of love with myself," he confessed with a tight smile, "and into it with someone else."

He couldn't bring himself to say it any clearer than that, because his heart hammered and his hands trembled with a strange anxiety—no—a happiness he had never known. *Good heavens*, thought James, *I love her so, this little spinster.*

Breathless, he felt like a silly dolt but could not laugh at himself again because she looked breathless, too. Knowing he would be gone for a time, he didn't think it inappropriate to show her how much he meant what he was trying to say. He leaned down to her full lips and watched her eyes flutter shut. Reaching for her hand, he squeezed it—

"Mr. Hathaway!" Mrs. Applewaite burst into the room so suddenly the door slapped the back of the wall. "Oops!" she chortled. He wondered if her outburst was because she'd pushed the door open too hard or because she'd caught him face to face with her daughter.

"How delightful to see you! We thought you would be off soon—today or tomorrow."

James casually repositioned himself on the settee but left his hand in Phoebe's grip. He pasted a friendly smile on his face and tried to act entertained while Mrs. Applewaite went on and on about his new adventure aboard the *Lily*. Rather than heartily agree as he usually would, he listened patiently while sneaking sideways glances at Phoebe who seemed bemused. Either that, he thought with an inward smile, or she was cooling down, too, and devastated to have missed his passionate-to-be farewell kiss.

ALTHOUGH JAMES CALLED to tell her goodbye before his ship's departure, Phoebe felt some sense of obligation to see the *Lily* off on her maiden voyage. The pomp and circumstance for the new vessel occurred at the shipyard, but Phoebe saw her leave from the blustery shore between the fort and the wharf. She slipped off her shoes with the sand a bit warmer now and watched the narrow pennant of the company's colors snap in the breeze as *Lily* drifted downriver and across the bay.

Try as she might, Phoebe could not imagine James standing at the helm with a captain or coxswain with a serious look on his face, but then again, she had seen facets of him the past few weeks that she never imagined. A sad, privileged little boy, quarantined to his room one illness after another, he'd found joy in the creeks and tributaries that gently stroked the peninsula of Charleston once he could escape his bed. On the water, he'd discovered animals, friends, fresh air, and freedom. She almost envied the stubborn resilience with which he pushed back against what the world expected of a planter's son.

Phoebe's heart burned at the thought of him. He was adorably handsome and always filled with some sort of enthusiasm, even for little things. With his slanted jaw and bright eyes, it was impossible not to look upon him without some tingle of admiration.

For someone who'd loitered around taverns and gaming tables for years, he had an impressive ethic when applied. She understood now the restrictive expectations of his future had held him down like a ship with a bowline in the water, spinning aimlessly with every wind. He seemed surer of his course now and radiated a different kind of confidence.

She squeezed her fingers into her palms. They were to be married. Stiff, uptight Phoebe Applewaite, who spoke haltingly around her peers, became rather clumsy at any attention, and had very little to recommend her except obsessive industriousness with a needle.

A smile tugged at her lips. He did not think of her that way. He spoke to her like she was his equal, took her dreams seriously, and had on more than one occasion called her handsome. Perhaps she was not as plain or peculiar as she had convinced herself throughout the years.

Her heart warmed at the distant view of *Lily* gliding out of the harbor. She felt excited. Happy for him. Happy for herself. She was in love.

*Love?* Phoebe's smile faded, her eyes blinded by the sun now well above the horizon. She closed them and took a deep breath. Yes, it was true. She had known it for some time, but now she could accept it and welcome the happiness that came with it.

Phoebe Applewaite would be all right. She would no longer be a burden on her family. She would soon have a shop to organize and run. And finally, she would not trudge throughout the rest of her life alone. She would have a husband, and yes, by the by, she just happened to have fallen head over heels for him—again.

# CHAPTER NINE

The *Lily* reached the glowing tropical isles of the West Indies within two weeks. It was everything James ever dreamed. He was aboard a ship, with a real post, and not under the watchful eye of Papa or Mr. Albermarle. They delivered their rice, cotton, and dry timber to two more ports of call, and after allowing the men and himself to enjoy the exotic benefits, including a pineapple to take to Phoebe and rum for Benjamin, the *Lily* turned northeast for her return to the States.

Elated with the adventures on white, sandy shores and not missing Sandy Bank at all, James rolled back and forth on the balls of his feet waiting for his shift to end. Captain Ogden had retired hours ago. The older man seemed happy to let James earn his epaulettes, but he must soon relieve him so James could sleep and rest.

He'd never slept so little, but the energy of the waves pulsed through him as they danced past the ship so he had no issue waking at odd hours to make his way to the top deck. He loved the men already. They were a good crew, industrious, and easy to get along with—an able group of God-fearing sailors in an assembly of colors and talents.

Two of them were not free men. They wore copper slave badges engraved with their identities and skills. It was cruel, thought James, as he'd only known the Africans in Charleston to wear them. He extended more patience and kindness to them than he did the others, although he could not bring himself to act stern and speak harshly to anyone. He left that to the bosun. All he wanted to do was manage the wind and the sails, and imagine life in the different places beyond the horizon. He wondered what New Holland was like on the far side of the world and if he'd ever have the chance to sail there.

Just as stars began to emerge from beneath the cover of daylight, James noticed a group of men crowded over the forward hatch. He ignored them for a time so they would not think him cross, but two of them jerked their heads back and looked his way so fast his gut tensed. He swept his gaze across the deck in search of Mr. Howe, but the bosun was nowhere to be seen.

Heads began to turn. Something was up. He called for the nearest ship's boy—Mr. Albermarle's son—who was knotting rope in an out-of-the-way place along the rail. The barefoot lad with bark-colored hair stuck out in all directions approached. He nibbled on a piece of rolled tobacco, his face pensive as he watched the men over the hatch.

James nodded toward the crew. "What's wrong with Mr. Rusk?"

The boy glanced toward the bow; he'd obviously been lost in his own thoughts, too. "I don't know, sir. I was below deck 'til just now." He hesitated and a guilty look crossed his face. "I..." he began, then looked away.

"Go on then. Find out what."

James hated to leave the con and insert himself in the commotion. He had not fully earned the men's trust, he knew, but they seemed to find him likeable enough despite his lack of experience. More men looked with concern toward the hatch.

James glanced up and saw some of the crew on the yardarms staring down. Drawing a breath of courage and hating to make a fuss, he squared his shoulders.

"What's that then?" he called in a firm tone. Young Albermarle was lost from view, surrounded by the men. Two of them dropped down the ladder as he approached, and he heard raised voices from below.

"Smoke," someone said just as the scent hit his nose. James inhaled sharply, pushed the crowd aside, and dropped down the ladder just as the bosun came up. His eyes were enormous, and a sheen of perspiration glistened on his forehead.

"There's fire in the hold," Mr. Howe snapped and then he began to shout: "The buckets! The alarm!" All at once, the deck exploded into action, but James froze at the top of the hatch.

Mr. Howe grabbed his arm and shook it. "Fire in the hold, I don't know how, but it's spreading fast." The smell of smoke was stronger now, and James began to feel dizzy. "What's your orders? Mr. Hathaway? Sir!"

James swallowed, expecting to see bright orange flames crackling in the darkness below him at any moment.

"Sir?"

*The ship. His post!* James took a breath and jumped, nearly shattering his ankles and knees. He grabbed a lantern and staggered down the passageway to another hatch that dropped to the next deck underneath. The air grew thick and the pungent odor of smoke, choking. A shadow burst up the ladder from below followed by two more men and empty buckets just as the ship's bell began to ring out in a pounding clatter.

"It's out of control," one cried, and the trio dashed past him. James felt a hot draft erupt from the hatch's mouth like the sinister breath of a volcano. His mind raced, unsure of what to do. He could not put out a fire alone. He didn't have the authority or the cowardice to scream for everyone to abandon ship.

James tried to think, to sort things out in an organized manner, but he was a man of action—spontaneous action, and trying to consider every detail paralyzed him. Perhaps that was what Papa had meant all along.

His mind clouded as the air became acrid. There was no room for mistakes. Eerily, he watched a red-orange glow emerge from the hold. It reminded him of light striking the locks of Phoebe's hair, and then pounding footfalls came up from behind. He found himself moving into a water bucket line as Mr. Howe screamed orders echoed by Captain Ogden above deck. It was no good.

James could feel heat from the boards beneath his feet. The far end of a bulwark where hammocks were slung burst into flames. Some of the men shouted in terror and scurried up the ladder into the night. The choking smoke became unbearable, and his coughs grew more ragged.

He stepped aside as licking fire moved along the deck at his feet and looked back in the near darkness. It was only him and a frantic Mr. Howe left, with the Albermarle boy at the foot of the ladder looking all around with rounded eyes. The boy shook his head like he could make it all go away by refusing to accept it, but someone had to...

James's eyes burned and began to seep. "Go!" he shouted, realizing they would all three burn to death if they did not escape now. He jerked Howe around and shoved him forward, and they stumbled their way to the ladder. The bosun grabbed young Albermarle by the neck and shoved him upward into someone's hands. There was no one waiting for James when he managed to drag himself out of the smoking hole. All around him everyone screamed orders at everyone else and lines whizzed through box and tackle as two small skiffs were lowered.

James crawled to his feet gasping for air. Captain Ogden towered over the helm shouting orders and shaking his fists, barely discernable in the twilight. Smoke leaked from all of the portholes, and the entire ship had a strange glow.

*The powder magazine!* remembered James, and he suddenly understood the panic. There were guns and gunpowder stored in the ship's magazine for protection. He dashed to the rail where men slid over, some with casks and others waiting for the second boat to drop. He raised an arm and shouted, "Captain!" toward Ogden. It was then he saw little Albermarle dashing back and forth like a frantic rabbit trying to follow orders from a dozen mouths.

"Boy!" he shouted, and then he remembered his name. "Zachariah!" he screamed.

The boy froze in his tracks, panting. James motioned him over, and he stumbled forward. Tears streamed down his face. "It wasn't me," he cried, but every other detail on his face suggested he'd had something to do with this.

James grabbed Zachariah by the shoulder. The second skiff was on its way down, half-full. Other members of the crew flung themselves over the ship's side, clinging to the ratlines like desperate spiders trying to stay in their webs.

*They can't swim*, he thought, remembering so many sailors could not. He looked back and saw Howe coming across the deck dragging a dazed Captain Ogden by the arm. When the captain saw James, he spat, "What have you done, Hathaway? What have you done?" Spittle sprayed from his mouth, and his eyes swelled like two moons.

It was all gibberish to James. The boy beside him put his arms over his head and ducked as a rumble threatened from the belly of the ship. "Zooks!" James cried, "she's going to blow!"

The sugar! If its dust had not started the fire, the flammable sweet powder would certainly turn the ship into a fireball. Heat rolled through the air in waves.

"Take the boy!" shouted Howe, who ignored the ranting captain, too.

"You go," ordered James, forcing himself to come to his senses. He'd asked for this job to prove himself. He could think fast in a canoe in the Cooper's mad currents. This was just a little more water if he focused only on what was happening around the ship. He might often scramble at the last minute, but he never overturned.

Zachariah went over the side, scrambling to catch the limp rigging, and James went after him. He barely held on tight enough to keep from falling into the sloshing water below. Grabbing the tail of the boy's shirt, he guided him down into a skiff attempting to push off. There was little room left.

The ship grumbled, threatening again, and a blast exploded on the port side. The ratlines trembled, and James looked up to see two more men coming down. He pushed Albermarle's son down hard, and with a scream, the boy fell the remaining distance into the boat, landing on the angry, frantic bodies of men.

"Wait!" James shouted as it began to pull away. The moment seemed surreal as a calm moon shined down on the scene.

Its silver rays reflected off the swaying sea. The ship rocked about in an odd motion, the gap between her hull and the departing skiff increased, and James heard Ogden scream in fury from overhead.

There was little choice but to let go and hope for the best. His instincts told him to hold fast, but he knew he was losing precious time. Flames climbed up the stern now. The taffrail and a mizzen sail caught fire.

With a deep breath, James jumped, his arms outstretched to catch the edge of the skiff as it floated away. He knew the instant his flying feet smacked the hard surface of the sea he'd missed his mark. The bosun and he would drown with the *Lily's* captain. He would never be wed to Phoebe Applewaite, and she would never know he loved her.

TWO WEEKS AFTER SHE stood on the oyster shell-strewn sand and waved goodbye, Phoebe realized she no longer obsessed over who would buy her goods in the marketplace. The new piles of handkerchiefs and delicately embroidered fichus had grown little by little, but the pressure to make a sale had eased if not evaporated. Her heart felt lighter. There was no schedule for her next shipment of embroidered goods so now was the time to focus on her shop's inventory.

Mama had insisted Phoebe wear her wedding gown, for Winnifred had refused it when she married Daniel. Being as it was of lovely ivory silk with bright green sprigs accented by peach, pink, and blue blossoms and that it had been only slightly altered once, Phoebe agreed. Mama was right, the colors would set off the auburn in her hair and make her apricot skin—as James called it—glow.

They found a mantua-maker in town who could fit them in with the wedding months away, but Phoebe insisted that she refashion the gown herself. True, she was weary of needlework, but she could not surrender to the thought that she should pay someone to do something she could do herself. She might have only been a child at the time, but the War of Independence had affected her in that way. For others, like Mama and Winnifred, it apparently had the opposite effect.

With clouds rolling across the dull sky in ominous swells, Phoebe pushed the pile of lush fabric aside and stood up from the settee. Charity had offered to bring her coffee, but she'd declined, thinking that a swift walk down to the market to purchase more thread would be a good opportunity to get some fresh air before the spring rain began.

Phoebe also refused Charity's offer to accompany her, and as was her habit, fetched a wool cape to keep away the damp. She hurried out, her pattens keeping her shoes above the sandy mud that lingered where the cobblestones had been unearthed. Soon, the holes in the street would be filled with salted puddles if the foreboding weather was any indication.

She scurried down to a dry goods shop on the corner of Broad Street, stamping her feet before she pulled open the door. A little brass bell tinkled, and she smiled to herself. Yes, she would have one, too, maybe a whole string of them to announce the arrival of her customers.

After scrutinizing the inventory arranged behind the counter, Phoebe shuffled up and down rows of displays on the other side of the store. A flat sweetgrass basket the size of a tabletop was filled with various shades of fine gossamer thread hetcheled from flax. It looked like the perfect thing to trim her reinvented wedding gown. Something new for something passed along from yesterday. She smiled faintly to herself.

"Oh, Miss Applewaite. How lovely you look this morning."

A familiar voice pulled her from her thoughts. Behind her stood Mr. Quinton. He doffed his hat, and she gave him a curtsey that almost faltered when she saw his married sister behind him. She forced herself to move her tongue. "Good morning to you, Mr. Quinton, despite your exaggerations. It's quite windy and damp and has blown my hat out of shape."

Alice Leonard stared. Phoebe curtsied with brittle knees. "Mrs. Leonard."

Mr. Quinton slanted his head and made a show of studying her. "My apologies, Mrs. Hathaway-to-be. I only saw the lovely locks draped over the collar of your cape and knew it was you."

Something in his tone sounded derisive, but Phoebe bit back a frown.

"I don't suppose you've heard from your intended?" Mr. Quinton continued. "He left a fortnight ago and forgot to say goodbye so there I sat at Shepheard's all by my lonesome."

"Though I'm sure you knew he was leaving," Phoebe guessed.

"Yes," admitted Mr. Quinton, "but I forgot the exact day."

"You poor man," managed Phoebe. She glanced down at the soft thread in her hand. "What have you come into Pilcher's for?" she asked. "I don't often see a man of your reputation traipsing around the market."

"Oh, I like the occasional visit, and my sister asked me to accompany her to town this week."

He smiled at Phoebe, but it didn't go very far. In fact, nothing polite about him went far. She wondered how much influence his tart sister had upon him. A few steps back, Mrs. Leonard watched with eyes narrowed in distaste. She looked impatient to move along.

"See, I was in Payne's," her brother boasted. He touched his neck, implying something mysterious about his tight cravat.

"He is the best tailor in Charleston," Phoebe declared. "We have used his shop for two generations."

"Yes, he has been around." Mr. Quinton could not meet her eyes for long. He shifted his gaze to the wall behind her as if examining the baskets and different-sized barrels.

Phoebe stole a glance at the counter where the line for customers had diminished. "Well, I—"

"Tell me," Mr. Quinton began again, "do you still intend to open your own shop? What with becoming mistress of Sandy Bank—eventually—I presume your ambitions have completely changed."

Mrs. Leonard made a choking noise that sounded like laughter.

"I have not," Phoebe replied. She ignored his sister's critical snort. "I've already found a suitable location, or my brother has, my brother-in-law, I mean."

Mr. Quinton looked mildly surprised as if her plans had been made up. "You will hire someone to manage it then, I presume."

She smiled, amazed at his penchant to believe women would never have time to pursue activities outside of marriage.

"Actually, Mr. Quinton," she explained, "I intend to manage it myself for the time being, as I won't be living at Sandy Bank for some time if ever."

"If ever?" He raised a brow.

"Surely, Mr. Hathaway has mentioned to you he has no intention of living out his days in the low country."

Mr. Quinton sniffed. "I'm sure he'll change his mind. At least in the heat of summer."

"Apparently I find the season as bearable in town as he does."

"Perhaps you don't know any better." Mrs. Leonard spoke at last. If Phoebe didn't know better, her pink cheeks could actually be colored from envy. No doubt she'd always adored her older brother's best friend.

Rather than smart at the flippant comment, Phoebe shrugged. "We have a small house up the Ashley River at Duck Point, Mr. Quinton, and I have spent time in the summer there. I'm afraid I don't find it any cooler than our home in town."

Mrs. Leonard rolled her eyes.

"You do have a few tall trees that offer shade," he observed. "I have seen your modest home on Beaufain. Lovely courtyard."

"Thank you."

"I don't suppose visits up the Ashley will be in order then," assumed Mr. Quinton, "since your sister and her husband are there. And you have a tract of land, too, I understand. I suppose there's a house?"

She shook her head in denial. "Yes, my father did set aside a few acres for me, but no, there is no house."

"How inconvenient." He studied her, his implausible smile dissolving. "I suspect it won't be long then with Mr. Hathaway's plans."

Phoebe felt her forehead wrinkle. "I wasn't aware James had plans." She stopped short so that she did not say she planned to sell it. She hadn't meant to share such personal details of her relationship with James, especially with this pair, and she certainly didn't want them to know she knew nothing of any other plans that had to do with her land.

"Nay, not James," Mrs. Leonard corrected her. "He meant his father. Mr. Hathaway is as enthusiastic as Mrs. Hathaway that you will wed. He's wanted a parcel of land up the Ashley for a long time now, not too far inland, and now he will have what he wants thanks to James."

Phoebe's mind froze even as she felt her composure drop away.

Mr. Quinton cleared his throat. "Oh, I'm sure it will be cleared for timber—and income—right away. No use in having it sit." He smiled at her but looked uneasy. "So you may have another house in the low country after all even if you do not like the heat."

Phoebe's heart tightened, and her jaw did, too. She wanted to explain that she intended to have it sold. It was the only way to mortgage her shop. She'd assumed James understood.

"You did not know?" Mr. Quinton guessed. "I am sorry, but don't worry, it probably slipped James's mind to mention it." He winked. "To be a captain aboard one of these blasted merchantmen is all he ever really cared about. He would be happy to be a common sailor if that was his lot."

Phoebe stared a few moments longer then managed to croak, "I do not find anything wrong with his ambitions."

"None? His ancestors didn't sacrifice all that only to have their descendants move backward. His papa has made a fortune in brick so his family would not have to dirty their hands."

Phoebe scowled.

"Well, aren't you a practical woman after all?" purred Mrs. Leonard. "So you must not mind that James only pursued you to please his papa. The old fellow did promise him a position if he settled down right away—and to make him captain soon if he won *you* over." With widened eyes, she tried to look innocent.

Phoebe felt her expression harden while the room behind Mrs. Leonard began to spin like time had sped up outside of their conversation. As if sensing her distress, Mr. Quinton coughed and made an odd gesture like he might pat her shoulder. Phoebe's mouth felt dry, her tongue as thick as marsh mud, but she managed to say with a plummeting heart, "Mr. Hathaway is only marrying me to be made captain?"

The man before her gave a single, swift nod as his sister laughed, "Of course that's why."

Mr. Quinton blurted, "With your mamas involved and encouraging it all—at least that was the tittle-tattle—I assumed it was understood."

"What was understood?" Phoebe heard her tone drop several ominous keys.

"That he would marry you to get a ship, and you would marry him to escape a life of spinsterhood." Mr. Quinton waved his hand like it was nothing. "Or, to get a shop." He gave her a polite smile although he'd just insulted her single state once again.

"I'm sure he is happy to fund it," Mrs. Leonard chimed, "although I don't know that his parents are aware of his intentions to let you move forward with such a common thing."

Phoebe stepped back into the shelf behind her, and the thread slipped from her weak grip. She could not take it anymore. The piercing words. The horrifying revelations.

Her mind swirled with smoking clouds that rumbled around in her skull like thunder. Lightning struck, and she snatched at her throat, pulling the clasp of her cloak undone. Balling the collar up in her fist, she managed to find the clarity to utter, "Good day, Mr. Quinton," before fleeing the shop. She could not speak to Mrs. Leonard; she would have struck her.

The storm outside had come, too. It threw down heavy curtains of rain from the sky. It flooded the streets, soaked her hat through, and blasted her heart to pieces.

PHOEBE SWITCHED BACK and forth between her bed and the shuttered window. Outside, a violent tempest had taken over the city. It pounded on the rooftops and seeped into the cracks of the Applewaites' home finding new weakened spots to leak through.

Her room was faring well, but Momma's at the back of the house was not. Phoebe heard her faint distraught cries now and then along with Charity's soothing tones. Their distress could not equal hers, she told herself. She'd been tricked into falling in love just so James could begin a career at sea.

*That's what it was about then.* She made herself accept it at last. *He did not love me.* But she could not bear to say it aloud. Not yet.

It became black as pitch in her chambers, much like it was outside—and in her heart. Earlier, she'd choked back tears until she reached the house, ignored everyone's concerns that she was wet and cold, and escaped beneath the quilt on her bed for the rest of the day. Charity snuck in with a bowl of broth littered with bits of colorful root vegetables, and though she was not ill, Phoebe played along. She could not hide her red, chapped face. It was braised and sore from salty tears. Mama did not notice. Charity did not ask.

Phoebe's eyes brimmed over again while she stood at the window watching the storm. What had she been thinking? Her destiny had been set, her path clear. Why had she let Mama's excitement over a flowering friendship with Mrs. Hathaway persuade her to listen to all of their encouragements? Although Mrs. Hathaway liked her—approved of her—despite the fact that she was not from a powerful family, it didn't mean she really wanted Phoebe for a daughter-in-law. James, or perhaps his father, had put that into her head.

Her heart dropped into another dark canyon. James had made quite the bargain with his father, she brooded. He would get a post on one of their ships if he quit gallivanting around Charleston like a fool and settle down. Phoebe had only been in the right place at the right time.

She swallowed a thick knot of pain and allowed thin tears to leak again. Her whole body throbbed with betrayal. She put a fist to her nose and sniffled. She'd had her heart bruised by disappointment before and yes, she'd shed a few tears for young men she fancied who'd overlooked her, but this man, this *beau garçon*, was nothing more than a pretty boy—one who saw an opportunity to get what he wanted and make everyone else around him happy, too. He hadn't changed at all.

She wiped her face long and hard then dried her damp palms on her robe. Sighing, she slipped into the seat of the ladder-backed chair at her small writing table. There was the tiniest glow from embers in the hearth. She laid her head on her arms and tried not to feel sick.

Had he really thought that she was so desperate to be married that she'd accept just anyone? She stirred around inside her heart trying to feel angry. There were embers in there, too, hot and glowing. Well, she had not wanted to be married at all, or desired his attention, until she found in him a friend. And what about his kindnesses and secret longings? Had it all been a remarkable charade to make her believe he actually had more depth than a thimble?

Phoebe sat back in her chair with a soft thump. He'd practically admitted the whole thing, she realized. She locked her arms across her stomach. James had told her he wanted to be a ship's captain. He'd joked about his parents' enthusiasm over their blossoming friendship. He never, she realized, said that he loved her although he'd hinted at it.

She sniffed back another round of tears. There would be no water left in her at this rate. Thank heavens she hadn't confessed to him how much she loved him. She'd been carried away by the secret yearnings of her heart. The romantic in her kept strictly under control had escaped, and she'd forgotten that she'd accepted a life without a partner or children.

Handsome, playful James Hathaway had changed her mind. He was the kind of boy every girl wanted but the sort of gentleman she would have never been avaricious enough to pursue without encouragement. And here she was. He'd hypnotized her like a Hindu snake charmer, and she'd fallen for it.

Phoebe let out a heavy, tired sigh. Tomorrow she would be angry. Tonight, she must keep from slipping into a deep hole of self-pity. *The poor Applewaite spinster*, she imagined everyone would say, *humiliated by that rake at Sandy Hall. Doesn't she know better at her age*? Mrs. Leonard would be happy to spread the news around.

"Silly, spoiled James Hathaway," Phoebe whispered with a scowl. Why, she wouldn't spend another day with that deceitful man much less an entire lifetime. Lightning struck the heavens and lit up the room. Phoebe saw the half-hemmed gown for her wedding folded neatly by the wardrobe. She set her jaw and straightened in the chair.

With luck, this storm would pass, and the *Lily* would return to Charleston soon. She couldn't wait to tell him. She must speak to him at once before she lost her nerve. The glowing embers inside of her burst into raging flames, and she lit a tall candle and pulled out her writing set.

IT WAS THE FIRST TIME in James's life that the Carolina coast looked unwelcoming. He felt exhausted to his very core. He wanted to go to sleep and never wake up. The deck of the *Regina* felt crowded. He moved to a vacant end, and the men around him stepped aside. No one spoke to him. His stomach rolled as the ship swayed, dipping in the white-washed sunlight.

After abandoning the burning *Lily*, James had swum beside the skiff holding onto the edge, while his captain and bosun bobbed along on the single cask Howe had thrown overboard. Ogden panicked every time Howe splashed and screamed about sharks, but the nightmares in James's head didn't appear. His breath froze in his chest every time he allowed himself to think of them, and he'd become too afraid to kick his legs and just held on.

Eventually, the men crowded one on top of the other, and a kind sailor took pity on him and pulled him from the water. The boat had groaned and sank lower. Complaints rumbled through some of the exhausted men, but no one threw him back. A Spanish privateer fished them out of the sea a few hours after dawn, and just in time, for a violent storm later blew in.

"Mr. Hathaway?" interrupted a small voice, and he looked down. Zachariah stood at his elbow. His trembling had stopped, but he looked like a sick cat. The boy offered him a broken piece of ship's biscuit.

"You eat it," James insisted even as his stomach complained. The boy looked reluctant for only a moment before closing his eyes and biting down. James let out a hoarse chuckle. They had not slept at all since leaving St. Augustine. He and the crew took shelter in a few rooms over a ramshackle inn at the quay. The swaying palm trees there reminded him of the islands they'd left behind, but the Atlantic surf looked different and darker, like his future.

James groaned under his breath and squinted to see if he could see a lighthouse to mark their progress. Every now and then, young Albermarle peered up at him with a pensive look. The boy had been inconsolable aboard the Spanish ship and then in the rented room he'd laid beside James and sobbed.

It wasn't hard to put together: the boy disappearing to the hold then returning with a roll of gnawed tobacco. He hadn't looked surprised when the men screamed *Fire!* Only horrified. Smoking was not allowed at sea. It was a foolish thing; something only a thoughtless boy would do. James could not bring himself to ask, but when he searched Zachariah's face the next morning, he could tell the child knew that he knew.

A bell sounded followed by stamping feet and shouted orders. The *Regina* prepared to enter the harbor mouth which came closer as the minutes rolled by. Zachariah stared again. James squeezed the rail. There were so many things on his mind. The ship. The fire. His papa's face and the reaction of the other investors when they learned about what happened. Why must it bring down a boy, too?

James thought of Mr. Albermarle should he learn his son had burned and sank the *Lily*. No, it would ruin the family. It would taint the boy forever. He exhaled heavily through his nose. "You mustn't say a word, Zachariah, if you had anything to do with the fire." He continued looking straight ahead so he could not read the boy's face. Zachariah became motionless.

"Tell the truth," James admonished him, "always tell the truth, but if you lit a pipe while down in the hold, you must leave that part out. You only checked on the cargo, chased a few rats, and then made your way back up topside."

The boy beside him remained stiff, but after a few seconds he said in a high pitched tone, "Yes, Mr. Hathaway."

James swallowed. Ogden had not come along on *Regina*, which had conveniently been in St. Augustine's port when they arrived. Perhaps the old captain was stowed away in some admiral's house on an impressive street, writing letters to Charleston to clear himself of the blame. He had, after all, been asleep in his quarters.

The distant outline of Fort Moultrie on Sullivan's Island came into view, and he peered further into the bay at the distant city of Charleston. Perhaps Phoebe stood on the shore, watching and waiting. The *Regina* had her money from her first shipment to the Indies, but had the news reached town? Did she know the *Lily* had sunk on her maiden voyage? He'd lost the pineapple he purchased for her in the fire.

Cursed fire, and what had he done? He'd been in command—daydreaming at the con and plotting ways to make the men adore him. Then he'd petrified to stone. He'd stood there like a little boy staring out his bed chamber's window, watching everyone else hurry and scurry below. There was no one to blame but himself.

Someone called his name, and he looked. One of the captain's officers waved a letter in the air for him. He raised a brow, curious. A mail packet ship had pulled alongside them in Savannah's waters. The crew had exchanged some cargo, and he'd stepped off for a short time to find a hot meal. He'd returned to his berth as soon as possible to keep an eye on Albermarle's boy.

"I'm sorry," apologized the officer. "This came for you in Savannah. You were off, and I forgot about it."

James gave him a reassuring nod. "It's no matter. Thank you." His stomach sank as he accepted it. Papa had wasted no time. Surely, he was furious with him. It would be the last straw. Even Mama could not save him now. It would be back to Sandy Bank or nothing.

James glanced down at the rather feminine handwriting with surprise. It didn't look familiar. Curious, he retired to his closet-sized quarters which had more space than anyone else's besides the captain and stood in the sunlight that radiated from the porthole. He opened his ivory pocket knife and slid it through the vermillion seal of a flourished capital *A* over the outline of a palmetto tree. Why, Applewaite, of course.

Feeling his heart surge with comfort that he should receive a personal missive from the one person in the world who would understand—and care—about what happened, he fumbled with the sheet of folded paper as he opened it as fast as he could.

*Dear Mr. Hathaway,*
*I'm writing to inform you...*

# CHAPTER TEN

The sun returned pale and watery to the early April sky. Phoebe could not shake off the gloom that hovered over her wherever she went. News trickled into the harbor that the *Lily* had been lost although the crew had saved themselves. She could hardly believe it. The thought James could have died was gutting, and Phoebe refused to consider it. No word came from Sandy Bank. Surely, he was still alive.

She did not tell Mama her intentions until after the letter was sent breaking off the engagement with James. The agreement had been an impetuous decision, she decided. Her change of heart should have been kept between James and herself for as long as possible. Even though they didn't know if James had received the letter, Phoebe's decision shattered Mama into pieces of shock, disappointment, and blame.

The very sight of her sent Mama into fits, so Phoebe stayed in her room as much as possible. It seemed that her feelings were not as important as what Charleston society thought—or how it would look for poor Mrs. Hathaway and nearly-killed James. More than once, Mama declared that Phoebe should go to the low country house at Duck Point, and Winnifred should come and live at home with her husband in town. It would have pleased Winnifred, but it was impossible with Daniel working the land there.

Phoebe hurried down the street with Charity trailing behind her carrying their basket. She tried not to see the sideways glances toward her since the gossip had spread that she'd ended it with Mr. Hathaway like a fickle filly. She slowed as she approached the narrow brick storefront of what had been a leather shop. It'd sold pieces of cowhide, deer skins, and leather accessories. It would still have a smell, she imagined, but Daniel had already approached them about purchasing the building outright if not to rent. She only needed his money for her plot of land up the Ashley. No need to clarify it with James or his father now.

There was the expected income from the Indies, too, that James promised one of the company's representatives would bring while he was away. She had not heard a thing; but that income she intended to turn over to Mama. It would bring her such comfort and help with the household—now that there would be no sharing in the spoils of James's inheritance.

Of course, Mama had spent wildly, too, exchanging letters with Mrs. Hathaway still living at Sandy Bank. The wedding would have been at the Congregational Church.

Phoebe idled in front of the abandoned leather shop, peering into the dusty windows to see if it had been emptied out. She planned to have Daniel's family assist with the carpentry and then hire out for painters. Her mind wandered down a lane of hope as she pictured a block printed cotton valance across the top window. It needed a seat below and a shelf to display her prettiest things. That would be Mama's fichus and Phoebe's best-dressed hats in felt, straw, and silk.

Charity had continued walking a few doors down. Hearing the call for fresh catches from the market's fishmonger, Phoebe looked for her and their eyes met. *Two*, she mouthed, holding up two fingers, and before she looked away she caught sight of her brother-in-law striding toward her from East Bay.

She raised a gloved hand, and he gave a sharp nod. He did not smile at all which was not like him. How could it be such a beautiful spring day and no one felt like smiling? It was humiliating that he would frown at her so like Mama did from sun up to sundown. He must have heard even if Sandy Bank had not.

Daniel was not often in town with the planting season underway upriver. They'd begun the third week of February, almost two months ago, and she hoped he had good news. "Phoebe," he greeted her, stopping to look up at the second floor of the brick store. "I received your message. I've just left the Exchange."

"Have you found a buyer for your crop this September? They should not mind you are new at it or that it's a small farm right now."

He said nothing but looked at her with reluctance in his eyes.

"Are you alright? Is Winnifred here?"

"She is with my family today. We planned to come to dine tomorrow. I thought your mother would have told you."

Phoebe tried to smile although her mind clouded with confusion. "She did not tell me you were back."

"We are, yes," he stammered then gave a half-laugh. "I'm not certain you will want me at your table when you hear my news."

Her fear at his censure for breaking off such an advantageous engagement was forgotten, and Phoebe lifted her brows with concern.

"The storm," he said, his shoulders sinking.

"It took away a few shutters in town," Phoebe informed him, "but Mama said she received a note from Winnifred you made it through unscathed for the most part."

"The house withstood it. I feared for some hours it was a hurricane, but the waters receded at last." Daniel hesitated then looked her in the eye. "The creek ran over. The rain came so hard and so fast and fell for so many hours and then there was the wind..." He shook his head in a defeated gesture.

"Oh no," said Phoebe with a gasp. "The crop!"

"Yes," he faltered. "It's gone. Everything was either washed away or blown off." A frown of disappointment smeared his cheeks. "The plants were too young, the soil too loose. I should have built up the creek bank, at least that's what my neighbor, Mr. Jackson, said, but he advised me of it after the fact."

Phoebe felt ill for him. "I'm so sorry," she murmured, resisting the urge to hug him though they stood in the street.

"Yes," he returned, "and I'm sorry, too. I might as well move back to town and join my father and brother again in the workshop."

She thought of her income; the sale from the portion of her land. "But you can replant," she insisted, "your field and maybe my land, too."

Daniel looked at Phoebe sadly and a chill ran down her spine. "That's it, you see. I cannot buy your land right now."

The air in her chest whooshed out. "But—" she gulped.

"I'm sorry, sister," said Daniel again, and he reached out to pat her clasped hands. "I had to buy more seed, and I hired an Irishman who's just worked off his indenture to come out and help us. He's going to live in the outbuilding behind the house."

Phoebe wagged her head back and forth in disbelief. It sounded like he had a solution for his problem but not hers. "So you can't buy my land?"

"Not right now, but I will," Daniel promised. "Someday." He glanced through the grimy window beside them. "There are other interested parties in this property, and I simply cannot come up with the money right now to help you buy it at this time."

Phoebe's bones, which had been aching for days, seemed to melt in her body. Her legs threatened to crumple to the ground. She did not breathe for so many seconds that it took a shaky gasp to force back the hysterical protests in her mind.

Daniel tried to comfort her. "Please don't be distraught. I know you must feel devastated."

Her mind scrambled for other solutions, for there were always some somewhere. "I'll just sell it to someone else," she sputtered. "The land, I mean."

"Your mama would never allow it," Daniel warned, "and of course, I must plead with you to give me more time."

Phoebe's violent determination to maintain her poise failed to keep despair from stinging her eyes. *I'm almost 27!* she wanted to scream. "I need to find my path," she whispered in a choked voice, "and decide my future."

"It will come," said Daniel, patting her arm. "I have no intention of pushing you out of your house."

Phoebe knew Winnifred would not hesitate, and besides, they would be back in the summer for a time and stay until the September harvest if the second round of planting was successful. "Your family has no room," Phoebe reminded him, "and your elder brother inherits everything." She swallowed with watery eyes that made the world looked glossy.

"I do not mind the third floor," he assured her, but the small cramped attic level of the home on Beaufain Street was a mishmash of storage and Charity's room.

Phoebe swallowed again so she did not cry. She was done with tears. "I have the bigger room, and I am happy to relinquish it to you and Winnifred should you move back home."

"I know your Mama intended the house to pass to you both, but we would never throw you out."

Phoebe knew after a time she would not be able to bear growing old in her own home if it was ruled by Winnifred and whatever children she brought into the world. Mama had already mentioned how Phoebe did not need it now with her living at Sandy Bank to come. But she would not marry James after all, and now the shop she hoped to open was gone.

Phoebe made herself look into the window and find things to criticize. "It's quite a small space," she said in a shaky voice, "and so dirty. Why, it's a long walk to the wharves from here. I would do better to be closer to the Exchange."

"Yes," said Daniel, pretending to agree with her. "We'll try again next year and find a better place."

"I should go," stuttered Phoebe. She turned to leave, but he put a hand on her elbow.

"Phoebe, I'm sorry. I did not want to tell you at dinner."

"It's no matter," she mumbled, but it did. It mattered more than anything in the world. She fumbled with her freshly-repaired parasol. "I'm finished with Mr. Payne and have what I need from the market. I should return home before it's too warm." She looked around for Charity.

Daniel hesitated. "Come, let me walk you."

She rattled her head no. "You were on the way to your father's house."

"I am sorry to disappoint you, but if you are going straight home..." His soft eyes studied her, and she understood her sister's attraction to the plain man. He was gentle and kind.

"Yes," she blurted, ignoring the pinch in her throat. She stared past him toward the wharves. He sighed and turned away, and she let him go.

Beyond him in the distance, her focus drew to a handsome, but rather haggard man with slumped shoulders crossing over the street. Her heart leaped into her throat.

James looked up as if to speak to his papa beside him. There was a stern-looking man at his elbow on the other side, and a young boy trailed behind them. As if feeling her gaze, James stumbled to a stop and peered her direction from beneath a dark cocked hat. His clothes looked disheveled; his hair was pulled back in a tight queue behind his head. The devil-may-care boyish grin was nowhere to be seen. He looked instead as if he were on his way to a funeral.

Phoebe's stomach clenched so hard at the sight of him she thought she would bend in half. *He was alive!* Her fingernails cut into her palms. Alive and safe, but her heart was still broken. She forced herself to turn about on her short heel, and with a face blazing with a fire that threatened to consume her, she hurried off. From the way that he'd gazed at her, she knew. He had received the letter. It was off.

Scorching tears threatened, but she kept her chin up as she strode down the street. It was a tragedy the *Lily* had been lost and on his first excursion, too, but he was no longer her concern. Her heart squeezed painfully, and she forced herself to take a sharp, jerky breath that ended in a sob she cut short with great effort.

James Hathaway had not drowned at sea. He was only drowning in land and wealth and privilege. Phoebe had her own problems to deal with, in addition to a heart he'd smashed into pieces.

AFTER A SERIES OF LONG interviews, which included a private conversation with Papa and Mr. Albermarle before the menacing investors who'd financed *Lily*, James fled the Exchange. He returned to his dusty apartment across from the wharf to collect his things. He would meet his father at the ferry the next morning, and his trunks, gig, and horse, would transfer across the river to Sandy Bank where his life would begin again—without Phoebe.

Seeing her on the street when he was at his absolute worst felt like a dagger to his splintered soul. He slept poorly, his mind obsessing over what he considered the most shameful moments of his life: the seconds he'd frozen at the mouth of the hatch as men shouted there was fire, the letter from Phoebe with its forbidding words and accusations, his father's disappointed face, and the furious expressions of the investors.

Captain Ogden sent a harsh letter from Spanish Florida to explain his tardiness—as if he was seeing to the company's jilted connections although their goods had been delivered. He adamantly refused to accept any responsibility for a ship he hardly knew, a crew he had not hired, and a first mate, who failed to sound the alarm and give orders when it was reported there were flames in the hold. Somehow, it was all James's fault unless he could produce a guiltier party.

James could have singled out young Albermarle. Once upon a time, it would have been easy to innocently lift his hands and shrug. What could one man do when a roaring fire raced through a wooden ship? The men had done their best, and he'd saved them all, hadn't he? Not a single life was lost. But that was because of the bosun, he admitted, who'd ensured the captain made it out alive. It could have been much worse.

The silence of the night was broken by the occasional ship's bell or jolting cries of laughter from the darkness outside. By dawn, James was dressed and sending things down to the gig. The heavier items went on ahead in a stacked chest by wagon.

His occasional valet promised to send over what remained, though there was little of consequence. James piled up his packet of papers and letters and stowed them under the gig's seat in a small lockbox. He knew before he even cracked the whip he would take a long, roundabout course to the northern dock where the ferryman waited.

A lingering early morning fog thinned as he looped back and forth through the streets. When he turned right onto Beaufain, all seemed quiet and peaceful, and he wondered if Phoebe was asleep. In her brief letter, she claimed to have been injured to learn that he would only marry her for a ship. Mr. Quinton, she informed him, had told her everything. She knew about James's and his papa's bargain and believed her heart to have been taken in bribery.

James could not believe that Benjamin would betray him so. His friend had never been happy for him to win at anything, much less have something he did not. It was selfish.

Without thinking, he slowed Dogberry as they passed the Applewaite house. The confined dwelling looked murky in the wispy, damp morning. Its black iron gate to the back gardens was locked tight, and upstairs, the long porch running down the side of the house seemed to sag with loneliness.

He brought the gig to a halt and searched the windows. They stared like blank eyes over the street. He'd never intended for Phoebe to know the truth. It had been a secret, and then before he knew it, the deal with his father hadn't mattered. He'd fallen in love with her anyway.

James released a bitter sigh. He'd only loved a woman once before, and she'd been beyond his reach, too, a cinnamon-toned servant in the main house on a neighboring plantation. With dark eyes and sweet plump lips, she'd stared through him and ignored his advances, inappropriate as they were. He pined for pretty Stella for years until she married someone and moved to the upstairs as a lady's maid or something like it. Had that even been love? He hadn't known her likes or dislikes, what made her laugh, or her opinions—about anything.

Any man could fall for Stella, but not everyone would take more than a passing notice of Phoebe. She put people off easily, but only those who did not take the time to get to know her. Perhaps, they deserved it then. She was worth knowing and had no time for false pretenses.

He was a walking false pretense if there ever was one.

Studying the quiet house and wishing he could see her, James knew that with friends like Mrs. Leonard and cads like himself, it was no wonder Phoebe took care of herself first. She'd had to step up as a child after her father died and care for her timid Mama and sister. And she'd never stopped. The responsibilities had made her fortify herself against the world and nobody could get in. But he had.

James swallowed the painful weight pushing on his chest. Phoebe had asked him not to write her a letter back. She didn't want a message. She didn't want to see him. She thought he was a fraud.

*Dash it all!* He wanted to see her, to explain and convince her that he'd never meant to mislead her and that he cared for her. Loved her. She must despise him now and think him a dreadful failure for losing the *Lily*. It was like being bound back in his bed in his room at Sandy Bank. He felt trapped and alone, with no one who understood or cared.

A movement on the porch upstairs made his breath catch. Why, there she was! She stood in the corner wrapped in blue peering down at him. With her long hair curling past her shoulders, she reminded him of a sea nymph scrutinizing the morning. Had she been watching him the entire time?

Their gazes clashed, and she stepped back as if she hoped he would not see her. He froze, unsure if he should touch his hat or climb out of the carriage and beg her to come out into the street. He opened his mouth to call out, but she shook her head in one swift movement and melted out of sight.

No, she did not want him. He was the laughing stock of Charleston now—a silly fool that pranced around in ruffles and lace singing drunken ditties at midnight in the alleys. The man who was given a post on a brand new merchantman—a man with no naval experience, just canoe races down the river—and he'd sunk it. With Ogden's help, they'd all think him a blustering imposter with no talent or ability at all. It was better to go back to his plantation with his tail between his legs and direct the family business from the study instead of getting his hands dirty.

James's cheeks tingled with shame. Phoebe didn't come back out. She was finished with him, and he deserved it. She was better off with a millinery shop than she was marrying the village idiot. He sniffed hard and cracked the whip before the tragic weight of it made his eyes wet. The gig lurched and pulled him away from Phoebe Applewaite for good.

A while later, he found Papa and Mr. Albermarle waiting for him at the river. As his belongings were loaded onto the ferry, he moved over to the rail and watched the sun rise over the eastern horizon beyond Sullivan's Island. The murmur of voices on the breeze mingled with the birds' complaints overhead. Nervous horses stamped and vibrated the boards beneath his feet.

He'd just released another cleansing breath of salt air when Albermarle joined him. James remained silent. The man had been furious with their loss. His loss. He'd built the *Lily* himself and almost sacrificed his son on the maiden voyage.

James pretended not to notice him, but Albermarle folded his arms with a heavy release of breath that reeked of disappointment and something worse. After a few moments, he said, "You have escaped responsibility with the inquiry board and the investors. I know your family is relieved."

When James said nothing, Albermarle continued. "You're a very lucky man, Mr. Hathaway." He looked sideways at him. "It comes as no surprise to me, none at all, since you are more adept at starting your own fires than you are putting them out."

James winced, but his fists curled with offense.

"I've watched your papa make excuses for you for years. I pity him." Albermarle shook his head in disgust, and James's face warmed. It was a sickening feeling of shame and anxiety that had already made him feel ill for weeks. He wanted to defend himself, but there was no point.

"I lost a great deal of my own money in this venture," Albermarle complained. "I don't suppose you have any intention of providing restitution to the other owners?"

James looked at him with heavy eyes. "You know I do not have enough money to cover a ship's cost. Besides," he muttered, "it was a risk. Every investment is."

Phoebe jumped into his mind, and he tried to push her away. Yes, he had invested heavily, too. Not with his money but with his heart. He'd lost wonderful possibilities with her, on top of faith and respect and his reputation.

"Well, it comes out of your pocket in the end," muttered Albermarle, meaning the Hathaway fortune, James suspected. The man's nerve prickled him. He hadn't approved of James since he was a boy, and now he was using this unimaginable tragedy to unload his unsavory feelings onto him.

Zachariah came up beside his father, and Albermarle put a hand on his shoulder. James studied the child then sensing he was being watched, returned to the water view.

"If it wasn't for my boy," said Albermarle, "I'd take you to a court for my losses, but I suppose there are more important things."

Zachariah glanced uncomfortably at his father then at James. James looked away. Their secret would be kept.

"I should thank you for saving his life," admitted Albermarle. Touching Zachariah on the shoulder again, he added, "But

I don't want to see you in the shipyard ever again. If you come to work under me—or over me—I will quit and never see your father or have anything to do with your family again."

James's breath hitched in his chest. Albermarle and Papa had been good friends for many years and very successful in business together. To be the cause of a wrecked friendship between them would break his heart. He gave a sharp nod.

After staring hard at James to make sure he understood, Albermarle steered his son away from him, and they walked back to the front of the ferry together. Papa stood silent and alone across the deck, lost in some grim thought. He did not speak to James the entire course of the river crossing.

THE HOUSE ON BEAUFAIN street felt like a smoking powder keg although April was deliciously breezy. Even when a messenger from the *Regina* brought the money and her papa's small trunk back from the exported handkerchiefs, it did not cool Mama's temper.

Phoebe sat in the front parlor and sewed until her head throbbed, expecting no visitors and retiring to her room whenever Mama stomped in with a frown to stare out the window for hours.

A few friends called, but Phoebe chose to escape outside into the blossoming garden or up to her room to avoid their disapproving frowns. For a woman who wanted to shroud their shame and avoid gossip, Mama was doing a fine job informing everyone in their acquaintance of Phoebe's hideous act.

The tragedy of it all made the days uncomfortable and the nights restless. Phoebe spent more hours on the covered porch in the moonlight than she cared to admit, watching the quiet world turn outside her house. She avoided the church, the market, and even the sandy shore where she liked to dawdle. When James stopped in front of the house two mornings after returning to Charleston, Phoebe was horrified to be caught moping on the balcony as if she was not the one who'd penned the letter.

Secretly, an enormous part of her hoped he'd leap from his gig and demand she come out and allow him to apologize. He had not, so she must have been right after all. There had been nothing real between them. She'd just been another shiny button on his coat.

Mama stormed into the parlor on Tuesday, making Phoebe jump like someone had poked her spine with a knitting needle. Fumbling with her hat strings, her mother threw her bergère angrily onto the settee rather than lifting the bench seat to store her things.

Phoebe stared in concern. "How were your morning calls?"

"My calls? Mine? Well, besides going out alone because of your situation, I was not let in at Mrs. Heyward's who claimed to have a headache."

Phoebe wrinkled her forehead. "Perhaps she did. 'Tis the season with so many of the trees flowering."

"Or perhaps it is because she is one of Mrs. Hathaway's oldest and dearest friends. And who am I to be let into that fine house?"

"They do have a fine home," agreed Phoebe, "but just because they are next door to the Russells and friends of the Hathaways—"

"How could you, Phoebe? How could you do this to me?"

"I did it to myself, Mama." Phoebe twisted the handkerchief she'd been decorating, poking her palm with the sharp needle. "Ow!" It did not help her temper. "Not to you. I did not do this *to* you."

"Mr. Hathaway has retired to Sandy Bank. Even he cannot bear the ridicule of what you have done."

"Mama," Phoebe warned. "He sank a company ship on its first voyage. Why they even let him aboard I cannot fathom, but—"

"Oh, Phoebe! That is mindless and cruel. The stupid boat caught fire. It was probably ill-built. That's what we've all decided. It certainly wasn't poor Mr. Hathaway's fault."

Phoebe raised her eyes to the ceiling at Mama's absurdity. It only served to stoke the ill feelings that blazed between them.

"How dare you behave as if I'm overreacting." Mama snapped her hands up onto her hips. "You have sulked around this house like a woman scorned while you're the one who refused the man. A Hathaway!" she cried. "You could have been a Hathaway!"

Phoebe grit her teeth. "You mean you could have been a Hathaway or related to one."

Mama's eyes widened. "Don't you dare judge me. I have fretted about this family since the day your Papa died. I did everything I could to make sure you had all you needed to be accepted in society."

Phoebe knew Mama was right, but how could she not mention Phoebe's sacrifices, either? Her mother wasn't finished. "There is no reason to drag us down so low we must cut gowns for our own neighbors. Before long I will be scrubbing floors!"

"There is nothing wrong with a little work," muttered Phoebe.

"There is nothing wrong with marrying a gentleman to secure a home and your mama!" Mama's eyes filled with tears. "I'm exhausted, Phoebe. I'm tired, and I want to rest now—to see you and Winnifred taken care of so I can sleep at night. Put me in the attic story if you wish, but I will not continue fretting over your future for the rest of mine."

"Then don't."

Mama let out a small gasp. "You thankless child!" The room felt like someone had lit an invisible fire.

Phoebe narrowed her eyes as she jumped to her feet. "I am not the ungrateful one, Mama! Have you ever thought that everything I do is to take care of you? I've done everything in my power to make you happy, and Winnifred, too. Have I complained that my younger sister came out right behind me before I wed? Did I avoid her wedding? Am I unfriendly to her husband?" Phoebe raised her voice to a shout. "Why don't you send me upriver and have them live here instead. It's what you and Winnifred want."

Mama stared in shock at Phoebe's outburst. It hung in the air like a noose between them, swaying between reason and regret. She wrung her hands still protected in her faded riding gloves. "That's not a terrible idea..."

Her reply made Phoebe's heart roar. The sizzling sensation traveled up her neck and into her head so fast and hot she couldn't think straight. "Then do it, Mama. Send your shameful spinster daughter to the low country and let her oversee the indigo. At least then I will be out of sight and out of mind!"

"Go," bade Mama in a hushed tone. "You do not like dinners or balls. You would rather sit inside all day and sew until your fingers bleed than make calls."

"Good gracious!" snapped Phoebe. She threw the ball of stitching in her hands to the floor. "I'll pack my things, and you can find a way to supplement the household income on your own." She thundered from the room, raced down the hall, and scrambled up the stairs.

"Go then," she heard Mama repeat as she turned on the first landing. "I won't need to worry about anything with Daniel here."

Phoebe's eyes watered as a moan rose in her chest. It pressed against her heart, but she forced it back down. To the low country then, with its swamps and flies and alligators. Even all of that sounded preferable to this.

She hurried to her chambers and slammed the door as hard as she could. She'd rather enjoyed her time at Sandy Bank, and this could be much like it if her brother-in-law had made improvements to the property. Only at Duck Point, there would be no market, no shops, and no harbor view. No dancing. No dinners. And unlike Sandy Bank, she would be quite alone.

# CHAPTER ELEVEN

The heaving barge mirrored Phoebe's feelings as she gripped the rail. Charity and she were escorted by a manservant the McClellans sent to help move them upriver. Mama was not well, which was to be expected with the dark cloud that settled over the house as plans were put into motion this late April.

It was all Phoebe could do not to wrap her arms around poor, sniffling Charity, who did not want to move out to this wild marshland. The water tossed and sighed as the river pilot sloshed them along with the ingoing tide. She was grateful she didn't eat, especially when Charity dashed to the rail and made a spectacle of losing whatever she'd put into her stomach that morning.

Stoic, Phoebe stared into the tree line along the distant shore. She had never known any home but the stone dwelling on Beaufain Street. It was a monumental change in her life, much like the closing of a book and the opening of another.

To her relief, the journey felt shorter than the excursion to Sandy Bank so many weeks ago. Or was it months? Spring had wallowed slowly into the first waves of sub-tropical heat that would swell until summer when it became unbearable in the afternoon. She wondered what it would be like in the countryside.

Finally, the maneuverings of the crew hinted they were near. She saw a long stretch of land ahead as they entered a channel. Duck Point. It was a narrow strip of island. Tall wheat-like grasses rippled on its shores. Across the water along a muddy bank, she watched towering pines go by on the mainland. Soon, they would reach a dock where her family crest was carved into a post, and she would be home.

There was no welcome party when they arrived. Trembling, Phoebe forced herself to stay calm when her escort helped her out onto the rickety landing. After a rather informal yet polite goodbye, the men left them there like wide-eyed lost sheep. Astonished, they paced the boards for a few minutes while Charity made nervous noises.

"Mr. Cadwell knows we are coming?" she hinted.

Phoebe refrained from exhaling in frustration. "Yes, I told you he expects us. I'm sure he'll be here soon." They moved into the shadows of lofty tree branches to hide from the sun. Phoebe's legs throbbed, her back hurt, and her heart felt shriveled and dry.

"I do prefer the city," said Charity in a high-pitched tone.

"Yes, as do I," agreed Phoebe. If only they could sit. A sudden buzzing in her ear made her jump, and she swatted at something invisible. Down the embankment, a few yards away from the dock, she saw a sturdy-looking log. It was not in the shade, but it would do until the sun grew too hot.

"Let us sit at least." Popping open her sturdy oil-cloth umbrella, Phoebe motioned for Charity to follow her. She'd just put one boot a few inches into the dark sand when the girl behind her let out a piercing scream, and the log turned and looked at them.

Phoebe did not look back at Charity, for she knew in an instant what had made her scream. The alligator, three meters long at least, stilled again, but she could see its round eye watching them. It did not move, not even a ripple, but the air felt charged as if lightning could strike at any moment.

Frozen in terror and hypnotized by the ogling eye beneath its brow, Phoebe couldn't move, either. A sudden jerk on her arm made her gasp as Charity pulled her back onto the bank. She didn't wait to be coaxed; both women grabbed hands and ran shrieking back to the dock where they cowered against a piling watching the giant dragon muse over what action to take next. It was no longer lying on the earth but standing on four stubby legs alerted to their presence, or perhaps, shuddered Phoebe, considering its next meal.

Beside her, Charity began to wheeze, and Phoebe squeezed her hand. "Don't," she urged between her own heavy breaths. Charity did not respond. In not so many words, she told Phoebe that this was her fault, for Phoebe had refused Mr. Hathaway, defied Mama, and insisted she leave town to escape society's censure. Now they would both die in the untamed countryside—a horrible death.

The creature shuffled in the sand, and Charity shrieked again. Phoebe's heart hammered in her chest as perspiration ran down her sides. She closed her eyes and prayed, while another part of her mind wondered how safe it would be to follow the obvious signs of a wagon trail inland. Then, as if it was a comforting sign from God, she heard bells jingling and the most beautiful sound of wagon wheels crunching along their direction.

Daniel, with a thin white man seated beside him, appeared through the trees as Charity dropped to her knees and praised heaven. Relief flooded over Phoebe making the world spin, but she raised her hand in a composed salutation. The alligator did not move as the wagon bounced by its sunning spot, but it watched.

With a grim nod its direction, Phoebe pointed toward the danger, hoping her knees would not give way. Both men looked at it then glanced at each other before throwing their heads back and howling with laughter. Charity stopped her sniffling and climbed to her feet. Phoebe stared.

"Oh, I see you've met Arnold!" her brother-in-law called. He motioned toward the animal. "Benedict Arnold," he said with a guffaw as the wagon came to a halt.

"It almost got us!" cried Charity, and both men laughed again.

Phoebe felt her face crumple with displeasure at their amusement but motioned toward the trunks waiting to be loaded. "I am happy you came along at last," she said in a steady voice that made her proud.

There was no reason for anyone to know she thought she might curl up and die if someone did not take her back to Charleston straight away.

HEAT RADIATED OFF THE kiln in waves.

Papa had situated the brickyard on the southeast end of the property, out of view of the main house, but close to the docks along the creek so it wasn't far to transport them once they were dried and fired. James wiped his forehead with his sleeve and looked down at his filthy breeches. The former over-seer had moved to the fields, and James took his place to super-vise the brick-making.

He hated the heat. He would not, however, sit astride a horse and bark orders. If he was going to make bricks, he was going to make them, so he moved from the mixing room to where they were cut, and then over to the rows to see them lined like tin soldiers and turned to dry in the sun. In the evenings, he helped cut wood for the kiln if he could still move.

The midday sun glowered down on Sandy Bank. It tempt-ed James to make everyone stop for water and vittles, although such a thing like that was not often done. It didn't seem fair for him to take cover while the work carried on around him. Mam-my's son and his childhood friend, Theodore was there, and he could not pretend to enjoy their circumstances. There was no respect for James now, no friendship. He felt lonely and inse-cure in this new role.

The echo of hooves drew his attention to the rutted road that connected the brickyard to the drive of the house. It was not Papa, but a familiar figure and horse. Benjamin brought the thoroughbred to a stop with a sharp jerk. His man—a shadow he called Michael—drew up behind him on his own mount.

"They said I could find you here." Benjamin took off his broad hat and ran his fingers through his dark curly hair. "You look like you've rolled around in the mud."

Indifferent to him now and uninterested in any games that might be afoot, James shrugged. When he didn't reply, Ben-jamin swung off the saddle and strode across the yard. "You did not answer my messages, and I sent one off a fortnight ago."

James kept his face impassive but polite. He wiped his caked gloves on his stained breeches. "I never received one. We came out straight away."

"After your inquiry," guessed Benjamin.

"Yes." James knew his tone sounded flat.

"So," said Benjamin, "I see you are busy, but I have not heard the story. Not from a reliable source. "

"What is there to hear?"

His partner in boyhood scandals widened his eyes. "You had a ship. You sank it."

"It burned," James corrected him. "We could not put it out and had to abandon ship."

"And that's the end of it? Boring," teased Benjamin. "I suppose it's a more exciting tragedy to tell if one was more invested."

"We were heavily invested," James reminded him.

Benjamin stared at him, hat dangling from his hands. Something in his eyes hinted at remorse. "I could use a drink. I did not want to bother your papa."

"Yes, well," said James, not bothering to look sorry, "I'm afraid I am otherwise engaged. You should hurry up to the house."

"I won't stay long," promised Benjamin, "just a few days if I am in your way. I wanted to see if you were content to be back."

He looked almost ashamed of himself, and James wondered if he was ready to confess that he had played a part in Phoebe's hurt and indignation. Things would never be the same now.

"Can we walk?" Benjamin asked with a furrowed brow.

James looked toward the dock. "I suppose I could check on the last load. I like them stacked just so."

"Yes," said Benjamin, "you can be particular."

They left the yard and walked across the crushed oyster shells and pebbles that lined the footpath to the creek. James looked across the water in the distance and watched an assertive ibis dash after its meal.

"You have abandoned us all together in town."

"My parents insist that I live at Sandy Bank for a time."

"And learn the family business, I suppose."

"Much as you had to once upon a time."

"Yes," agreed Benjamin, "but as you know, I am not so hands-on." He gave a dry chuckle.

"We do not have much faith in an army of overseers—especially cruel and lazy ones."

"No, your father is a particular man himself."

Finally, James could stand it no longer. He did not want intruders here. He had mind-numbing responsibilities, not to mention his own loneliness. "Why have you come? Do I owe you a game? A debt?"

"No," said Benjamin, "I owe you one."

James thought back. "I'm sure we were even the last time I left Shepheard's."

"We were." They came to the dock where the barges floated empty and high on the water. It sloshed against the pilings and made a pleasant sound. "I owe you an apology."

James inhaled. So, it was true. When Benjamin did not elaborate, he pressed him. "I assume you mean Miss Applewaite."

Benjamin looked as if he did not want to meet James's eye. "You know then. I'm sorry."

"I'm sure it is all over town by now. Mama is furious with me as if I jilted Phoebe rather than the other way around." He gave Benjamin a hard stare. "That you would tell a virtuous young woman she was only proposed to in order for me to get my way. It was shameful for me to even think it, yes, but you did not have to humiliate her or hurt her feelings, if she ever had any for me at all."

"Oh, she has feelings," Benjamin assured him. "I saw her face. She looked like my sister slapped her when—"

"Your sister?" James's hands clenched.

"Alice, of course. Her ancient and dull husband begged me to take her to town, and we had just walked into Pilcher's when I spied Miss Applewaite there."

"And your sister told her? She knew?"

Benjamin looked guilty. "I suppose I told her, yes, at some inopportune moment when I was in my cups. Your engagement was a shock to me. To think that Miss Applewaite would even acknowledge two rogues like us."

James closed his eyes. "Now, that I can believe. We have always joked we would never allow the other to settle, but I never thought you'd hinder me if I changed my mind."

"I'm sorry," stammered Benjamin. "There was nothing I could do. She looked horrified and humiliated."

"I suppose everyone heard."

"In the shop, yes."

"And then I lost a new ship and came home to be rejected twice."

Benjamin winced. "I'm so sorry, my friend. I know you came to care for her in a way."

James looked up at him in surprise. "Actually, Benji, I loved her, and there's nothing I can do about it now because she won't see me. What she said in her letter was right. I am a disgrace."

"You're no disgrace," snorted Benjamin. "If there was anything I could do, I would, but as you probably know, she's..." He looked at James.

"What?" James braced himself. Had she fallen ill? Chosen someone else?

"She's been sent to live on the family land upriver. It's not too far south of my place, remember?" Benjamin raised his eyebrows in a show of disbelief. "Her mama shipped her out to the low country and pretends like she never existed at all."

"She what?" James could not believe his ears. "They sent her away? Because of me? She hates the low country! Especially there. What about her shop?"

"Oh, there's no shop," Benjamin assured him. "The only sowing she's doing is with seeds."

BENJAMIN MADE AN EFFORT to be helpful in the brick-yard two days in a row before he found other reasons to ride around the property or visit the house. He confided in James in-between distractions that he had a word with Mr. Leonard and spoke to Alice himself, informing them that if another unkind word passed to Miss Applewaite or anyone of her relation, it would be the end of his escorting her about Charleston in place of her elderly and often sickly husband. Amused, James could forgive his boredom after that.

As the week neared its end, Benjamin admitted to James he planned to return to the city for a concert with the young and widowed Mrs. Roberts, who had no wish to remarry but enjoyed handsome company. He was sure the early crop at home was coming along fine without his help.

After entertaining a subdued Mama in her drawing room, they settled in the rather masculine meeting room upstairs. It smelled faintly of tobacco and leather, and the chairs were as comfortable as they had been in early spring.

"You clean up well," Benjamin flattered him. "Why not come with me to town?"

James shook his head. "I have an order to finish. Perhaps next month I will float down with it on the barges."

His friend was not interested in drink. There had been enough port and coffee. He leaned back and crossed his boots, putting his hands behind his head. "If you are certain you are in love with Miss Applewaite, why waste about here?"

A painful sting needled James in the heart. "I regret that I confided in as much to you. She is gone now anyway, is she not? And if she were still at home, she would slam the door in my face."

"Yes, well," mused Benjamin, "she did refuse you a dance, but she came around the next time, didn't she?"

James looked past him out the window. The view allowed him to see the treetops and coppery sunlight that meant the sun would soon slip away. He'd never been so tired in all his life. His boots felt like lead during the day, but when he collapsed at night he could not sleep. Over and over, his mind considered every decision he'd made since Twelfth Night.

"You do look poorly, my friend," admitted Benjamin. "You're melancholy and dull and even I wouldn't dance with you."

James felt his lips crease into a faint smile. "I'm sorry I have not been good company. I do not want to disappoint Papa in the brickyard."

"Blast the bricks," Benjamin shot back. "You never wanted to run this place. You know what you want to do."

James studied the wine-colored spines of the row of agricultural journals stacked neatly on a second shelf. What he wanted didn't seem to matter.

"If you want a boat that bad, brother, come manage my barges for me." Benjamin flicked a small bit of paper across the table. "We've let the last captain go, he made such a muddle of things. The man stopped to visit his friends and folk along the way while the rice sat on the river for a week." He shook his head in disgust.

As ludicrous as it was, Benjamin's suggestion sparked something like life in James's chest. He studied Benjamin's face. "You need a river captain?"

"I have four barges. Two quite large. It's already time to move early produce into town, not to mention, I have some livestock that needs transporting." He broke into laughter. "If you really want to abandon the family business and lower yourself..."

James sat back in his chair. Just considering it made him want to laugh, too, but the possibility of being on the water was a soothing thought. He would love to do such a thing—run supplies up and downriver studying the current and watching the sand bars dotted with birds and the occasional alligator go by.

"Are you seriously considering it?" Benjamin sounded like he might explode with laughter. He loved a good joke.

Treading with care, James asked, "Where would I stay?"

"At the house, of course."

"I couldn't do that."

"Why? Because you'd be a hireling? Not any good then? Well, Mama and the girls might agree, but we could arrange some proper living quarters for you until you find another boat to manage."

"Ship," James whispered. He'd had a wonderful time aboard *Lily*, and yet he'd only been first mate. This could be a new beginning. It was far beneath him and his family name, but if it was the only way...

Why, if Phoebe Applewaite could refuse an advantageous marriage to a plantation heir to pursue her own ambitions, he could certainly refuse a living at Sandy Bank to earn a ship. He'd just have to start at the bottom like any other man.

"A river captain it is," he said, looking at Benjamin with a thumping heart. It was madness, but someday they'd admire him for it. More importantly, he'd admire himself. That was something. He'd never have Phoebe back, but he could be on the water again.

Benjamin's wide-eyed surprise stretched into a broad grin.

TO HER CREDIT, WINNIFRED was helpful in the little garden behind the house planted to provide vegetables for the pantry. She spoke of little other than returning to Charleston.

Over and over, she spoke of when she could leave the musty house to Phoebe and Charity with the hired Mr. Suter to watch over the crops.

Besides Daniel and his overseer, there were only three workers to tend to the modest field that had been replanted with cotton. It would be late if it produced at all; the indigo had washed away.

"Perhaps," suggested Winnifred, as she plucked a few leaves off her cabbages, "you can come to town at the harvest when Daniel comes back out."

Phoebe shrugged from her crouched position with her hands in soil up to her wrists. "I suppose it is up to Mama. She recommended I live here, and I agreed."

"That doesn't mean you have to stay out here forever like an old swamp witch."

Despite her humor hardening until there was little left to make her smile, Phoebe almost giggled. "Though," she admitted, "that's pretty much what lies ahead of me now." She glanced over her shoulder at Charity hacking at peas like she despised them.

"Maybe Charity should go back with you."

"I'd like that, but Mama wrote she must stay with you." Raven-haired Winnifred with her beautiful expressive eyes pressed the leaves flat in her hands. "I so miss the market and the shops." She stopped. "Oh, I'm sorry," she stammered, "that you didn't — don't have one."

Phoebe looked away. "It doesn't matter now I suppose. And I didn't want to sew gowns, you remember. I wanted the whole whale: hats and trimmings and yards of silks even Mr. Payne would admire."

"Well," her sister prattled on, "I am glad you are over that now and do seem to like it out here as long as old Arnold isn't around."

"I cannot believe you named that beast," grumbled Phoebe. She stood and stretched while doing a slow turn to survey the property. "If I see that monster anywhere near this place, I'll shoot him myself."

Her sister laughed. "Not if Mr. Suter has his way. I think he is fond of him."

Phoebe shuddered. As Winnifred beckoned Charity to follow her inside for something to eat, Phoebe stayed in the garden, pressing together her unraveling bergère as she estimated the time left before the sun drooped over the trees. Her dyed cotton gown, now soft and thinning from several washes, was hardly blue anymore. She hitched it up to cool her hot legs but not for long with the burrowing, biting bugs about.

It seemed a little cool this morning, less muggy than town but not that much less. Phoebe ached for the cobbled streets of Charleston. She'd tried to accept her circumstances—harsh, lonely, and demanding—but she could not make her peace. She did love the flowing creek that ran along the property and even the dark and suspicious waters of the channel. The view across the water to Duck Point was divine, but there was little else in this undeveloped low country, just dirt and labor. And then of course, the ever-present dangers of alligators and wild cats creeping up the banks, and snakes, spiders, and the infuriating mosquitoes that tormented her if she forgot to apply her rosemary oil.

She wasn't cut out for it, no more than Winnifred, but at least her sister had Daniel. They would go back to town soon, and maybe someday, somehow, Phoebe would learn to love the strange quiet and impenetrable darkness here.

For someone who preferred the corner as opposed to the center of a room, she missed people—their stories, their voices, their laughter, and all of the different things that could happen from day to day. She felt restless with her pretty complaining sister who could not love it here either, but soon she'd be gone, and Daniel, too, the only calm in the midst of their storm. Not that Phoebe minded Mr. Suter, but he kept his distance or to his old wooden hut with its dirt floors. He was aloof but polite. Perhaps he'd heard gossip about her, too.

She wet her lower chapped lip with her tongue and winced. It was difficult to stay clean and in good looks out here. She wondered what James would think if he could see her now. The heavy ache in her heart returned, and she let it brew, too fatigued to push it away.

Why did she think of him still? Why did she hurt herself so? He'd never loved her, and she had moved on. Left. Walked away. Or sailed away, upriver. She'd forced herself to leave. Him. Everything.

Phoebe's throat tightened as she tried to keep the gnawing pain at bay. It would take a while, she told herself. People recovered from heartaches all the time, and James was so far down-river she didn't have to see or hear of him. Except she couldn't help thinking about him. She wondered if he'd been given another ship or if he was back at the Exchange by day and haunting the taverns at night.

Such a silly man, she told herself, but he wasn't, and she knew it. She thought fondly of Sandy Bank then stopped herself. It was even further from town. She'd only enjoyed it so because of the beautiful house and gardens. Then there was her handsome master, but no, it was too late and pointless to pine for him.

She let a sobbing noise escape from her throat then sat back on her heels to get herself under control. Tears were for the nighttime when no one was listening. Soon, she'd be alone here, and she could cry all she wanted. No one would know.

It would take a long, long time to forget about James Hathaway—if she ever forgot about him at all.

JAMES FELT LIKE A COWARD packing to leave for the Quinton's plantation before telling his parents. Mama was unusually quiet at dinner, so he suspected the servants had talked, and she knew he was up to something.

Papa questioned him about the progress in the brickyard. "The order is complete," James assured him, and they discussed further plans to get the bricks floated downriver to the port.

He waited until the three of them were in the drawing room, Mama with her coffee, and Papa calm and relaxed after a glass of port at the cleared table. Mama stared into the empty hearth. There was no need for a fire tonight. Spring was in her last days. It'd grown hot quickly.

James cleared his throat. "Now that this order is finished," he began then hesitated to see if he had Papa's attention.

"Smithfield is next," Papa mumbled without lifting his gaze from a book.

"I know," James continued, "there is always another order to begin when one ends."

"That's how we keep mouths fed," said Papa. He glanced up at James.

"Yes, Papa, I know. It's just that, well, you can move Mr. Tingey back over from the fields because I am going away."

"Back to Charleston?" queried Mama.

"We've closed up the town house until July," Papa reminded him.

"Yes, I know," said James, somewhat irritated that his father seemed to be doing whatever he could to keep his son trapped here. James caught Mama's worried look. Worry lines around her eyes seemed to have increased as the months went by. He hoped it was age and not his conduct. "I'm going to stay at Benjamin's home—Quinton Plantation."

Mama's brows rose in surprise and disappointment flashed in her eyes. "Mr. Quinton? Why waste a good season there when Sandy Bank is just as nice?"

"You mean to quit working for me then?" Papa's voice was a blend of disbelief, irritation, and surrender.

"You know I don't want to run a brickyard," muttered James. "I don't mind the work, but I miss the sea and since I don't intend to keep up this end of the business in the future, I don't see the point in managing it."

"In the future?" A glint of humor lit up Papa's face. "You mean when I'm gone?" He tilted his head and studied James. "Pray tell, what will you do to keep Sandy Bank running then?"

James took a breath before he spoke. "I've thought it through, Papa, and I still want to pursue a captain's command."

Momma made a sniffing noise of disbelief.

"You gave that route a go, and it didn't work out." Papa sounded somber.

"It worked out fine. The fire was not my fault," James insisted. "It was a terrible accident, and I did the best I could under the circumstances."

His father's critical stare made James's hands hot. Papa was not a man of great temper, but his parents' disapproval that once easily guilted him into obedience now exasperated him.

"I confess I have not been the most responsible son," he admitted, and the heat in his hands raced to his cheeks. "I did set my own mindless pursuits before any assignments from the shipping company. I did not use my allowance responsibly."

Papa's face softened, and embarrassed, James looked down at the scarlet fringes of a rug. "In the future, I intend to run Sandy Bank as nothing more than a family farm that sustains itself. With a ship under my command, I should bring in more than enough to maintain basic expenses."

"And where will you get a ship?," wondered Papa. "You most certainly won't find a position here."

James was ready. "I've agreed to fulfill a period of employment for the Quintons."

"They don't have a ship."

James squeezed his fists. "Actually, they have several barges that bring their exports downriver."

"Well, those aren't ships," interjected Mama. She sounded breathless with suspicion.

"They are boats. So I am moving to Quinton Plantation to work as a river captain until I can find something a step up."

"A river captain? A dirty, wet boatman?" Mama's voice went up three octaves at least. Papa's face clouded with fascination.

"It's no dirtier than helping in the brickyard," James declared, "and it won't be for long."

Papa chimed in. "You have a plantation here with the choice to manage the fields or the yard, or there are calls to make at the shipyard and Exchange."

"You have excused me from town and from taking another post on one of our ships." James tried not to sound blameful. It was the investors' doing, too. "This is something I have done for myself, and it's decided. I'm leaving in the morning."

"A Hathaway does not work for a Quinton," Mama argued as she came to her feet. Her silk layers swished as she crossed the room, and James thought for a moment she might snatch him up by the shoulders and shake him, but she began to pace instead.

"A riverboat is a common career, not that I don't admire your intentions to make your own way," began Papa, "but what about the Navy?"

Mama gasped.

The idea sounded titillating to James, but he shook his head. "I've already considered that. Of course, it could be an option, but should I join, I would start at the bottom there just as I must now."

"But a riverboat!" repeated Mama in horror. "Your grandparents did not come to this country so their descendants could paddle vegetables and cows up and down the Ashley!"

"Why not?" demanded James, his voice rising to match her own. "They came in homespun shirts and dresses, didn't they? Your great-grandfather was an indentured man." Mama's face colored.

"James," warned Papa in a low tone, but he left off.

James took another breath. He shifted his gaze from one parent to the other, pleading for them to understand. "I only mean they turned the earth of this land we live on with their own hands. Why should I be any different and not soil mine?"

"You can soil your hands in a pair of good gloves all day long in our fields or stables," snapped Mama, "but you do not have to go work like a filthy dockhand for the Quinton family."

"Well..." said James, rising to his feet prepared to leave, "that is my intention, and I hope someday you'll understand and be proud of me."

"Ugh!" Mama gasped and stomped across the rug. She pointed at Papa. "You talk to him. He is your son!" She exited with a slam of the door.

"Sit down," ordered Papa as the echo of her fury faded away.

James folded himself back onto the long velvet settee. He stared at his hands.

"You have always been her son," said Papa in the quiet, "but of late you have become mine."

James felt his cheek twitch and tried not to smile. "I am trying to do what's right and be responsible, Papa, and this is the path I choose."

His father cleared his throat, and with a rush of courage James looked up to meet his eyes. "You understand I am disappointed."

James bobbed his head, his twisted stomach sinking deeper into his gut.

"However, *I* chose bricks," admitted Papa. "I much prefer it over the fuss and risk of rice and indigo. Everyone is building in this country, from the north to the south. It's made me a very rich man, even more than you know, but I understand if working the land or standing over a kiln does not satisfy you."

Papa sounded sad, and it made a lump form in James's throat.

"Your boyhood was strictly regulated. That's why I let you out with Theodore as soon as the doctors suspected it would do more good than harm. Mammy always had you cleaned up before your Mama could see you all wet and muddy, and she was right. You've grown up strong and healthy."

"You always allowed me on the river; even gave me my first pirogue."

Papa smiled. "You are much like great-grandfather Hath-away. Long before he invested in ships, he loved to sail them, too."

"He was in the Navy."

"The Royal Navy, yes. Stationed in the West Indies, remember? Which is how the family found its way to the Carolina coast. I guess it's in your blood."

Papa smiled, and James's eyes threatened to glisten as the knot in his throat tightened. "Then you understand?"

"I'm trying to. For your mother, it will be difficult. She hoped to have grandchildren by now, and she was very fond of Miss Applewaite this time around."

Phoebe's name struck James's heart like a musket ball. How many hearts had he toyed with and broken? And now he was the wrecked one. It shattered the comforting thoughts his father had shared with him. To James's horror, his eyes began to mist, and he looked away to concentrate on his grandmother's portrait over the mantel.

"Did you really like her?" wondered Papa.

James swallowed the painful lump down and nodded.

"A good woman. I'm sorry to hear it."

James cleared his throat. "She's more than that. Phoebe is thoughtful and a good listener. She's quite well-humored although she hides it from many. Anyone would be lucky to have her."

"My," uttered Papa. He leaned back in his chair and patted his pocket as if searching for his pipe. "You did seem to get on well."

"Yes." James wondered if the sickness he felt showed on his face. "We got on beautifully, but I'm afraid she didn't take kindly to being second to my desire for a captain's post. The word of my 'bargain' with you got out."

"So, that's what happened. Well, you lost the *Lily*," Papa pointed out, "do you still want her?"

The question startled James. He had come to understand that his wants could be petty and selfish, and so he hadn't asked himself that. "I love her." His cheeks flamed.

"Well, my goodness," mused Papa. He fell quiet for a few minutes while James studied the old portrait with a searing face.

"Have you apologized? Have you told her you love her even without a command?"

James shook his head.

"Why not?"

"I humiliated her, and besides, she's never been one to succumb to my charms. I've certainly never been convincing."

"I don't know about that. She agreed to marry you once."

James pressed his lips together and considered it.

Papa rambled on. "While it's good you are looking to begin a new career you are so passionate about, and all on your own, it would be foolish to lose another thing that moves you in the same way. Especially if she is why you have been so uncharacteristically solemn and wretched these past few weeks."

James looked over, curious. What did his father mean?

Finding his empty pipe, Papa stuck it between his teeth and gnawed. "You have always been one to find a way to get what you wanted. We could never keep you in bed when you were ill or from the water if we let you outside. I don't see why Miss Applewaite doesn't deserve the same determination."

He was right. James knew it. As much as his cheeks burned that Papa should know his most intimate feelings and regrets, James realized that his father only wanted what was best for him, not just in life, but in love.

"I still love her," he choked out, "and I haven't had the courage to explain myself and tell her that things haven't changed. After losing the *Lily*, I thought perhaps she was better off with someone else."

Papa nibbled on his pipe stem then said in the quiet, "Go on to the Quinton's then. I suppose you can't explain yourself to her if you're wandering around here in the brickyard."

"Thank you, Papa. I leave for the Ashley tomorrow. Though I doubt my paths will cross with hers, at least we'll be along the same river." James's eyes teared with appreciation.

"Make it so, Mr. Hathaway," Papa urged with a soft smile.

# CHAPTER TWELVE

As the days of May passed away, Mr. Suter drove Phoebe to the Jacksons' home for another dinner. It was the second time she'd dined with her neighbors at Duck Point, and she suspected it would become a regular occurrence since they'd offered the same hospitality to her sister and brother-in-law.

The Jacksons were older than her by several years, had two children, and a house and yard full of servants and enslaved persons. Considering the hypocrisy of their fundamental Christian values and the threat of slave uprisings in the thick, camouflaged low country, Phoebe found it hard to be comfortable there with her burgeoning interest in the anti-slavery pamphlets trickling down from Philadelphia.

After politely withdrawing from their small drawing room afterward, Mr. Suter and Charity met her with the wagon at the stoop, and she clambered up. Charity had insisted she accompany Mr. Suter on the ride, and they'd both enjoyed a small meal in the kitchen house.

Phoebe swatted at mosquitoes clinging to her hat's netting as they bobbled along. "I'm glad you enjoyed your dinner," she remarked. "I'm sorry mine ran on for so long. Mrs. Jackson is lonesome, I think. She did a great deal of talking and for quite a length of time once her husband grew bored with us."

Mr. Suter made a noise of amusement. "He was quite friendly with Mr. Cadwell and may miss dispensing advice."

"Now that it's grown hot, he wouldn't have seen them often anyway. Winnifred cannot bear the heat after late morning and would have never come out of her room."

Charity sniffed. "I'm sure she is happy to be back in town at home, Miss."

"Yes, I'm sure she is," begrudged Phoebe. How she missed town, but she would not complain. *Comme on faict son lict, on le treuve*—she had made her bed and must lie in it now. "She will miss being close to the river," Phoebe guessed, "and the ducks and her garden. How much better everything grows out this way."

"More room," Mr. Suter offered.

She raised her chin in agreement.

Along the way home, a sentry of pines and towering cottonwoods lined either side of the make-shift road then thinned into the edges of a cypress swamp. The road inclined past salt flats and stunted grasses while Phoebe watched for alligators and the channel's bank began to widen and reveal the dark strip of beach near the dock.

"Poor Mr. Arnold must be lonesome," she jested, and Charity made a noise of dissent. "I think Daniel may come back for him if he comes back for any of us at all." Phoebe kept a stingy thought to herself—that she would do anything to return home where she could walk to the market, see the wideopen ocean, and perhaps, dip a polite curtsey to Mr. Hathaway if he happened to pass by in his jaunty gig. As bruised and broken as she felt, she missed him and what had been.

With his weathered hands on the reigns, Mr. Suter motioned with his chin toward the channel. "That won't be Mr. Cadwell, I'd wager, as they're coming from upriver."

Phoebe peered ahead. A large boat, almost too wide to navigate the shallows of the channel, slid carefully down on the current toward her dock. She squinted. "Why would they come around this side of the river and risk getting stranded?"

Suter kept silent, saying he did not know. He slowed the wagon when they passed the dock, and Phoebe put a glove on his arm. "Stop," she said in a low tone. Although it was faster, it made little sense for anyone to come through the channel in a wide barge unless they were looking to stop along the mainland's shore to hunt ducks or fish. She certainly did not want strangers on her land.

Glancing around for Arnold and not seeing the sinister alligator lurking about, she scuttled down from the wagon and strode over to the pilings. The mark of her family crest was still there, deeply engraved into the hearty pine. She pressed the mosquito netting to her face so she could see better and pinched it at her neck to protect herself from the dreadful insects.

The boat drew nearer. It was loaded with grain sacks and casks of different sizes, as well as a few dark-colored men, most likely enslaved. Three white men were also aboard: two at the front, and one aft, stroking a long, thick oar with an enormous paddle. Two of them noticed the wagon, or perhaps her, at the edge of the dock.

It was all Phoebe could do not to put her hands on her hips, but she waited quietly, her heart thrumming with anxious curiosity. How could Mama suggest she live out here practically alone? The lonely low country was not always safe, not with runaways, smugglers, and God forbid, pirates.

One of them, sturdy and square-shouldered, pushed up a cocked hat to see better, and she knew him instantly even though her mind flapped back in surprise like a startled bird. He signaled to the man in the back and called at the others, and then remarkably, the craft changed direction and slinked toward the bank almost brushing the pilings as they managed to heave to and stop.

James Hathaway leaped up beside her as nimble as a young buck. A faint smile glowed on his face where his once-fair complexion had darkened to an interesting shade of pecan. Phoebe took a step away fighting jumbled desires to either embrace him or push him back into the water.

His basil-green stare swirled with some kind of reticence despite his overly-familiar demeanor. He caught himself and bowed. "Miss Applewaite?" His glance flitted toward the wagon and stopped on Mr. Suter. After a painful pause, he said, "It is still Miss Applewaite, isn't it?"

*Of course, you idiot.* Instead of speaking her first thought, Phoebe forced something different to come out of her dry mouth. "It is. This is Applewaite land. I'm afraid we are not accustomed to such large boats coming through the channel from upriver."

"Ah," he responded in a polite tone although his eyes drank her in. She could feel his probing stare trying to find its way through the netting that protected her expression and spinning emotions.

"I, uh," he stammered then motioned toward the other men, "it's a barge. From the Quinton's land. We are moving some exports downriver to Charleston."

Phoebe tore her eyes away from his penetrating gaze and scanned his plain attire which appeared only suitable for paddling down waterways. If she hadn't known he was a Hathaway, she would have never guessed it. His bare hands looked red and rough.

"You are working on the river now?" She tried to keep the surprise out of her tone.

"Yes, as a river captain," he conceded. "I tried the brickyard, but I missed the water, so I am..." He glanced over his shoulder then turned back to her with a sheepish grin. "I am learning to pilot the Ashley which is why we took the channel."

"Oh," replied Phoebe as her mind tried to comprehend what this meant. Unable to restrain herself, she queried in a discreet tone, "Have your parents cut you off?"

James chuckled. "No, but they are not willing to help me secure a career at sea so I am on my own."

"A river captain," Phoebe murmured. For someone who showed little interest in getting his hands dirty for so many years, he'd certainly changed his colors.

"It doesn't bring in a great deal of income," James admitted, "but I see Mr. Quinton on occasion, and the job keeps a roof over my head."

"That's very nice," Phoebe answered, not knowing what else to say. Gracious! Where did a river captain even sleep? It made no sense that a gentleman of James's reputation would leave his home, especially one as fine as Sandy Point, and work as a common laborer on a river barge.

"You looked confused," he observed.

"I am, but you look... happy."

His smile stiffened. "Not completely. I am satisfied to have my mind made up even if I have to start on a barge, but—" He looked at her, his stare piercing the netting and sinking deep into her eyes as he'd done on the banks of Rathall Creek. "I'm not completely happy."

She could not allow herself to believe he meant her. Those hopes were long burned to ashes. Phoebe cleared her throat and looked away. "I'm sorry it did not work out for you on the *Lily.*" James did not answer, and the moment became so strained she turned back to his examination.

"Miss Applewaite," he blurted. "Please allow me to apologize. I—"

Phoebe held up a gloved hand. Her plastered smile felt so tight it hurt. She could not speak of it. It was long past and people lingered nearby listening. "Please, don't," she mouthed.

"But I—"

"It's not necessary." She squared her shoulders. "It's lovely here, isn't it? I'm quite content. We have a good house up the way, and there's a freshwater spring off a little creek which is cool and tastes wonderful." She forced a good-humored smile. "We have a lovely garden, too," and she motioned toward Charity and Mr. Suter.

With his mouth falling into a straight line, James looked past her and gave the others in the wagon a small gesture of acknowledgment. "Then you are satisfied."

"Enough," fibbed Phoebe, "and I am out of Mama's way. Daniel and Winnifred will return in August when harvest time is near." Try as she might, she could not ignore his handsome face, tanned neck, and fine, broad shoulders.

Her resolve to withstand this first meeting wilted with her heart. Phoebe gulped. It was unbearable the next thing she must do, but she had to be polite. "Would you like to come with us for some refreshment, though you must have a schedule to keep?" she hinted.

James turned his hat over in his hands then swiped at an enormous mosquito flitting around his ear. "Thank you, no," he mumbled.

"Well then," she managed, "it was – it was good to see you."

"And you," came the swift reply. She saw remorse flash in his eyes and knew he was sorry for what he did; or sorry for something. She stared bravely, wishing he would leap back into his boat and leave before she started to cry.

With one last look, James turned to the piling but before he climbed back into the barge, he said, "I did not get my captain's post, Phoebe, and I did not get you, but you must know, please believe me, that it was you I wanted most of all." Then he leaped into the vessel without another word.

His words struck her like she was a bell, and she stood immobilized as they rang in her ears. Her heart pulsed with a strange relief as she watched the barge continue down the channel, but she quieted it. The quivering in her legs that began when she first saw him became violent trembling. What had he said? Did he mean it? Her mind swam.

Just as the barge went around the bend, James raised an arm in the air in a sweet, poignant signal of goodbye. Phoebe flicked her hand up in return. When he was out of sight, she tried to clear the gnarled emotions trapped in her throat, but it set loose a hornet's nest of agonizing anxieties that allowed a sob to escape. She covered her mouth and trapped them in her hand.

The wagon soon returned to the house, and without a word to Mr. Suter or Charity, Phoebe walked to her room and shut the door before collapsing onto the musty bed. She let the hurt she'd so carefully controlled stream out in rivulets. Now they could both go on. He had formally told her goodbye.

JAMES'S STOMACH BEGAN to roll once the barge broke free of the swift-moving channel and rejoined the heaving river that made them toss back and forth like a lazy, lumbering cow. At one point, he found himself leaning over the side to mist his face to help him keep from being sick. He was an object of ridicule to the others.

After they reached Charleston, James watched the men unload the barrels and sacks as he waited for the dockmaster. It was his third trip downriver, and he knew the charts by heart. Already, he felt like the Ashley had grown from a good acquaintance to a trusted friend. Soon, with a little more experience with the weather and tides, she would be as familiar as a lover. Until then, he was just a Hathaway, an entitled newcomer.

James leaned back on a post, his mind returning to the sight of Phoebe keeping watch from her family dock like a castle guard. His reaction upon seeing her had been stupefied although he'd known the Applewaite's land was somewhere along the river bank. Papa had pointed it out on a channel map, but James had not paid as close attention as he should have. When he saw her there, he did not know her at first from the netting dripping from her hat, but the sight of her striking *en garde* stance and the slim figure beneath the printed cotton gown arrested his gaze. His heart had prickled, and he just *knew*.

James wet his lips, drowning out the noise of men and squawking gulls around him. His attraction to her had not waned and neither had his admiration. He was still in love, dash it all. It hadn't gone away like a cold. He couldn't forget about her the way he had forgotten others.

Phoebe did not want him anymore. James felt his shoulders drop. It was clear—and unfair. She believed he'd only proposed to get aboard the *Lily* and that simply wasn't *wholly* true. Yes, it had motivated him in the beginning, but when he kissed her and asked for her hand, he'd meant it more honestly, more solidly, and more genuinely than he'd ever meant anything in his life.

His stomach rolled over again, and James grunted. He needed to put something in it before he was sick. Since he would take a room over the *Blue Porpoise*, he decided to head up the street and catch a late supper. The barge had arrived at the tail end of dusk, and soon the quay would be loud and boisterous. He knew he didn't want any of that and wondered if he'd suddenly somehow turned a hundred years old.

At last, James finished up business with a handshake, ignoring the surprise of the officials loitering around with raised brows. Why? It was old news now. Hathaway had left the Exchange and was getting his feet wet.

James resettled his hat. His hands felt stiff and cold as he found himself stumbling fatigued toward the inn. When he spied Mr. Albermarle at the end of the quay under a blazing torch, he almost groaned aloud.

Albermarle dropped his chin in a slow, deep nod, but James stiffened his shoulders and decided he had no desire to converse. The man greeted him again as he walked by, so he replied, "G' evening," in a taut tone. Before he could escape, a heavy hand landed on his shoulder, and he spun around on the defense.

"Mr. Hathaway," repeated Albermarle, eyes glinting with amusement.

"I said hello," James countered. "Do you have a message from my father, or do you just want to insult me again?"

"No," replied the man, his face guarded. "I would like to speak to you," he explained. "Are you heading to the *Blue Porpoise* with the other men? I'd like to buy you a drink if you would allow it."

James stared in surprise. "I am a bit dirty and damp, Mr. Albermarle, but that is where I plan to stay for the night."

"Until you return upriver?"

"That's right."

Albermarle studied him. Now curious, James added somewhat reluctantly, "I am thirsty enough and planned to get something to eat if you want to come along."

The man made a noise of agreement, and they walked side by side the remaining distance to a dark blue tavern with a porpoise-shaped sign swinging over the door. Settling at a vacant table crammed with rickety chairs, they sat across from one another, and Albermarle ordered fish and oysters along with corn fritters and two pint-sized tankards.

James's stomach growled in anticipation, and he nearly fainted with relief when the drink came right away. He took a long swallow and then a deep breath, waiting for Albermarle to unload his thoughts on him. He'd done so freely in the past, but the man looked hesitant, almost tired.

"So you don't have a message from Papa?" James clarified.

Albermarle cupped both hands around his drink. "I'm here about Zachariah."

James had just found this job working for Benjamin. Did the man want him to get his boy on with the Quintons, too?

Albermarle glanced around then lowered his eyes and voice. "I understand there is more to the story of the *Lily's* fire."

Startled, James remained silent. Albermarle gave a swift, jerking nod. "He has told me, finally, the whole truth, at least I like to think so." His bushy brows sank into a straight line.

"What did he say exactly?" James couldn't imagine the boy would lie and lay all of the blame on his shoulders.

"My son likes to smoke. I don't approve, of course, and neither does his mother. He's finally decided to find another pastime since nearly burning to death at sea, but his spirits haven't much improved until we had a conversation last week."

"I see." James waited.

In a near-whisper, Albermarle said, "I understand you were aware my son was smoking in the hold before the fire started."

"I was."

"And you didn't report it?"

"There was no time when it came to my attention." James pitied Zachariah. It was honorable of him to confess, but that didn't mean James would be a party to his punishment. "Besides," he added, "after all was said and done, no one perished, and I didn't see the point in dragging down an absentminded boy. I've been in his position."

Albermarle didn't reply, and James watched his faded gray eyes become less cold as if touched with gratitude. Clearing his throat, the man mumbled, "So you took the blame and keel-hauled your own reputation rather than speak out."

"I could have reacted faster; given orders sooner. I deserve some rebuke."

"Yet you have been banned from the shipyard."

James hiked his shoulders in a swift shrug.

"I owe you the deepest and most regretful apology," Albermarle admitted, "and I thank you."

He did not have to say that the brunt of the financial losses could have been demanded from him; that his family and his livelihood could have been ruined forever. And the boy. Zachariah could have been severely punished to the point of losing his life.

To dismiss the uncomfortable accolades, James took a long drink from his foaming ale and found it filled places inside of him that had felt parched for a long time. An invisible weight lifted from his shoulders. He was acquitted, at least in Albermarle's mind, and Papa would probably learn of it, too. This pleased James. It was enough.

"I'm happy your son is an honest one." He wiped his top lip with the back of his hand. Wouldn't Mama be appalled? Wasn't he a simple, honest sailor now in Albermarle's eyes?

The man across from him opened his mouth, but their vittles came before he could speak. They both ate ravenously from steaming plates until their appetites waned.

Half-finished, Albermarle pushed his plate away and rested his elbows on the table. He looked in better spirits now and seemed more friendly. "Your kindness and good cheer have always impressed me, Mr. Hathaway."

Now, this was a surprise.

"You are a young man, with privilege, but you do not rush to judgment or look for opportunities to use your position to hold others down."

James nearly choked. He didn't know how to take a compliment from hawk-eyed Albermarle. With his mouth full, he gave him a tight-lipped smile from over his plate.

"I have a proposal for you," said Albermarle. Something sparkled in his dull eyes, and James swallowed everything in one quick lump. What could this man offer better than floating up and down the river all week long?

Albermarle looked at him and a soft, fatherly smile spread over his face. "I have a cousin in Savannah, who has a small ship..."

PHOEBE FELT SO RESTLESS after helping Charity weed the kitchen garden, she toweled down her neck, washed her face again, tugged on her old leather boots, and marched down the wooden planks of the porch's rickety stairs. With a pointed walking stick in one hand and her widest parasol in the other, she stared down the property's drive to the opening in the tilted split rail fence. It would be too hot to do anything later, so now was the only time she would find any privacy unless she stayed in her room. Out here at Duck Point, Charity followed Phoebe everywhere like a lonely puppy and only brightened when Mr. Suter came around.

Since speaking with James on the docks, Phoebe had felt herself withdraw even further into her dreary mind, getting lost for long periods of time. Her list of grievances against him had dwindled, and they'd mysteriously faded for Mama, too. Emotions that once consumed her had metamorphosized from a dark angry caterpillar into a sleeping, numb cocoon.

Phoebe was not angry anymore but anxious to find her wings. She knew she must press forward despite having feelings that would likely never go away. Since James's appearance at the dock, they'd returned as fiercely as if he'd turned back time.

She exhaled in surrender while ambling down the road toward a row of trees casting late-morning shadows. Her alert gaze roamed ahead should Benedict Arnold decide to leave his beach and strut across her property for bigger prey than fish and ducks. When she'd last dined with the Jacksons, Mr. Jackson had made her blood run cold recounting one evening how there was a clatter at the door and his housekeeper opened it to almost be eaten alive. Benedict Arnold had climbed his way up the Jackson's porch stairs and appeared to be trying to climb up the house. Perhaps to the windows, Mr. Jackson said shaking his fist, where the baby slept in an upstairs room with the shutters unlocked.

It was a beastly tale, and yet the beast was real. Phoebe was surprised the alligator had not attacked anyone or taken up residence closer to the road within reach of horses and wagons. Yet.

At that thought, she halted at the end of the drive and looked carefully up and down each side of the road in both directions. The scent of cypress trees floated along the morning air. She inhaled, listening to the distant water gurgling along in the channel.

Well, she did have the thick and pointy walking stick Mr. Suter carved for her, and it was not that far to the dock. Scolding the Jacksons for filling her head with tales of horror, she strolled along the middle of the road, tapping the stick in front of her like it would seek out danger and alert her before it was too late.

The fresh air blowing off the channel felt like a happy embrace. The golden sunshine, inspirational. It was time to live. She must not fear alligators anymore, Phoebe told herself, or drown in the depths of despair over seeing James again. After all, she'd endured a war, a hungry, frightening childhood, and her beloved Papa's death. She'd survived pain from being teased about her homely childhood, the disdain of popular young women, and the humiliation of being single at her little sister's wedding.

Yes, Phoebe would survive this, too. It was just a broken heart, and like a ripped seam, time would mend it up again. Perhaps she could become better friends with Mrs. Jackson if she tried harder, or maybe her situation with Charity could be ignored. Why should they live so far out in a wild country and carry on as servant and mistress when they could be closer companions?

Phoebe exhaled and tried not to feel sorry for herself. Would she have friends again? Mama had written her the sweetest letter begging her forgiveness and insisting she missed her so, but would Phoebe ever feel comfortable enough to return to Charleston?

She slowed her gait as she realized the birds and crickets around her had fallen silent. Her heart began to thump as she came to a halt. She'd almost reached the dock. Looking sideways into the swampy brush and then back to the channel below, she realized it was eerily quiet. Benedict Arnold was nowhere in sight.

The sound of her heartbeat echoed in her ears. Phoebe held her breath. Behind her. That was the one direction she had missed. She could sense him, almost feel his hungry stare. Her throat became painfully parched. Phoebe clenched the handle of the parasol as her courage waned.

Suddenly there was a splash nearby, and her brain shouted a hundred instructions at once. She could see the monster—mouth gaping, teeth flashing, and jaws snapping just inches away—all in her mind's eye. Phoebe screamed and almost stumbled headfirst into the sandy dirt, but she caught herself and took off at a ferocious run. With eyes wide and ears straining to hear its shuffling gait behind her, she prayed the alligator couldn't run faster than a woman laced up in stiff stays.

The world began to shrink into a dark tunnel as Phoebe sucked in air in sharp, strangled breaths. Her legs felt weak as pudding, and tears pricked her eyelids when she realized she was not as strong as she had believed. She could not run more than a Charleston block at this pace. What a horrible way to die.

She stumbled as her strength gave out and a terrified bawl escaped when she looked back to see how much time she had to brace herself. Tripping over her feet, she fell backward onto her backside with a painful crunch.

*Nothing.*

She nearly fainted with relief when she saw nothing there. Not even in the distance. The fall had jerked her head back and wrung her neck. Gasping and clutching at the ground for support, Phoebe raised her eyes to heaven and cried out in relief.

She would have prayed in gratitude right then and there, but she heard her name. Reigning in the madness, she forced herself to get a grip on her hysteria and looked down the road. She'd run right past the dock, and there was a man.

He stared.

She panted for air.

Then like a vision, James Hathaway vaulted across the dock and dashed up the road. "Are you hurt?" When he reached her, he dropped to his knees, seized her elbows, and pulled her into him.

Phoebe clung to him as the world spun in and out. James. He was an angel in the middle of this swampland. With a stroke of courage, she peeked down the road. Still no alligator. James took her by the chin and lifted her head. "What is it? Smugglers? Poachers?"

Phoebe caught her breath and looked into his eyes. Her mouth tried to form words, but he hushed them by planting a gentle kiss on her lips without asking. "Tell me," he said in an urgent whisper. Now she was burning and tingling from head to toe.

"It's... I thought I—" she stuttered. Phoebe peeked around him again then closed her eyes and dropped her head back. She forced herself to breathe in and out before she fainted. When she looked again, his face hovered just inches away.

"I thought I heard something behind me," she faltered in a trembling voice. "I thought it was following me." She squeezed his arms as she regained her composure. He looked confused. "I thought an alligator was chasing me," she explained.

James's jaw relaxed. Phoebe realized how ridiculous it sounded and dropped against his chest as a laugh of relief burbled out.

"I thought Benedict Arnold was going to eat me," she quipped. A laugh followed in high-pitched titters, and she felt a hum in James's chest grow against her cheek as his own chuckles erupted. He fell beside her, breaking into guffaws, and she completely lost all self-control, dissolving into hysterical laughter. They crowed together until her ribs hurt, and she had to hold them.

"By jove!" he chortled with delight. "I heard a scream and there you came like a cannon blast, throwing things left and right with your skirts held so high I thought your boots were on fire."

Phoebe swiped at the tears in her eyes and allowed two more spurting giggles. "What a spectacle," she exclaimed, throwing up her hands, "and what a dignified sight I must be now." She took another deep breath, unable to stop smiling. She was alive and here was James very real and holding her tight.

He did not let go of her hand but crawled to his feet. He lifted her up and drew her against his chest again. "Are you well then? I don't need to call for reinforcements?"

Phoebe wobbled her head no and glanced toward the dock. "Are you alone?"

The same barge he'd descended the river on a few days ago bounced against the current from its line knotted against a piling. "I'm not," James replied. "I've sent them off—to rest or fish if they want. Just for a little while."

"I hope they will be very careful then."

"The channel is fast-moving for alligators."

"But not for Arnold," Phoebe insisted. "He comes back and forth between the beach and the cypress swamp all the time. We've even seen him swim over from the island."

"The men have guns," James assured her, taking her hand and walking her toward the barge. "Would you like to see the bolts of silk and sheer embroidered muslins I'm taking back to the Quintons? They're quite lovely."

She eyed him with curiosity. "You want to show me your shipment?"

James hesitated like she'd said something wrong. A flush rose on his cheeks, and his face tightened. "Actually," he said at last, "I intended to come up to the house to call." He paused. "If you'd welcome me."

Phoebe tried to push back the ardent hope that flooded her heart. Here he was, no ship, no plantation, not even his fancy gig, and he wanted to see her.

"Of course you're welcome." She searched his face, aching to find the courage to plead with him to be frank and honest with her this time. Then it dawned on her that he probably only stopped at Duck Point to see if she had any handkerchiefs ready to send to the Indies.

James removed his hat. "I'm happy to hear that, and look, I brought you something."

Phoebe looked to where he pointed. Balanced on top of one of the pilings was a giant, golden pineapple. She gasped in surprise. "You remembered. Oh, how thoughtful! You are very much enjoying this river business, aren't you? I suppose you have come about handkerchiefs?"

He reached for her arm and pulled her close again. Intimately close. Quite inappropriately close for a barge captain. A light breeze riffled through his hair. "Actually, the only business I have to discuss with you is my heart."

Phoebe's breath caught in her chest, and she thought she would swoon if she heard the words he'd whispered in her dreams.

"My hopes haven't changed," he confessed in a quiet voice that melted her. "But my reasons have and only for the better."

"Miss Applewaite—Phoebe, I have admired you all my life and adored you since you refused to dance with me on Twelfth Night. To be frank, I must tell you..." He squeezed her hand as the healthy glow on his cheeks receded. "I was indeed encouraged by my parents to court you, and it was promised I would have a position aboard one of the company ships if I settled, but... How it all came about was that I – I fell very much in love with you and thought the position aboard *Lily* only as an additional gift. What they said, what they say now, is not true at all."

Phoebe searched his eyes for earnestness and found it there. Her eyes seeped with tears of happiness. She wanted to confess her joy but found she could not speak.

A smile bloomed across James's face as if he felt her bliss. "I would have asked you to be my wife if I'd only been promised a kiln."

She laughed lightly, her face aching from the depths of her deep smile.

"Say you believe me," pleaded James. "Say you believe *in* me." He waited with a hungry look for her response.

"James Hathaway, I never once believed you could not be anything you wanted to be." She swallowed. "And I have loved you, I think, since my coming out and our first dance, but I admit I gave up on it—until now."

He smiled with pleasure. "And I am very much in love with you and do not want to sail to any place in the world without knowing I've secured your affection." He gazed at her with hope. Phoebe nodded to urge him, her heart burning and cheeks flaming with the possibility that this could all be true.

"You will marry me, won't you? Change your mind? Despite my lack of interest in agriculture or bricks or—" He stopped short, and she saw he was near breathless with despair.

Giddy happiness coursed through Phoebe like a river. "Of course I will," she promised, eyes overflowing.

His gaze trailed down her face to her lips. As if in a dream, she let her eyes flutter shut. James knew exactly what she wished for and took her into his arms, unraveling her into a pile of helpless cotton and lace.

When the echo of men's voices snatched her from their private delight, she pulled back and whispered more encouragement. "It does not matter what you choose to do as long as we do it together," she promised. "There are no issues as far as I'm concerned if you want to captain a riverboat."

Inches from her lips, James's mouth parted into a sly and sultry smile. It was an inviting look she was beginning to know well. "Why, Miss Applewaite," he murmured, "I have been offered a small trading ship that takes short jaunts up and down the coast." His eyes shined with exhilaration. "So you will be a captain's bride after all."

She gasped with joy for him and threw her arms around his neck to hug him tight. He hung back his head and laughed then danced her around in a circle with his hands around her waist.

Phoebe dropped her head onto his shoulder. *At last.* Gazing down the rippling channel, she saw an old familiar log on the bank. A smile escaped as a tear slipped down her cheek.

Benedict Arnold, the traitor, if he had been following her at all, had made his way down to the cool water and was standing in it up to his wrinkled old elbows watching her soak in all the future happiness James Hathaway had offered.

# EPILOGUE

I n beautiful gold calligraphy, *Mrs. Hathaway's Millineries and Fine Goods* announced itself as the most recent shop to open on the corner of Queen Street and East Bay. Painted as blue as a robin's egg, a ray of early summer sunshine bounced off its window and made a rainbow in Charleston's sea air.

Phoebe smiled in satisfaction. She stepped back to the far side of the cobbled street to examine her display from left to right, finding the hats particularly attractive bookends for her clocks and jewelry resting between them.

"And just what are you grinning about?" called a familiar voice. She spun around with a delighted cry to see her husband. He was clad in his sea coat and handsome cocked hat with fine white trim. His striking grin made her heart spin, too. She dashed across the remaining distance between them and flew into his arms. He embraced her for long seconds before pulling back.

"You are not excited I'm home again?" They swayed together ignoring the looks of others passing by in carriages and wagons.

Phoebe pecked him on the cheek. "I just returned from the beach. Did you see me? I waved you in."

"Past the fort? Yes, I saw you there looking like a damsel in distress."

"A white handkerchief was all I had, and I assure you, I was not in distress."

"I see you are not. Is that a new clock there in the shop?"

Phoebe bobbed her head in assent. "I purchased a dozen and already sold two this week—one to Mrs. Leonard who hurried out before I could thank her."

"Amazing," her husband murmured. "She must have wanted it badly. I suppose Mr. Quinton brought her in?"

"He's been very kind, you know."

"He is grateful you accepted his apology."

"I was happy to accept."

James pulled back and examined Phoebe's eyes, nose, and then her lips. "We should hurry along home," he suggested, and she flushed.

"You might as well kiss me here since I can deduce your intentions."

He grinned like an imp. "That's only the half of them, my lady."

She raised her brows and tapped him on the arm. "Come see the clock," she pleaded, "and my new bolt of white muslin. How fast it goes these days."

"French fashion," sniffed James, and Phoebe giggled. She led him to the window dodging a wagon pulling fishy-smelling barrels.

"See here," she exclaimed, "none of this would have been possible without your generosity or your parents, but..."

She then forgot what she was saying and admired their reflections in the window. Husband and wife now, they looked much older, she thought, and wiser, but it had only been a year.

James met her eyes in a windowpane. "I'm sorry, what? I only see a goddess in the glass."

She elbowed him. "Don't be silly." Glowing from his compliments and something more, Phoebe noted, "It's already hot. I've written to your Mama about June. We'll close down the town house when you next depart, and I will go out to Sandy Bank for the summer."

James wrapped an arm around her waist, still watching her in the window. "She's looking forward to it, and happy you are bringing your mama, too. I suppose you're happy not to be returning to Duck Point, although there's work aplenty with Daniel clearing our land now."

"So am I, more than you know," she agreed. "I even suggested to Winnifred that she join us at Sandy Bank for a time if she wishes. It would be grand to have her there with Mama and me to rest and relax.

He took her hand and slid it inside his arm to guide her down the street. "Come, walk with me to the water," he begged, and she allowed him to take her away although her assistant—the proud and independent Mrs. Charity Suter—would be wondering where she'd wandered off to. Sea air licked over them like puppy kisses, and she sighed with contentment.

"And what are you looking forward to at Sandy Bank besides relief from the heat?"

Phoebe glanced at James sideways through her lashes. "Only some extra rest for a few weeks as I find myself fatigued more than usual."

He studied her face with concern. "Are you ill? I thought you seemed thinner."

She chuckled at the fretting tone in his voice. "Don't worry, sweeting. I'm as healthy as anyone. I'll outlive you all."

He let out a dry laugh. "Then don't frighten me so. I know what it's like to be sickly, and it's no fun."

"Well," she admitted, "I've had a taste of it these past few weeks."

James looked at her with a question in his eye as they dropped off the street and tramped down onto the sandy shore.

"It won't last," she reassured him. "With a little rest and some quiet dinners at Sandy Bank, I'm sure I'll recover eventually—although I may be a little more plump than you are used to having me."

They stopped when their shoes sank into the sand but close enough to hear the gentle lap of the waves onto the shore. "But you're so much thinner now," he said with a confused frown.

Phoebe couldn't hold back a grin as she patted her stomach through her long, muslin gown. "Not everywhere," she winked.

His eyes went from her belly to her face and back down again.

A giggle escaped, and Phoebe exclaimed, "I'm going to have a child, you dolt. I thought you were raised on a farm."

James met her gaze with his mouth hanging open. She burst into laughter.

"A brickyard, really," he managed at last, then he laughed as his eyes flooded with tears. It made Phoebe wrap her arms around his neck.

"Well, your shopkeeper is going to have a baby," she murmured, and he piled kisses across her cheek. "Another Hathaway. Another Applewaite," she whispered to the man she loved with all her heart and soul.

James laughed with happiness then stumbled back, tossed his hat up into the air, and spun her about until all Phoebe saw were blurs of happiness and ever after on the distant horizon.

## THE END

## Don't miss Book Three

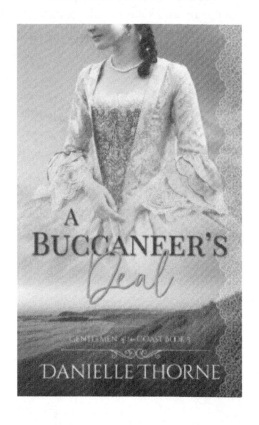

## Get your copy at Amazon.com.

# AUTHOR'S NOTE

HI. I'VE NEVER LEFT a note in a work of fiction before, but I wanted to share the fun I had writing this book with you. I don't know how I lived in the South my entire life and never visited Charleston. During research for *A Captain's Bride*, I spent three days in this beautiful city. It was cold and rainy, but its haunting charm mesmerized me. The history is both astounding and regretful. The architecture is to die for. If you ever have a chance to visit, I highly recommend it. There's a really cool restaurant nearby called *Poe's Tavern*. There are awesome tours inside historical homes and on preserved plantations. The International African American Museum will open there in 2022.

Did you know Phoebe Applewaite was a real person? While working on my family history, I came across a Phoebe Applewaite born in 1741 in Virginia. She is my sixth cousin eight times removed and though we're distant, I instantly felt a connection to her when I read her lovely name. Creating her aloof namesake in this book came naturally because I've struggled with shyness and anxiety my entire life. I know what it's like to feel, "crushed against the window panes, separated from all of the buzzing conversations like she was trapped alone in a glass jar." We're not all fans of being in the spotlight, even if we want to be successful!

James? Mr. Hathaway was fun to write, too. I thought it was interesting watching him mature and change. I was blessed to have many friends growing up in Nashville—especially young men who were like brothers to me. How I love a cheerful, funny boy. In fact, I married one!

A huge "thank you" to my beta readers who helped me through the publishing process once I had the first draft down. Special thanks to Dawn Pearson, who is a stellar reader and belongs in the copyediting business. Thank you to my review team. I appreciate you! And last but first in my heart, thanks to my family who put up with my crazy hours during the first draft and the final copy. I know there will be errors, but I do everything possible to make my stories historically accurate and error-free.

I hope you enjoyed this romance story and join me again for book 3, *A Buccaneer's Deal*. Thank you for reading my books, leaving reviews, and sending me notes. Your support means everything.

Best wishes,

**Danielle Thorne**

# MORE BOOKS
# BY DANIELLE THORNE

### Historical

*The Privateer of San Madrid*

*A Pirate at Pembroke*

*Proper Attire*

*Josette*

### Holiday

*Brushstrokes and Blessings*

*Henry's Holiday Charade*

*Garland's Christmas Romance*

*Valentine Gold*

### Contemporary

*Turtle Soup*

*By Heart and Compass*

*Death Cheater*

*Cheated*

### Non-fiction

*Southern Girl, Yankee Roots*

*The Story of Andrew Jackson*

*The Story of Illinois Becoming a State*

*The Story of Queen Victoria 200 Years After Her Birth*

# About the Author

Danielle Thorne writes historical and contemporary romance from south of Atlanta, Georgia. Married for thirty years to the same fellow, she's the mother of four boys, two daughters-in-law, and she has two grandbabies. There are also cats involved.

Danielle is a graduate of Ricks College and BYU-Idaho. Besides writing pursuits, she's active in her church and community. Free time is filled with books, movies, too much yardwork, and not enough wandering the country or cruising the beautiful, blue seas. She's worked as an editor for Solstice and Desert Breeze Publishing and is the author of non-fiction for young adults.

Her first book with Harlequin's Love Inspired line will be out July 2020.

**Visit Danielle at www.daniellethorne.com**
You can also connect with Danielle at Facebook (Author Danielle Thorne), Twitter (@DanielleThorne), or Instagram (@authordaniellethorne).

# Dear Reader, Before you go...

Please visit Amazon.com to share your thoughts and review this book. Thank you!

Made in the USA
Las Vegas, NV
05 February 2024

85369981R00152